UNEXPECTED

PUBLIC RELATIONS BOOK 2

LIZA GAINES

Edited by
RHONDA MERWARTH
Cover Art by
CROCO DESIGNS

For JLH

CHAPTER 1

GWEN

THAT MOTHERFUCKING no-good son of a bitch.

Gaping at Mac, my tears drying on my cheeks, I'm stunned into an angry calm by his laughter. It isn't just a nervous chuckle, like he thinks I might be pulling an awful prank, either. No, that bastard is bent over, bracing himself on the counter, shoulders shaking, eyes watering laughing. "This isn't a joke."

"I'm sorry." Turning toward me, he swallows his humor and pulls me against his chest. "I know it's not, but you have to admit, it's a little bit funny. We must be the most incompetent people in the world when it comes to birth control."

We. Unexpected relief rushes through me, leaving me unsteady on my feet. There are no questions about if it's his. No blame because I must've messed up my pills. No accusations that I did it on purpose. Just we. "We weren't incompetent the first time, we were irresponsible idiots. This time I...I don't know what happened. I took my pill every morning—I know I didn't miss any. But maybe with all the travel, the time zones, the weird hours...I don't know, maybe I took

"

some late and didn't even realize it, but whatever happened, it's pretty clearly my fault and I'm so, so sorry." My breath hitches and my eyes are starting to burn so I look away, cheek pressed to his bare chest, and struggle to keep my tears at bay. Even more, hoping he won't notice them if I fail.

"Hey, don't do that." He squeezes me tighter, smoothing his hands over my back. "We'll figure this out, okay?"

"Okay." I nod, and his hands skim lower to squeeze my ass through the fluffy white hotel towel I wrapped myself in after my shower. It's amazing the way my body reacts to his touch, even in my current state of turmoil, but I ignore the goose bumps prickling my skin and croak, "What are you doing?"

Mac dips his head, his warm breath puffing against the side of my neck. Gathering the towel with both hands, he tugs until the knot loosens and falls to the floor. His lips tickle the soft skin under my ear when he asks, "What do you think I'm doing?"

My knees wobble, and I lean against his chest for balance, squeezing my eyes closed, trying to focus. It doesn't work. The arousal slowly building in my center is just one more emotion...one more thing, spinning wildly with all my other thoughts and worries, and I can't concentrate on any of them. It's too much, too many conflicting feelings, and I don't know how to untangle them. "We can't. I can't. We have to talk about this." My voice is thick, and I feel like I'm suffo- cating. Like the room is closing in around me. Shaking my head in frustration, I try again, going straight for the most important ques- tion. "What are we going to do?"

"I don't know." Mac straightens, his gaze meeting mine. He cradles my jaw in one palm, his thumb stroking my cheek. "I promise we'll talk, but right now, I'm not even sure what I think, let alone what to say or where to start, except that I know I need you."

Ever since noticing my period is late, I've been unable to get out of my own mixed-up head long enough to really notice him. Now, it's like seeing him for the first time. The stress lines at the corners of his eyes, the furrow of his brow, the set of his jaw, the earnest timbre of his voice. He's trying to handle this in the best way he knows how, just like I am, and I understand the impulse to be close. To be together. I feel it too. "Okay, but—"

"No buts." Mac shakes his head and presses one finger to my lips. With his other hand on my hip, he turns me until my backside is pressed against the bathroom counter.

His expression is still so serious, his dark eyes turbulent, and a hard lump of guilt lodges in my throat. I did this to him. *Again.* "Mac, I—"

He interrupts again, his lips quirking in a small, teasing smile. "You really can't be quiet, can you?"

Despite everything else, and to my complete surprise, I laugh. It's soft and feeble, but it's real and it feels like a life preserver. Like maybe this isn't terrible, or it is, but we'll get through it anyway. After so many years of facing every obstacle alone, it's hard to accept this time might be different. But God, do I want it to be different.

Bracing both hands on the edge of the counter, I boost myself up to sit on it and spread my knees. It's as much a silent declaration that I can be quiet as it is an invitation. It turns out I need this moment as much as he does, and now that I've come around to the idea, I'm impatient. Desperate. I want these few minutes of escape before we have to confront the reality of our situation.

Mac drops his towel and by the time it hits the floor, I've hooked one leg around his hip, drawing him closer. He arches one brow, his mouth curving in a lopsided smile, but he doesn't resist. Wrapping one arm around me, his hand splayed across the small of my back, he dips his head to kiss me and guides his erection between my legs.

Over a dozen years, we've spent a combined total of six or seven months together. We've made the most of it, at least in the sack, but no matter how many times we've had sex, the first slide of his cock inside me never fails to make my breath catch in my throat, my pulse pound in my ears. And then he kisses me, and a soft moan slips from my mouth to his mouth.

Neither of us speaks; I guess he doesn't know what to say any more than I do but it doesn't matter. We don't need to. Balanced on the edge of the counter with my legs around his waist and my hands on his shoulders, we rock together, hands and mouths exploring. In some strange, indefinable way, it's unfamiliar, as if we're learning each other in entirely new ways. Maybe I'm a foolish romantic, maybe I'm setting myself up for heartbreak, maybe it's just pregnancy hormones, but this almost feels like the beginning of a future.

On top of everything else, his soft kisses and tender touches are too much, too overwhelming. I feel like an exposed nerve, raw and defenseless, every sensation amplified by my vulnerability and we're both surprised by the abrupt arrival of my orgasm and the tears it leaves in its wake. With an array of low shushing sounds, he gathers me tighter to his chest, his lips gliding over my damp cheeks like he can erase the salty tracks of water with kisses. His voice is gruff, his warm breath puffing against my temple, when he says, "Don't cry, baby. I've got you."

"Just don't stop." Even I'm not sure what I'm asking of him. Don't stop making love to me on the bathroom counter? Don't stop holding me together when I feel like everything's falling apart? Don't stop being here?

Whatever I meant, he seems to understand because he strokes my cheek with his thumb and nods. "I won't. I promise."

"You okay?"

No longer weak-kneed and panting, we'd made our way back to bed and Mac's stretched out on his back next to me. His tone is casual, like it's an offhand question of little importance, but the sidelong look he's giving me suggests otherwise. He's probably worried asking might make me cry again.

I nod and give him what I hope is a reassuring smile. "It's just a lot. I'm sorry."

"It is a lot," he agrees with a sigh and reaches for me, pulling me closer until I'm draped over his chest. He has one arm locked around my waist, holding me there, while he strokes and pets me like an orphaned kitten. I'd gotten my tears under control earlier, but my nose is beginning to burn again. Cuddling with Mac just feels so *right*.

I can hear his heartbeat, strong and steady, and I concentrate on its reassuring thud and his solid presence instead of the creeping worries threatening to disrupt my nebulous calm and the alarming tender feelings I have for him. Neither of us says anything, and I don't know if he's intentionally giving me the space to collect myself or if he just doesn't know what to say either, but I appreciate it. Still, we can't ignore this forever and my voice is strong if quiet when I finally gather the courage to ask, "What are we going to do?"

Mac grunts, his fingers flexing over the curve of my ass, and the silence stretches so long it startles me when he says, "First, you're going to take a test."

"I already know what the test will say." And I do, because it's not just the late period.

My breasts are sore, I've been feeling bloated, and I'm always tired, all things I'd written off as a combination of PMS, my recent bout of the flu, and my hectic schedule. Poor diet too, if I'm being honest. I eat like shit when we're on the road. But as soon as I realized I was late, I knew in my gut my assumptions had been wrong. Yes, a lot of that felt like PMS, but it's different too. Familiar. Like when I was pregnant the first time. I hadn't recognized it then, of course, but I do now.

"Humor me. I haven't done this before."

It's not an unreasonable request, so I nod, rubbing my cheek against his chest. "Okay. Kim's schedule is really tight today, but I'll see if I can find a minute to get away and pick one up."

"I'll take care of it."

It's kind of him to offer, but it seems like a bad idea. "How will you do it without Cece or Alex noticing?"

"How will you?"

That is, unfortunately, a fair point. Campaign events are always chaotic but it's not like we have scheduled stops at a pharmacy. If either of us tries to sneak away someone—most likely Cece—is bound to notice.

"Wait, I have an idea." Chin to his chest, Mac looks down at me, studying my face, his own expression revealing nothing. "Do you trust me?"

Well that sounds ominous. Even I can hear the hesitation in my voice when I answer. "Yeah. What is it?"

"Just give me a second." Mac grabs his phone off the nightstand.

"What are you doing? Amazon will take three days—we'll be in another state. I don't remember which one, but a different one...by then." An unfortunate side effect of our frenetic travel schedule is that it's simply too hard for me to remember it all. I'd never be in the right place at the right time if it weren't for Cece managing the details. I consider it a win if I know what state I'm actually in, never mind where I'm headed next.

But Mac doesn't reply, instead placing a call. I can't hear the other person when they answer so I don't know who it is, but he doesn't bother with a greeting. "Hey, are you going to be at Kim's meet-and-greet at that diner today?" This time when he pauses, I can hear the other voice enough to recognize it's a woman, but I can't make out the words or tell who it is. "Great, I need a favor... Ha, yeah, I know, but no, this is totally off the record... No really, this is personal, not work."

Who the hell is he talking to?

"Thanks. I need you to pick up a pregnancy test and discreetly pass it to Gwen. I'll pay you back." He laughs—I'm really starting to hate his laugh—and then adds, "Nope, not joking. Can you do it or not?" The person must agree, because after a short pause Mac says, "Perfect, thanks."

"Who the hell was that?" I demand, pushing up on his chest to look at him.

He tosses his phone aside. "Stef. She'll—"

"Are you out of your mind?" I sit up, straddling him with both hands braced on his chest, and my voice rises with each word. "I don't want anyone to know about this, and you go and tell a reporter, who also happens to be your ex-girlfriend, and enlist her to buy a test for me?" By the time I've finished, I'm more or less yelling in his face.

If I had to guess, he prefers being shouted at over being cried on and, to his credit, he doesn't flinch. "Okay, first of all, she isn't my ex-girlfriend. We just—"

"You do not want to finish that sentence."

"Fair enough." Mac has the gall to smile before adding, "Second of all, you can trust her, I promise. She won't breathe a word to anyone."

"Do you have any idea how uncomfortable this is for me? How would you like it if I made you get condoms from my ex?"

"Uh, I'm pretty sure there's no way I can answer either of those questions without pissing you off more." His hands are on my thighs, his thumbs gently rubbing back and forth over my skin. It's going to take a lot more than that to soothe my temper.

"I am pissed off that you are breathing right now."

"My point exactly." Mac grins, totally unintimidated, and leans up to kiss the side of my neck before rolling out from under me, sending me sprawling across the mattress. "Come on, we've got to get going. We're already late for breakfast, and Kim has that radio interview in an hour."

"I hate you," I sputter and climb out of bed, but the bastard just shrugs and disappears back into the bathroom, like he knows I don't really mean it. And if that's what he thinks, he's right. As upset as I am right now, there's something comforting about his nonchalant mood.

I definitely would have preferred he didn't drag Stef into this, but all things considered, it could be so much worse. I feel like I've been spinning out of control all morning, and his unruffled reactions have been the only thing that kept me from completely losing it. Even his ill-timed laughter, as irritating as it was, grounded me, and I almost wonder if he did it on purpose. Does he know that being angry with him is easier than confronting all my other out-of-control emotions head-on?

Probably not. His unflappable response to our predicament is almost certainly because he doesn't think I'm actually pregnant. Once I take a test and he can see the proof with his own eyes, shit's probably going to get really ugly, really fast.

GWEN

BY THE TIME we reach the diner where Kim is scheduled to eat lunch, press palms, and give a short speech, I'm resigned to the fact that Mac was right, we needed help to accomplish what should've been a simple task. Traveling with Kim to all of her events means riding in a caravan of chauffeured SUVs. Sure, Mac or I could ask them to stop somewhere along the way and they would, if time allowed, but the entire group would be aware of the detour. How the hell would we explain it? And it'll be almost a week until we get back home, allowing one of us to easily sneak away on our errand.

So yes, I can concede that as pathetic as it is, we need help, but why Stef? Reporter or not, if Mac says I can trust her not to gossip, I can accept that, because I do trust his judgment. But still, why did it have to be her? Why couldn't he have called in a favor with someone he hasn't slept with? Is that really so much to ask?

Kim is about halfway through her lunch when Stef arrives. She's standing in a group of reporters near the entrance and doesn't look at me for a long time. When our eyes do meet, she smiles and waves, like an acquaintance offering a friendly greeting from across the room. It seems perfectly natural, just like it does a few minutes later when she excuses herself from her group and heads for the bathroom. After waiting a few more minutes, I do the same; Cece is fortunately too absorbed in conversation with Mac to notice. I'll have to thank him later for providing such a good distraction.

When I enter the bathroom, Stef is standing in front of the sink, reapplying her lipstick. Meeting my eyes in the mirror, she caps the tube, drops it in her purse, and turns around, thrusting a brown paper bag at me.

"Nothing to say?" I ask, having braced myself for some kind of drama.

"We've all been there at one time or another." Stef shrugs, and her freshly glossed lips lift in a warm smile.

Okay, this is good. I can do this. Unrolling the top of the bag, I peek inside and find three pregnancy tests, all different brands. Surprised, I look up. "Three?"

"When it happened to me, I was young and broke, so I only bought one. It was negative, but then I worried there was something wrong with the test. Maybe it malfunctioned or something, you know? So I went and bought another one. That one was negative too, but I'd have bought a third one if I hadn't gotten my period before I could get back to the store. I figured I'd save you the hassle."

"Heh, thanks, I wouldn't have thought of that. Do you think..." Realizing I'm about to make a slightly weird encounter super awkward, I don't finish my question.

"What?" Stef raises both brows, her mouth pursed with curiosity.

It's a little rich, asking for her advice after I got so mad at Mac for involving her, and this has gone okay so far. I probably shouldn't push my luck. And yet...it's not like I want to talk to my sisters about this. Or Cece. *Oh, what the hell.* "I'm just trying to decide if I should do this now or wait until I'm back at the hotel tonight," I blurt, wincing as I say it.

"Oh, hmm." She frowns, tapping a finger on her chin while she thinks it over. "I guess that depends on how you're going to react to the results. And how you think Mac's going to react. He seemed pretty chill about the whole thing on the phone but I wouldn't blame you if you didn't want him hovering over your shoulder while you do it."

This is surreal. Not just because I'm having this conversation with a woman Mac was sleeping with in the not-nearly-distant-enough past, but also because it's actually helpful. Who'd have guessed? "Yeah, he was. I think because he's expecting it to be negative."

"But you expect otherwise."

It was a statement rather than a question, but I answer anyway. "I've already had a baby. I've been pregnant before. I'm pretty sure about this and I'm afraid when the test confirms it, he's going to…" What? I don't know, so I borrow Stef's word. "He's going to lose his chill."

After this morning, I'm not particularly worried he'll bolt, but there's a wide range of potential reactions between accepting reality with aplomb and abandonment. It's hard to guess where he'll land on that spectrum, especially since some of the calm I found earlier is evaporating with each passing minute. I don't exactly trust my own judgment at the moment.

"Is it cowardly if I do it now?"

"Girl, no. You want to do it now, do it now, and if he has a problem with that, tell him to go fuck himself. And if he's still being a dickweed about it, remind him that if he'd fucked himself instead of you in the first place, you wouldn't be in this situation. Game over, you win."

"Irrefutable logic." We both laugh and after a moment's hesitation, I add, "Is it weird if I ask you to stay?" It's bad enough that I'm hiding in a drab public restroom with a broken soap dispenser and an overflowing trash can to take a pregnancy test but I don't want to do it alone.

"Nope, I'm happy to hang out for a few minutes. This is a job for girlfriends and in this case, I can see why you don't want to involve Cece."

"Are we girlfriends?" I gesture between us before setting the bag on the counter and retrieving the boxes. Lining them up on the counter, I pretend my hands aren't shaking.

"Sure, why not? Unless it's weird for you, and I understand if it is."

Is it weird for me? I give her side-eye in the mirror and consider it while she helps me open all the packages.

I really, really expected this whole thing to be uncomfortable, but it isn't, mostly I think because Stef isn't. She's warm and friendly and doesn't seem at all resentful or jealous about my relationship with Mac. He insisted it was only sex and that they were friends, but I didn't really believe him, or rather, I didn't think he knew what he was talking about. Just because he believed they were friends with benefits didn't mean she believed it, even if she said she did. But maybe I'm projecting. Mac and I never had a traditional relationship and a lot of our connection did revolve around sex, but there was always something more than that too, even if I never could really identify what it was. That doesn't mean it's like that for everyone.

"Honestly," I say, "I thought this would be weird and I was pretty mad at Mac when he called you. You've been pretty cool, though, so yeah, I don't see why we can't be friends."

We've gotten all the boxes open and I'm halfway to the stall, the tests clutched in one hand, when Stef says, "That dipshit. He called me without talking to you first?"

"Right?" Smiling to myself, I close myself in the stall. "He acted like I was some kind of weirdo for being upset about it."

"Did you kick him in the balls? You should kick him in the balls."

"I didn't kick him in the balls. I like his balls." Juggling three tests while peeing and trying not to drop them in the toilet, all while also carrying on a conversation, is more challenging than I expected, and I nearly fumble the second one into the bowl. "Shit!"

"You okay?" She takes a step closer to the stall, her heels clicking on the tile floor.

"Sorry, everything's fine. I almost dropped one, but we're good." Remembering what I was saying right before my near miss, I ask, "Did I just make things awkward?"

"Not awkward. It's pretty obvious you like the man's equipment or we wouldn't be here right now," Stef points out with an amused chuckle.

When I emerge, Stef has already cleaned up all my trash, stuffing the empty boxes and other packaging in her purse so we won't leave any evidence behind. Smart. She watches without comment while I lay the tests out on the counter and set a timer on my phone. With that done I'm left with nothing to do but just stand there, staring at the tests, and Stef puts her hands on my shoulders, gently turning me away from the counter.

"A watched pot never boils and all that bullshit," she murmurs, giving my arms a gentle squeeze before letting go. "So, what do you think about working on the campaign? I think someone said this is your first?"

It's obvious she's trying to distract me, but I don't mind. It's better than standing here staring like an idiot, trying to will the tests to be negative. And it's certainly better than the worry and fear that will only ramp up if left to my own devices. "I like it. It's more exciting than I expected, and it's actually fun to interact with the people who come to see her, but the long hours and insane travel aren't awesome."

"Yeah, I hear you. When I was a little girl, I used to daydream about seeing the world." For a split second she seems girlish, with a faraway look in her eyes and a soft smile, but then she shakes it off, her smile becoming unnaturally bright. "By the end of my second election season, I'd crossed all fifty states off my list, so I don't mind."

"Me too. Half the time I don't even know which state I'm in though, so I'm not sure if it really counts. When I first started, I thought it was a little weird that Mac's PA travels with the team, but I get it now. If it weren't for Cece, the three of us would probably be wandering aimlessly, hungry and disheveled all the time."

"Oh, yeah, Cece is a lifesaver. A couple of years ago I was covering this stupid story about the mayor of D.C. who decided to give a lame-ass speech outside in February. I slipped on the ice and got a run in my nylons. Mac and Cece were there because they were doing some work with the mayor, so I asked Cece if she happened to have some clear nail polish. She didn't, but she had a backup pair of nylons, which she gave me. Then when I was bitching about the wind, she gave me a spare scarf. I swear she carries a whole department store in that shoulder bag of hers."

"No joke, she has everything you could ever need," I say, nodding knowingly. "A stash of protein bars, tampons, a sewing kit, a first aid kit, probably her own damn nuclear arsenal. If you have an emergency, or even a mild inconvenience, Cece will solve it or no one can."

The alarm on my phone beeps, overly loud in the near empty bathroom, and Stef's lips twitch. She gestures toward the counter. "Except emergency pregnancy tests."

"Yeah, except that." I blow out a loud breath and force a smile. There's no point in dilly-dallying when I already know what they're going to say. Still, the results hit me like a kick to the gut. *I'm pregnant.* Panic skitters through me, settling in the pit of my stomach like an itchy, clawing animal. My chest is tight and heavy, and I probably sound like I've run a marathon when I whisper, "All positive."

"Looks that way," she agrees and I jerk, startled, when she lays a hand on my back.

I thought I was prepared for this. After all, the tests are only confirming what I already know. But maybe in some small, unacknowledged place, I was harboring the fragile hope that I was wrong, and that just adds another worry to my growing list of them. If it's hitting me this hard when it's exactly the result I expected, how will it impact Mac?

With shaking hands, I use my phone to take a picture of the tests. I'm unsteady enough that the photo comes out a little blurry, but there's no mistaking the results, and I fire off a text before I can change my mind. "Well, I just sent him a picture, so I guess we'll see—"

I'm interrupted by the opening bathroom door. In a scramble, Stef snatches all three tests off the counter, holding them behind her back as we both whirl toward the door. We probably couldn't have looked more guilty if we tried, but Stef recovers quickly and thank God she does, because it's Cece.

"Oh, there you are! I was starting to wonder where you'd disappeared to," Cece says with a frown, her eyes darting between Stef and me.

"Sorry, that's my fault. I was holding Gwen hostage with girl talk, since we don't have Mac hanging over our shoulders for once. We were just talking about how he does this thing with his tongue that—"

"Eww." Cece scrunches up her face and raises both hands, her pointer fingers crossed like she's warding off a vampire. "Do not say another word."

"Okay, but it's your loss." Stef shrugs.

"I'll take your word for it," Cece grumbles, turning toward one of the stalls.

As soon as the door closes behind her, Stef wordlessly passes the tests to me, and I shove them in my purse. We share a brief silent exchange where I thank her and she hugs me and then I'm alone, waiting for Cece to finish in the stall and waiting for Mac to respond to my message.

∼

MAC

"That's really cool. Does she plan to—" I'm interrupted by the buzz of my cell phone vibrating on the orange tabletop next to my plate. Forcing myself to ignore it, I finish my thought. "Does she plan to get another degree?"

Cece and I have been chatting about her mom's recent return to college. Sharon retired last year, but apparently she's already bored and has begun taking classes to keep herself busy. I've met her several times—she and Cece are basically joined at the hip—and I can't say this development surprises me much. She's one of those people who just can't be still.

"I don't know. I don't think she knows." Cece shrugs and gestures at my phone. It's beeped again, reminding me I have an unread message. "You going to read that or just stare at your phone all day?"

Good question. The preview on my lock screen informed me it's an image message from Gwen. I didn't realize I was staring until Cece pointed it out but…yeah, I guess I am. It was so much easier to manage my feelings in the safe cocoon of our hotel room this morning. That is, if manage means ignore. She was so upset, it was simple to concentrate all my energy on her. Besides, I could convince myself it's possible…likely, even…that she isn't actually pregnant, but that's becoming increasingly difficult. Her strained smiles and jittery anxiety, even in the midst of another hectic day on the campaign trail, are wearing me down, upsetting my carefully cultivated denial, and now the definitive answer is probably just a swipe and a tap away. *Maybe she sent a picture of funny bathroom graffiti.*

Blowing out a harsh breath, I unlock the screen and navigate to my messages. Cece is excusing herself to use the restroom, and a faint alarm pings at the edges of my awareness. I should stop her, or at least slow her down, in case Gwen needs more time, but the photo has resolved on my screen and I'm apparently no longer capable of speech. Three little white sticks are lined up on a dingy gray counter. Two say pregnant, and the third shows a plus sign. Even disoriented as I am, I've seen enough commercials on TV to know exactly what that means.

Fuck. Fuck. Fuck. Motherfucking fuck.

My chest aches and my lungs are burning—perfectly normal, since I'm not breathing—and I clench my fists under the table as a series of rapid-fire questions assault my brain. How did this happen? What will we do? Does she want to have another baby? With me? Can I handle it if she does?

"Seriously?"

Alex's incredulous question from across the table jerks me off the merry-go-round of panic, and my wildly careening thoughts come to a shuddering halt. "What?"

He gestures to the empty plate in front of me, and I frown. I could've sworn I still had a handful of onion rings and half a reuben left, which he confirms when he says, "I ate the rest of your lunch, and you didn't even notice."

Under normal circumstances we're both good eaters, and that twerp fucking knows better than to take food off my plate. When I was about Tristan's age, we got into a wrestling match at the dining room table because Alex pulled a similar stunt. I lost my PlayStation for a month and it was worth it, but now I can't bring myself to care. I probably wasn't going to finish it anyway. My stomach feels stretched taut, like the surface of a trampoline, and I'm pretty certain if I tried to eat, the food would bounce back up just as quickly as it went down. It's a shame too, because that was a damn good sandwich.

"What the hell is wrong with you?" His head is tipped to one side, his lips curled down in a concerned frown.

"Sorry, I'm distracted today." Pushing the plate away, I add, "And not that hungry."

Alex scoots his chair away from the table, the metal legs scraping on the cement floor. "Gwen didn't give you the flu, did she?"

"I'm fine. Just a lot on my mind."

He leans away from the table, eyes narrowing with suspicion. I suppose it's hard for him to understand, since nothing ever puts him off his feed. That's probably why he's so tall. Fortunately, he doesn't press, instead deciding to change the subject. "Has Brian gotten the latest internal polls yet?"

"Sometime today," I answer absently. The bathroom door has swung open, and Stef exits to rejoin a small cluster of reporters without so much as a glance in my direction.

Alex hasn't noticed my wandering attention—or he's chosen to ignore it—and his voice sounds as if it's coming from a distance when he says, "I'm anxious to see them. Hopefully her numbers have improved against Hennessey. I think he's our only real primary threat and—"

He's still talking, but I've entirely tuned him out. Gwen's emerged from the restroom, Cece trailing after her, and I can't seem to take my eyes off her. She's been pale all day, her fine features pulled into a weary, tight expression, but now she's...wrecked. There's no other word for it. Her shoulders droop, and her plump lips are pressed into a thin line. Even her hair, normally a glossy, golden curtain around her shoulders, seems to have lost its luster. Impossible, of course, for that to be true. It's probably a trick of the cheap fluorescent lights, but her distress is so obvious it seems plausible.

And then her gaze finds mine and it's worse than receiving the text. The rush of panic when I saw the test results was about me, really. About my own fears and worries and insecurities. Seeing those same things in her expression is ten times—a thousand times—worse. It's agonizing, and I want to fix this for her, to make her feel better so she won't ever look at me this way again. Only, I don't know how or if it's even possible. And if I try... Well, odds are, I'll fuck up and make things worse, not better.

There won't be an opportunity for us to be alone and talk until late tonight, after Kim's rally. It isn't ideal and I loathe leaving her to stew in her misery all day, but maybe I can use this time to figure out what to say to her, because right now? I have no idea.

Slipping my phone under the table, I tap out a quick text to Gwen. *It's going to be okay.* That doesn't actually feel true and there is so much more we both need to say, but it's the best I can do under the circumstance. Hopefully, it'll be enough to reassure her until we can have a private conversation.

CHAPTER 3

GWEN

After returning to the hotel, I've been tasked with sorting through correspondence Kim has received from supporters, looking for any she might like to write back to. The number of people who've actually gone to the trouble of writing real letters instead of just sending an email is surprising, but it isn't an unpleasant job. It's inspiring to read about all the ways she's touched people's lives, and it's a nice distraction from my own troubles at the moment. Not that it's actually working.

"Have I told you I'm glad to have you back? I was starting to miss my shadow," Kim teases and slides into the chair next to me. There's a hint of concern in her eyes, and she rests one hand on my forearm when she adds, "You still look sort of awful, though. Are you sure you're over the flu?"

"I'm fine, I promise. I just..." Unsure how to finish that sentence, I let it hang.

I've never missed my own mother much. She wasn't a kind or loving person, even in her best moments. But there have been times I longed for a maternal figure in my life, someone comforting and supportive, and this is one of them.

It would be so easy to tell Kim too. She's the kind of person who makes others feel at ease, as evidenced by the stack of heartfelt letters in front of me. Combined with her own personal experience with unplanned pregnancies, it's tempting to unload on her. But I haven't known her very long and, with their longstanding friendship, she belongs to Mac, not me. If either of us is going to seek her guidance, it should be him.

Besides, I'm not without other people to lean on. I have my sisters, or I could call Lindsey. And there's Cece, of course, except much like Kim, talking to her might put her in an awkward position. I could probably even call Stef, a development I never would have expected in a million years. But it isn't the same, and it's hard not to be angry at my mom all over again for failing to be the kind of parent I need.

"You just what?" Kim presses, straightening in her seat.

"Nothing. I have a lot on my mind, that's all." *And I'll feel better once I've talked to Mac.* Other than a single short text meant to assure me everything will be fine, he hasn't acknowledged our situation and his poker face is superb. It's unfair of me to expect anything else. We're on the clock and now isn't the time for dealing with our personal issues but part of me can't help but worry his detached demeanor might be more meaningful than that.

"Well, just to be safe, why don't you skip the rally tonight? You can get some rest and ease back into the breakneck pace of the campaign," Kim suggests, folding her hands on the table.

It's an appealing thought, but this is my job, and I won't shirk my professional responsibilities just because my personal life is a dumpster fire. Besides, I probably wouldn't get any rest, anyway. Alone time would just give my churning worries more opportunity to overwhelm me. Especially since there is no chance Mac might skip the rally.

I don't need time alone right now, I need him. And more specifically, I need to know where his head is. His supportive response this morning was encouraging, but it's hard to say how he'll be feeling once he's had some time to think it through. "Thank you, but that's not necessary."

"I appreciate your work ethic, Gwen, but you won't be doing me or my campaign any good if you push yourself too hard, too fast." She sounds like a boss, practical and upfront, but her expression is every bit one of maternal concern, like she's giving me an eye-hug or something.

"I'm not sick anymore," I insist, inwardly cringing at the whiny note in my voice. *Christ, I sound like Tris.*

My stomach lurches. *Tristan.*

If I have another baby, what will he think? He always said he wanted a little brother and he must be pretty serious about it, because he said as much to Mac within minutes of their meeting. But would he still welcome a new sibling when so much has already changed so suddenly? How would it make him feel? Would it affect his relationship with Mac? With me?

Kim interrupts my thoughts, helpfully preventing them from spiraling out of control. "Maybe not, but something is wrong. Would it help to talk about it?"

"I don't know," I admit, careful not to look at her. If her expression matches the quiet concern in her voice, I'll spill my guts whether I want to or not. "But I shouldn't talk about it with you, anyway."

"Oh, so this is about Mac?" Of course she wouldn't need me to tell her that much. Kim is perceptive, a trait that unfortunately only makes me want to confide in her more. She would give good, helpful advice.

"Sort of, and I don't want to put you in the middle." Mac and I aren't, as of yet, at odds, but we might be before this is over. If that's the case, working together will be difficult enough—maybe impossible—and putting Kim in the middle would only make it worse.

"Come on," Kim says, pushing out of her chair and looking at me expectantly.

"Where?" I ask, but I'm already rising to follow her. She used her mom voice, stern but warm, and even though I'm a grown woman and she isn't *my* mother, it can't be ignored.

Kim doesn't answer, but it isn't hard to guess. She's taking me into the bedroom, the one place in her suite where we can be assured of a private conversation. No one else seems to notice our departure. Mac is on the phone, his brow furrowed as he has what appears to be a heated conversation with someone back at the DC office. Alex is deep in conversation with someone from the communications team, and Cece is taking notes for them.

Closing the bedroom door behind us, Kim takes a seat on the end of the bed, patting the mattress next to her. "What's going on?"

There isn't much point in delaying the inevitable. Kim is persuasive and now that she's got me alone, it's only a matter of time before she gets the truth out of me. Besides, if I'm being honest, I want to tell her. She knows from personal experience exactly what I'm going through and I want her advice. I want her to tell me what to do.

"I'm pregnant," I say, still standing by the door.

Kim's eyes widen and her lips part, her surprise evident, but she doesn't say anything. It's a little scary, wondering what she's thinking, and I lean back against the door, my hands clenched so tight my nails dig into my palms. "I take it this wasn't planned?" she asks, her expression settling into more neutral territory.

"Of course not."

"Does Mac know?"

Her question is proof of Mac's excellent acting skills and, not for the first time, I'm reminded how much he's changed. When he was younger, Mac never would have been able to disguise his emotions so well, especially not from someone he was so close with.

Or maybe he's just not that upset?

No. If that's true, it's only because it still seems unreal to him. Mac never wanted children and, though he's doing well with Tristan, it's just not possible he will be anything less than devastated once reality sets in.

"Yes, but we haven't really had a chance to talk about it. I'm afraid he's going to—"

"No, don't think about what he's going to do," Kim interrupts gruffly. "He's a grown man, and he can take care of himself. You need to focus on what's best for you."

"But—"

"No."

Frowning, I toss my head back in frustration, banging it against the door behind me. It's impossible not to think about how he's going to react, and not just for my own sake. It's his relationship with Tristan I'm most worried about. Things have been going so well between the two of them, and I'll never forgive myself if my getting knocked up again has a negative impact on that. "Can I ask you something?"

"Anything," Kim answers with a nod. "I've been where you are. It was one of the most difficult times in my life, but I don't regret the choices I made then, and I don't want you to regret whatever choices you make now. So, if it will help, I'm an open book."

"Even if Mac doesn't like whatever decision I make?" There's a part of me that wants her to backpedal and withdraw her offer. It seems like he has so few people who are unreservedly in his corner. He can't even rely on his family for that kind of unwavering support, and while I might long for a mother's guidance, my sisters will always have my back. I'm greedy for Kim's advice, but maybe he needs her more than I do.

"Even then." Kim folds her hands in her lap, rubbing the palm of her left hand with her thumb. Her voice is quiet but firm, her gaze steady on mine when she adds, "Mac is stronger and more capable than he thinks. Ever since he was a boy, he's always underestimated himself. Don't you make the same mistake."

"Okay." I nod, chastened, because she's right. Instead of lamenting that Mac should have someone in his corner, maybe I need to be that someone.

It's a terrifying thought, especially now. My heartbeat quickens, and I lean more heavily against the door on account of my suddenly wobbly knees. The only people I've ever given that kind of loyalty are my sisters and my son, and I've never questioned that they are equally dedicated to me. We're family, after all, and even my mother's abuse and eventual abandonment didn't dissuade me from my commitment to them. But Mac? That's different, because I'm not so sure he feels the same way. In fact, I'm pretty sure he doesn't, and this pregnancy only makes things more complicated.

"Good. Now, how can I help?"

"You could tell me what to do, because I have no idea."

Kim smiles softly and shakes her head. "I can't do that. You're the only one who knows if you want to have another baby."

"But I don't know—that's the problem."

"What was your first thought when you realized you were pregnant?"

"That Mac was going to hate me."

"And your second thought?"

"That Tristan would hate me. And that this might ruin their relationship. They've only just met and are starting to love each other. It all feels so fragile."

Kim sighs and gets up, coming to stand in front of me. "Tristan loves you, and children are more resilient than we give them credit for. He'll be fine. And Mac's problems are just that. Mac's problems. You're centering the two of them in a decision that is ultimately about you."

"But what kind of mother and…whatever I am to Mac…would I be if I didn't consider what was best for them too?"

"I'm not telling you to ignore them. But you need to decide what you want first. Once you know that, you can figure out how it will impact them and what, if anything, you should do about it. So, I'll ask again. Do you want to have this baby?"

Her question takes me off guard and confuses me. I've been so anxious about the ramifications of another accidental pregnancy that, as silly as it sounds, I haven't stopped to consider if I want another baby. *Do I?*

Lately, I've been mourning Tristan's maturity. Missing the cuddles and kisses and being needed. But at the same time, I have more freedom now than I did when he was small. As much as I miss having a little one to snuggle, I'm enjoying that too, and I don't know if I want to give it up again.

Especially considering I'm probably resetting the clock on another eighteen years of single motherhood. Because even if Mac isn't angry with me, even if he wants to be involved with this baby from the start, we aren't ever going to be a traditional family, and it will be hard. In some ways, harder than the first time. Mac's participation would mean I won't have sole control this time, which is for sure a selfish consideration, but it wouldn't be easy to give up. And maybe I'm just too tired for diapers and colic and teething again. *Maybe.*

"I don't know." My eyes burn with unshed tears, my voice quivering with frustrated confusion. I never expected to be facing this situation again, and I'm completely unprepared. Although it's cowardly and weak, I just want someone to make the decision for me.

A weird choking sound escapes my throat before the tears spill over, and Kim gives me a sympathetic look. Pulling me into her arms, she presses my face to her shoulder and makes soothing, shushing sounds, like I've done for Tristan and my sisters a thousand times. Like my dad used to do for me before he died. It should be strange to lean on Kim in this way, but it's such a welcome comfort I've been missing for so long, and it feels too good to let someone else be the strong one for once.

Kim guides me over to the bed and, still holding me and rubbing my back, we sit on the edge of the mattress. She waits patiently while I cry, whispering encouraging words and promising everything will be all right until it subsides.

I straighten, wiping my face with shaking hands.

With a smile, she tucks my hair behind my ears. "Feeling better?"

"Yeah. I still don't know what to do, but I guess I needed that. Thank you."

"Anytime. I remember when Jess told me she was pregnant with Amy. I was beside myself, because I felt like she was repeating the same mistakes I made, having a baby so young. I didn't want her to have to struggle the way I had in the early years, and I spent the better part of two days crying on Arnie's shoulder. Sometimes, you just need to let it all out, and then your next steps become clearer."

I don't know if it will work that way for me, but I do feel better. Like someone's opened the release valve on the pressure cooker and let some of the steam out of me. "No one ever talks about Amy's dad. Is he still in the picture?"

"That's a story for another day," Kim says, glancing toward the door and patting my knee. "For now, you and I need to get back to work. But I do want you to skip the rally tonight."

"But—"

Kim shakes her head, refusing to hear my objections. "You need some time to sort yourself out. We'll survive one rally without you."

They've already survived several rallies without me while I had the flu, and I feel guilty about missing another so soon, but I don't press. What would be the point? Her mind is made up. "Okay," I concede, but not without one last contrary complaint. "But I don't really think it will help."

"Maybe not, but it won't hurt." Kim pulls me in for one more hug before we rejoin the crowd on the other side of the door. Squeezing me tight she says, "I know it doesn't seem that way right now, but this is going to work out just fine. Focus on what you really want before you start worrying about Mac and Tristan, and you'll find your way through this, okay? And I'm here any time if you want to talk again."

I agree with a weak nod against her shoulder. But as thankful as I am for her generosity, I'm not nearly as convinced as she is about the eventual outcome.

CHAPTER 4

GWEN

WHATEVER KIM INTENDED when she ordered me to stay home from
the rally, it didn't work. Unless she actually wanted me to eat room
service in my pajamas while binge watching the latest season of *Project
Runway*. If that's the case, it's been a smashing success, but it certainly
isn't a productive use of my time. Then again, neither is thinking
about my current dilemma. That just makes me cry.

When it's time for Kim's speech, I'm unable to resist flipping the
TV over to one of the twenty-four-hour news channels. She might be
able to forbid me from attending the rally, but she can't stop me from
watching and I enjoy seeing the real time reactions on social media.

Tonight's event is being held in a packed gymnasium and she's
already at the podium talking about her education initiatives. The
camera pans the cheering crowd and I catch a glimpse of Mac
standing off to one side of the stage. He's smiling and laughing with
Cece and Kim's campaign manager, Brian, and my heart flutters. Mac
is so handsome when he's happy, his often-stern expression and
angular features softened by high spirits.

These days, that's a side of him I see most often with Tristan. At least, that's when he seems to be at his most relaxed and easygoing. Whatever his reservations were about parenthood, he's a good dad, and I can't help but wonder what he might have been like when Tris was small. Or what he might be like with a new baby.

Hoping to divert myself from that thought—and the warm mushy sensation it's prompted in my chest—I grab my work phone off the nightstand and open Twitter. If anything can distract me, it will, especially because there are several direct messages waiting for me. There's nothing out of the ordinary with the first few but I pause, my finger hovering over the screen, at the fourth message. The preview says @NoOneYouKnow83 sent me a photo. With a username like that, it probably isn't anything I want to see, but one more dick pic isn't going to kill me. On the off chance it's a legitimate message from a supporter, I open it with a resigned sigh. *Why does the internet have to be so awful?*

But instead of a gross closeup of some loser's penis, a bunch of college-aged kids fill my screen. It looks like a house party. No, a frat party. The high percentage of University of Georgia baseball caps and T-shirts are a dead giveaway. But what does this have to do with Kim or her campaign? Why would someone send it to us? There's no accompanying message explaining @NoOneYouKnow83's motives and it's just a bunch of kids having a good time, like they do every weekend in college towns around the globe.

As far as I know, no one close to Kim has any connection to the University of Georgia. Or Georgia at all, for that matter, and on first glance, none of these people look familiar. The intended subjects of the photo are the two girls at its center. One Black and one white, with their arms looped around each other and red plastic cups in their other hand, they are clearly having a very good time and I am one hundred percent certain I've never seen either of them before. I'll have to show it to Kim and the others to be sure, of course, but I don't think those girls are the reason we received the picture.

Bending close to my phone, I study the faces in the periphery of the photo, the people who just happened to be caught in the background, and my gaze snags on a couple on the right-hand side of the photo. They're so focused on one another that they stand out from the crowd around them. Two boys—young men—standing toe to toe, and my initial impression is that they're about to fight because the intensity between them is just so…much. But that's not right. They're too close; it's too intimate. The way their heads are angled, their lips just inches apart, and one of them—the shorter one, with shaggy blond hair—has his hands on the taller boy's hips, his thumbs hooked in the waistband of tall boy's cargo shorts. And tall boy…

Oh. My. God. I do *know tall boy.* That's Sean Hennessey. A much-younger version of him, yes, but that's him. The brown hair and slanted cheekbones are recognizable enough and the jagged scar on his chin is newer, fresher, but unmistakable just the same. I once saw an interview where he was asked about it and he blew the question off with a charming smile and a quip about the misadventures of youth.

It's obvious now why the picture was sent. Sean Hennessey is a candidate for President of the United States, and someone wants to stop him. Whoever they are, it's vile that they would sink to these kinds of depths to do it and my stomach contracts into a hard ball. The room service burger I ate earlier, which was amazing at the time, is now an indigestible rock.

I'll have to show this to Mac and Kim. Probably her campaign manager Brian too. But they won't use it. I wouldn't be working on this campaign if they were the kind of people who would and, to be honest, I'm not sure this picture is the bombshell @NoOneYou-Know83 thinks it is. Ten years ago? Definitely. But now? I could be wrong—I'm probably wrong—but there's reason to hope that democratic voters wouldn't be swayed by something that so clearly has nothing to do with his qualifications. The world is changing. Not fast enough, but it is changing.

But what if there's more? Maybe this photo is meant to be a teaser. Maybe whatever else @NoOneYouKnow83 has is more damaging. I'm tempted to reply to the message and ask why it was sent, just to see what kind of response I get, but I refrain. I'm way out of my depth here and I can't do anything until I've shown the others. They'll know what to do.

❧

BY THE TIME MAC RETURNS, it's almost one in the morning and he seems surprised to find me awake. I've turned the TV off and gotten in bed but I've left the lights on, and sleep still feels a long way off, if it's coming at all tonight.

His tie has been loosened already and his long fingers go to his throat, deftly unknotting it as he comes to stand at the edge of the bed, one brow arched. "You're still up."

"I got a weird DM on Kim's account tonight. I can't stop thinking about it."

"Another dick pic? One that's actually good?" One corner of his mouth kicks up in a tired smile and he tosses his tie onto the nearby chair. His coat soon follows.

"There's no such thing as a good dick pic."

"You only say that because I've never sent you one."

"Please don't. Your dick has gotten me in enough trouble already." It's a joke but considering our current situation it lands all wrong, and he pauses in unbuttoning his shirt to stare at me. "I'm sorry, I didn't… I mean, I was kidding."

"I know." Mac nods briskly and returns his attention to undressing. "So what was this DM?"

"A picture of Sean Hennessey. When he was in college, I think, and it pretty strongly implies he's making out with another guy." I sit up in bed and reach for my phone. "Do you want to see?"

He waves me off and shrugs out of his shirt. "In the morning. What did they say? Did you respond?"

"They didn't say anything and no, I didn't reply. I figured that was above my pay grade without talking to you or Brian first."

He nods and sits on the edge of the bed, his back to me, to take off his shoes. "We'll figure it out in the morning. Kim won't use it, but she might want to give Hennessey a heads up that someone is up to dirty tricks."

Although I was certain we wouldn't sink to that level, I'm nonetheless relieved by his confirmation, and it's good to hear they might warn Hennessey. It isn't required but it would be the decent thing to do.

Having told Mac is a weight off my shoulders. This isn't something I need to worry about. Senior staff will handle it, leaving me free to worry about other, far more personal problems. His thoughts must be moving in the same direction, because he glances over his shoulder at me before he stands to step out of his pants. "I guess we have a lot to figure out, don't we?"

I stiffen, my voice tight. "You want to talk about that now?"

"Will you be able to sleep if we don't?" He's naked now, and I allow myself to hate him for just a second. The way he looks, it just isn't fair. He occasionally gets up early to go for a run, even more rarely he'll check out the hotel gym, and he eats like a starving man who can only be saved by fast food and vending machines, yet he still looks like *that*.

His tattoos highlight rather than hide the definition of his arms, the ridges of his abdomen are men's magazine perfect, the muscles of his thighs bunching as he bends over the bed to throw back the covers on his side. His body is a work of art and in a few months I'm going to look like—

With an undignified sound, I stop that train of thought in its tracks. I don't know what I'm going to look like in a few months, because I don't know what I'm going to do. But Mac is still looking at me, one brow arched in question, so maybe now is the time to start figuring that out.

"Doubtful," I admit. I'm not actually sure having the discussion will help. This feels like one of those nights where I'll get very little sleep, no matter what I do.

"Same, so we might as well." There's an edge of anxiety in his voice as he stretches out next to me and rolls on his side. He hooks one arm over me, pulling me closer, and the solid, warm press of his body next to mine gives me courage.

"Well, it's going to be a pretty short conversation, because I was thinking about it today and it only seems fair, since I had to do it all last time, you have to do it all this time. Well, the parts you can do. All the thinky parts."

"Cute," Mac huffs with strained humor, his warm breath blowing across my shoulder. "But we both know the first decision is all yours."

I appreciate the gesture and wouldn't hesitate to veto him, but I still want to hear his thoughts. I *need* to hear his thoughts. "What do you think, though?"

"I think you're the only one who knows what's best for you and if that's what's best, it shouldn't matter what I think about it." He sounds so calm, like we're talking about where to have dinner or what movie to see, but it isn't lost on me that we're having this conversation in vague terms, neither of us apparently willing to identify the subject more precisely. Maybe that's a clue to what his opinion really is but if so, I wish he'd come right out and say it.

"That's not fair. I get that it's ultimately my decision, but I want to be able to talk to you about it. I want your opinion even if I end up making a different choice." It comes out heated, like I'm angry, and I guess I am. Isn't that the whole point of telling him? Of experiencing this together? It's a bitter pill to swallow that he's right here next to me and I might still have to do this alone. I refuse to accept that.

Mac nuzzles into my hair until his lips brush my neck just below my ear. His voice is barely a whisper and the soft caress of his breath makes me shiver when he says, "I don't know what I think. Partly because there's too much I don't know. Can I ask a few questions?"

"Yeah, of course." The agitation has drained from my voice and I close my eyes. The importance of this conversation has made me jitter with anxiety and I have to concentrate all my energy on remaining still.

"Are there any medical issues in play?"

It's a reasonable question—it even makes sense that it's his first question, but it still makes me laugh. It's a reluctant, surprised sound. As unexpected as it is welcome after all my worry. "Nope, healthy as a horse as far as I know."

"A week ago, if someone had asked if you wanted more kids, what would you have said?"

"I'd have said I was indifferent."

Mac snorts and nips at my earlobe, giving it a quick, stinging bite that makes me smile. "How could you be indifferent about something like that?"

"It's always been a black-and-white question for you and that's fine —it is for a lot of people, but not me. I've never had some driving need to have more babies, but I've never been opposed to the idea either, if the circumstances were right." When Tristan was little, I assumed someday I'd get married and have another baby or two, but as he got older it seemed less likely, and that was okay too.

"That's fair." He pauses long enough to drag in a deep breath before asking, "Did you consider it the first time you were pregnant?"

"Of course."

"Why didn't you do it?" His voice is so fraught with emotions I can't identify, my stomach clenches. It's strange the way having another person to talk about it with helps in some ways and makes it harder in others.

"Honestly, it was mostly inertia. At the time, not making an active decision was easier than facing it head-on, even if that led to a more difficult outcome." Also, I wanted to hold on to a piece of Mac, but I'll never share that detail with him.

He's quiet for several minutes, long enough that I might have wondered if he'd fallen asleep if he weren't tracing the line of my collarbone with the tips of two fingers. I'm about to ask what he's thinking when he blows out a loud breath and breaks the silence. "That would obviously be the simplest solution, but I don't know if it's the right one. You're right, I was always very certain I didn't want kids, and then all a sudden I had one and he's fucking amazing, and that makes me think maybe it wouldn't be such a bad thing to have another. All the things I missed with Tristan, I wouldn't have to miss them this time and that's tempting."

My heart skips two beats, the first with regret and the second with burgeoning excitement. I can never make up for the years Mac and

Tristan missed together and I will go to my grave grieving for what I cost them both with all the foolish, wrong choices I made when I was younger. But this could be a second chance for both of us and it *is* tempting. I can't get ahead of myself though. That alone isn't reason enough to have another baby, and I can feel his unspoken words hanging in the air, so I give him a gentle prod. "But…"

"But then I remember the reasons I didn't want kids in the first place, and none of that has changed. And then I think, sure, that's all still true, but I already have one kid anyway, so does it really matter if there's one more? But what about you and me? We're kind of a mess. Like, even if we both definitely wanted another kid, I don't think we're in a place together where we would do it on purpose right now, are we?" I shake my head, and he tightens his arm around me, pulling my back against his chest. "Right. And all of that boils down to what I've already said. I have no idea what you should do."

"It's a lot to think about," I murmur, but I don't really mean it. Mac might not be able to put all his feelings to words, but one thing he said distilled the situation down to its most basic elements for me.

Even if we both definitely wanted another kid, I don't think we're in a place together where we would do it on purpose right now, are we?

We aren't. Everything is still so new and fragile, both between us and between him and Tristan. Adding a new baby to the mix would be a mistake. Except… "When I found out I was pregnant with Tristan, it was the lowest point of my life. I'd just become responsible for my sisters and I was poor and uneducated and so fucking scared, and I had him anyway. What would it say about me if I didn't have this baby when it would be so much easier now?"

With an irritated sound, Mac shifts, pushing me down on my back and looming over me in the dark. Bracketing my jaw between his thumb and forefinger, forcing me to look at him, he brings his face close to mine. "It wouldn't say anything about you. Yes, a lot has changed since you had Tris, much of it for the better, but there are still plenty of reasons you might not want another baby now. He's closer to college than diapers, for one thing and, for another, I have it on good authority your baby daddy is kind of an asshole. No one would blame you if you don't want to extend your tour of duty with him."

"Tour of duty." I repeat the phrase with a snort and despite the serious conversation, I smile.

"The only person you have to justify your decision to is yourself. And whatever you decide, we'll figure out the next steps together, okay?" Mac murmurs, brushing his lips over mine. It's barely even a kiss, but the little hairs on my arms stand up, and my heart skips what feels like several beats.

Whatever you decide, we'll figure out the next steps together. He said something similar this morning, but I guess I didn't really believe him then. I do now, and it gives me the courage to make the choice I want. If he's telling the truth, if we really will face the consequences together, if we are a team, it will be all right.

"Mac?"

"Hmm?" He's adjusted his position again, his growing erection pressed against my thigh as he kisses a path down my neck.

"I want to keep the baby."

"I know." He's moved lower, palming one breast while licking and kissing the other. His tongue flicks my nipple, and my answering shudder of arousal makes it difficult to concentrate on the conversation.

Already breathless, I look down at him, my brows furrowed. "You do?"

Mac hums, then raises his head, his gaze meeting mine. "I figured you were struggling because you were worried that wasn't the right thing, and probably because you didn't know how I'd react, not because you didn't know what you wanted."

In the end, that was exactly the problem, and maybe it had been all along. "How do you feel?" I ask hesitantly.

"I'm...okay-ish." Mac grins, his teeth white in the dark. "Right now, it's my job to reassure you everything is going to be okay. I can't promise you won't need to return that favor in the near future, though."

"I can do that."

"See? We're going to be awesome at this," he grins before dipping his head and closing his lips around my nipple. It's hardened into a stiff peak, and the gentle suction of his mouth sends pleasure racing to my core.

"Oh, God, Mac, wait…" I gasp, pressing my breast against his mouth and threading my fingers in his hair.

He releases my nipple with a pop and leans closer until we're almost nose to nose. "We still have a lot to figure out, I know, but the next discussion is going to be an enormous fight and I am going to be an enormous dick about it, so let's not tonight, okay?" His tone isn't without humor, but there's truth there too. He's talking about money, he has to be, and he's right—it's going to be a battle royale.

There have been a few small skirmishes in that war already, like when we discussed his—and apparently now my—housekeeper, Juana. Mostly, though, he keeps bringing it up, and I keep avoiding it. With a new baby on the way, I won't be able to put him off forever. But tonight, for once, he is the one who doesn't want to talk about it. I'm not about to force the issue.

Spreading my legs, I elevate my hips, a silent answer and invitation Mac ignores. Instead, shifting lower, he leaves a hot trail of kisses over my ribs and abdomen until he reaches my bellybutton. Pausing there, he raises his head again to ask, "When will this start to feel real?"

It isn't surprising that it seems abstract to him. I felt that way too with Tris for a while. But I don't know how to answer his question, because it was the subtle changes to my body that sharpened the idea of pregnancy into reality for me. It will be different for him. "I'm not sure," I answer honestly, pushing up on my elbows. "Maybe not until I start showing or you can feel the baby move."

Mac nods once, satisfied by that answer, and drops a kiss on my hip before moving lower still. With one hand on the inside of my thigh, he pushes my leg up, holding me open while he uses the fingers of his other hand to part my folds. His tongue is hot as a brand when he dips his head and licks my slit from bottom to top, my hips jerking reflexively. That isn't what Mac wants, though, and he pins me to the mattress with both hands, forcing me to be still so he can lavish my pussy with attention.

In an unhurried, meandering assault on my senses, Mac licks and sucks at the throbbing bundle of nerves between my legs. Every swipe of his tongue brings me closer to the orgasm my trembling body aches for, but he takes his time, demanding I indulge in each piece of kindling he adds to the growing fire. It's more than I can stand, and I'm pulling his hair and mewling pathetically by the time he finally pushes me into the void with a gentle scrape of teeth and the thrust of his tongue.

Apparently having expended all his patience on torturing me, Mac rises up and buries his cock in my spasming center with one hard thrust. The satisfying sense of fullness and the pleasurable stretch of my body around his heighten and draw out my climax. This morning's more reserved lovemaking on the bathroom counter was about reassurance and comfort. This is different, rougher, like we're both trying to burn off our worry and doubt with an all-consuming fuck. The kind that will leave us both in a blissful fog when it's over.

Bucking and arching under him, I meet each driving rock of his hips with soft, greedy pleas. *More. Harder.* Mac grunts in answer, shoving one of my legs higher so he can get deeper, the wet sounds of our bodies crashing together loud in the dark hotel room. His hands and mouth are everywhere, kissing and biting and petting every part of me he can reach, and I cling to him, relishing the feel of his flexing muscles under my hands and the mild heat of his five o'clock shadow on my skin.

I'm teetering on the edge of another orgasm, my blood rushing in my ears and every muscle in my body quivering with anticipation, when Mac grabs my chin and kisses me. His mouth is hard, demanding, possessive, and his weight presses me deeper into the mattress, his tempo wavering. My skin feels taut, like it can barely contain the climax blooming in my center, and he groans, long and low, as we both come.

He's still panting from exertion, and his voice is muffled against my neck when he says, "I think I might be able to sleep now."

"Same." I'm not quite there yet, but I will be soon, once my racing pulse slows and my overheated, sweaty skin cools. I don't know if it was the conversation or the sex—maybe both—but my earlier pessimism was unwarranted. Already my limbs are unwieldy, my mind muddled by the haze of impending sleep. But when Mac tries to roll away from me, I cling to him, locking my legs around his narrow hips and splaying my hands across his powerful back, relishing the way his muscles ripple and flex beneath my palms.

"Lemme go." His voice is slurred with imminent sleep, and he makes a halfhearted attempt to dislodge himself from my embrace. "I'm too heavy, baby."

He is, but just now, I don't mind. His body stretched over mine is like an anchor, keeping me in this moment with him, and I'm afraid if I release him, all my other concerns will come stampeding back. The decision we made tonight has only created more questions I can't answer. More worries I don't know how to resolve. More fears I have to learn to conquer. I'm not ready to face any of that yet, and I'd rather be crushed by his weight than that of my own anxiety.

I press my face to his shoulder, inhaling his sweaty, sexy scent, then whisper, "Just a little longer."

Mac grunts his ascent and shifts, his body relaxing into mine, and the last thought I have before I plunge into sleep is that I never want to let him go.

CHAPTER 5

MAC

THIS WAS A MISTAKE. Gwen and I are both idiots, and this was an epic mistake.

We decided we would wait as long as we could to tell anyone she's pregnant, not just for the usual reasons people wait, but also because we wanted time to ease Tristan into the idea. Up until now, we've really only treated each other like friends in front of him, but she has assured me that Tristan understands where babies come from. According to her, once he knows we're having another baby, he'll see through the amicable facade and realize we've been hiding things. So the plan is to gradually introduce him to the idea that we're a couple, even if that isn't precisely what we are.

Since we were on the road, it started with our video calls with him each evening. We sat closer together, or I draped my arm across her shoulders. When a knock on our door interrupted one call, I kissed the top of her head before I left to answer it. Once we got home, we started holding hands and sharing the occasional chaste kiss in front of him. Tristan took it all in without comment, but he definitely noticed. It almost felt as if he was studying us like an experiment in science class, for as closely as he watched. But he didn't seem upset, and I liked being able to touch Gwen when I wanted to without worry that we're giving him the wrong idea. It was nice.

After two weeks of what seemed like success, we took what felt like a reasonable next step. Tristan and Olivia were on spring break, and we had a trip to Milwaukee scheduled for the first four days of their vacation, so we asked Tristan if he wanted to come with us. I'm not sure if he was more excited about traveling with us or about flying for the first time, but either way, his response was instant and enthusiastic. I wanted to reserve a suite so Gwen and I could share the bedroom and Tristan could sleep on the pullout couch, but Gwen was worried that would be too much too fast, so we had Cece reserve a standard room with two double beds. The idea was that Gwen and I would sleep in separate beds and Tristan could sleep wherever he landed.

It was a sensible plan that seemed even more sensible once Olivia got wind of it. She wanted to come too. Gwen was resistant at first, but I didn't much care. I wasn't going to be getting laid either way, and though it wasn't really any of my business, I felt like the girl's interest in politics should be encouraged. After all, she's planning to major in Government when she goes to William and Mary in the fall. Spending some time with Kim's campaign would be an excellent experience for her before she heads off to college.

It's a good thing I didn't mind, because she wore her older sister down in short order and it was settled. Gwen and Olivia would share one bed, and Tristan and I would share the other. Aside from the fact that Gwen wouldn't be riding my dick for the next four days, I couldn't see a flaw in the plan.

But there was a flaw, one Gwen at least should have foreseen. For the third morning in a row I'm standing in the middle of a hotel room in flannel pajama pants and an old Foo Fighters T-shirt while Tristan and Olivia stare at me expectantly and we all listen to Gwen eject the contents of her stomach into the toilet. The first two mornings Gwen played it off, saying she must have eaten something that didn't agree with her, but from the looks on their faces, that excuse is wearing thin fast.

What a fucking time for morning sickness. Christ.

"So...?" Olivia raises both brows and presses her lips together in a futile attempt to hide a smile. She obviously thinks she knows what's going on, but all I give her is a blank stare, because seriously, what the fuck am I supposed to say right now?

Tristan comes to stand in front of me, his brow creased with worry that isn't so easy to ignore. "What's wrong with Mom?"

"She probably just picked up a little bug or something," I explain, and I can even justify the lie, at least in my own head. According to Gwen, the baby is about the size of a blueberry. There are bugs the size of a blueberry. Bug. Blueberry. Bug. That's good enough as far as my guilty conscious is concerned.

Apparently sensing my dishonesty, he narrows his eyes. "Is she going to be okay?"

"Of course she is," I say, ruffling his hair in what I hope is a reassuring gesture, because he shouldn't worry about this, even if I can't tell him why just yet.

"I'm fine, Tris, really." Gwen emerges from the bathroom and she does look mostly fine, although her smile is a little shaky. "You need to get in the shower. We can't be late today."

Tristan opens his mouth like he might argue, but Gwen shakes her head and gives him a stern look that sends him scampering for the bathroom. It's possibly the fastest I've ever seen him move when there wasn't food involved.

"So, seriously, are we going to talk about the elephant in the room, or am I just supposed to keep pretending to be stupid?" Olivia asks as soon as the sound of the shower filters out of the bathroom. Gwen gives her a sour look, and Olivia points at me, her eyes wide. "Wait, does he not know?"

Not cool, Liv. Not cool. I don't know if she thinks Gwen hasn't told me or if she really believes I'm that clueless. Either way, it's a little insulting. I mean, all this pregnancy stuff might be new to me, but I'd like to think I would have figured it out on my own by now.

"Mind your own business," Gwen says to her sister as she flops backward on the bed. Then, rolling her head to look at me she adds, "We have to accelerate the plan."

"Could we maybe talk about this when we don't have an audience?" I ask, but I shouldn't have bothered. Olivia talks right over me.

"Ohhh, there's a plan? What is it? Are you getting married?"

Christ on a crutch, what is it with this girl?

I like Olivia, I really do, and after three days of her near-constant presence I feel like I know her pretty well. She's intelligent, funny, and —my favorite thing about her—she adores Tristan, though she likes to pretend she doesn't. Gwen has worked hard to give Liv every chance in life, and she's the kind of kid who'll grab that opportunity with both hands and set the world on fire. But right this second, she's giving me a goddamn headache.

"We aren't getting married," I answer when Gwen just lays there, silently staring at the ceiling.

"Why not?" Olivia directs the question to her sister.

"Would you marry that?" She flails one arm in my direction.

"Well, no, but I also wouldn't keep having kids with him, so…"

Look, I don't want to get married. I want that even less than I want another kid. Fuck, I'd have a dozen more kids before I walked down the damn aisle with Gwen or anyone else. But being talked about like defective produce in the day-old bin at the supermarket is not cool, and my wounded pride demands I speak up. "For the record, I never asked."

"Why not?" Olivia swings around to face me.

"Because—" I'm interrupted by my ringing phone, and that's really for the best. I probably wouldn't score any points with either of them if I made my position on that topic clear. But unfortunately, the call is from my mother. With Easter next weekend, I've been expecting to hear from her. I'm just not sure I'm any more prepared for a conversation with her than I am with the Pierce sisters.

Turning my back on them, I stare out the window and answer the phone. "Hey, Mom."

"Good morning," she chirps in my ear. "How are things going? Where are you now?"

"Milwaukee, and things are going great. How are you?" I could give her the detailed rundown of the latest with the campaign, but she really isn't interested. Mom cares about politics about as much as I care about scrapbooking, a hobby she has determinedly held onto despite everyone else in the world making the move to digital.

"Oh, fine, but I'm worried about your father. He's been working so hard lately, and he never came home last night."

Screwing my eyes shut and clenching my jaw, I take a deep breath before answering. "I'm sure it will be fine." It isn't, of course, because these days, *working hard* and not coming home at night means Dad has a new girlfriend. Actually, that's pretty much what it always meant, but I can't very well say that to my mom. Once, when I was a kid, I overheard them arguing about his cheating, but I don't know if she realizes he's never stopped and I'm absolutely certain she isn't interested in my opinions about him.

"How's Alex? I called him yesterday, and he hasn't called me back."

That at least I have a legitimate explanation for. "He will, but I've got him working on a special side project, and it's keeping him pretty busy."

That side project is scouring the background of anyone even remotely qualified to be Vice President. If Kim wins the nomination, we'll be ready with an in-depth profile on anyone she might choose.

"When will you be home? You boys will be back for Easter, won't you, Will?" The thought that we might not be there has put a discordant note in her voice and I cringe against the guilt that presses on my shoulders.

"Yeah, of course, we'll both be there. For dinner." I add the clarification before she can ask what I know would otherwise be her next question. Church. *No, thanks.*

"You should bring Tristan. Don't you think it's time we meet our grandson?"

No, no, I don't. Not that I have any real hesitations about introducing him to my mom. She's generally wonderful, if a little prone to maternal guilt. But my dad? I'd happily let Tristan go his whole life without meeting him. Unfortunately, there's no good way to accomplish that without also keeping him from Mom, and that hardly seems fair. Besides, Dad would never harm Tristan. My kid will probably be met with the same smarmy charm Dad uses on my mother and brother. At worst, he'll be indifferent. All the vitriol gets saved for me.

"I'll have to talk to Gwen," I hedge. "They might have plans already."

"Well, she's had a decade of holidays with him. You haven't." From anyone else, that would have felt like a not-so-subtle dig at Gwen, but Mom doesn't mean it that way, she's just stating the facts, and her voice warms as she continues, "But I can understand. I wouldn't have wanted to let you and Alex go when you were little, either. Bring her too."

"I'll talk to her, but no promises."

One thing I know about Gwen is she won't want to leave her sisters alone for the holiday. Never mind that Willie is grown and Olivia nearly so, she's not going to abandon them to spend the day with my family. If I mentioned that to my mother, she'd want me to bring the whole damn lot of them, which seems particularly ill-advised. Willa would be fine, but Olivia and my dad would be like oil and water. She just might be the only other person besides me who could get under his skin enough to crack his mask.

When I've hung up the phone, I turn around to find Gwen and Liv sitting side by side at the foot of their bed, both staring at me.

"I heard my name," Gwen says suspiciously.

No point beating around the bush. "That was my mom. She wants me to bring Tris—and you if you want—to Easter dinner Sunday."

"That's...maybe not a bad idea." Gwen chews her lip, considering it. "Don't you think it will be better if we introduce them to Tris before we have to tell them...?" When she leaves the sentence hanging Liv rolls her eyes but doesn't say anything.

"Well, yeah, I guess." She does have a point—I'll have to stop dragging my feet on this soon. But I'm still not convinced Easter is the time to do it. "I'd kind of rather do it on more neutral turf. It's going to be overwhelming enough for Tris, and I don't want him to be uncomfortable at their house."

"We could have dinner at our apartment, and you could bring your family. That would definitely be easier for Tristan," Olivia suggests, and it isn't a bad idea. There's still the possibility that Olivia might push my dad to his breaking point with her cheerful questions and bubbly personality, but under the right circumstances, I could maybe enjoy rubbernecking that train wreck.

"No," Gwen says firmly. "Our apartment is too small. Remember how crowded it was the other week when Mac and Diane were both at dinner? But..." Gwen looks up at me, the corners of her eyes wrinkling. She doesn't think I'm going to like whatever she's about to suggest. "What about your place? It's certainly big enough for everyone, and you have a whole dining room I'll bet you've never even used."

She's right, I don't like it, but that doesn't make it a terrible idea. Tristan might not be as comfortable at my place as he would be at home, but he's been there before, and it would definitely be better than my parents' house. But... "No one wants me to make Easter dinner, unless they want takeout." It's not that I'm a bad cook—I can feed myself just fine. I even enjoy doing it sometimes, and I can make a killer plate of nachos. But cooking a holiday meal for what would be eight—maybe nine, if Willie brings Diane—that's well beyond my skill set.

"We could cook." Olivia gestures between herself and Gwen.

"We?" Gwen's giving her sister some pretty impressive side-eye.

"Well—" Olivia starts, but as soon as she does, the sound of the shower cuts off and Gwen interrupts her.

"Not a word about whatever you think you've figured out in front of Tristan. Not a word."

"Yes, ma'am," Olivia says with a smirk. "But I don't think anything. I know."

"Whatever," Gwen huffs and rolls her eyes before looking back to me. "So, Easter?"

"Fine with me," I agree. And the more I think about it, the more I like the idea. It allows me to introduce Tris to my family in a setting he's at least a little familiar with, in a situation where there is plenty of distraction because it's a holiday, and his mom and aunts will all be there, adding an extra layer of comforting familiarity for him. It probably can't be much better than that.

~

GWEN

OLIVIA IS beside herself with glee. Kim has an interview on the local TV station's morning show and a friendly intern has taken Olivia under her wing, giving her a backstage tour and introducing her around. Tristan and I are waiting in the green room with some of the other campaign staff. He's sitting next to me playing Pokémon Go on my personal phone while I tweet with some of Kim's followers, who are surprisingly interested in the picture I posted of her in the makeup chair. Apparently Olivia isn't the only one fascinated by the behind-the-scenes details.

"Well, hello."

I look up at the sound of an unfamiliar voice, surprised to see Sean Hennessey and three of his staff entering the room.

"Good to see you again, Sean," Brian says, rising from his chair to shake hands. "I take it they're having you on this morning too?"

"Hmm, yes, and Carpenter after me from what I gather," Hennessey replies conversationally, but when he sees Tristan he comes over to squat in front of us, smiling as he asks, "And who might you be?"

"My name is Tristan Pierce." He puffs out his chest and offers a toothy smile.

Hennessey chuckles, his voice warm as he says, "And I guess you must work on Representative Dunn's campaign?"

"No, I'm just a kid." Tris giggles and rolls his eyes like he can't believe this grownup is so silly.

"Ah, well, then maybe we can be friends after all. I'm Sean Hennessey." He offers Tristan his hand and it's clear he likes children and is good with them. Either that or he's honed the skill to woo voters. Kissing babies is a lot more effective when the babies aren't screaming their heads off. *God, Mac is turning me into such a cynic.*

"Wait…" Tristan looks up at me, ignoring Hennessey's extended hand. He must have recognized the name from listening to Mac and I talk about work, because he asks, "Is this the guy Dad says might backstab us?"

My cheeks heat with embarrassment and I offer Hennessey an apologetic look. Last weekend, Mac and I were talking about *the picture* while Tristan ate his breakfast and watched cartoons. Kim wanted to alert Hennessey that we received it—a decision we all agreed with—but she felt it needed to be handled in person and scheduling a meeting between two busy campaigns was all but impossible. The delay was starting to make everyone antsy and Mac wondered aloud, with his characteristic bluntness, if Hennessey would go to this much effort if the tables were turned. Who would have guessed Tris was actually paying attention?

"Who's your dad?" Hennessey asks, an amused smile playing on his lips.

"I am," Mac says from the doorway. Judging by the grin splitting his face he overheard the whole thing. I guess I'm the only one flustered by Tristan's blunder.

"Mac, good to see you." Hennessey straightens as he greets him and it seems genuine. "I didn't realize you were a family man."

"I'm a work in progress," Mac says with a shrug. "You're early. The producer said you wouldn't be arriving until after we'd cleared out."

They seem to be sizing each other up, both of them wary but not unfriendly. According to Mac, they've met a few times before, mostly at various events around D.C., so I wouldn't have anticipated them to be quite this leery of one another. Then again, being in direct competition changes things a lot.

"I was hoping to catch you, actually. Jim says you and Brian have been trying to set up a meeting."

Interesting. They'd been pestering Hennessey's campaign manager Jim and both Mac and Brian had the impression he was blowing them off. Apparently their message reached the big boss after all.

"You want to do this here?" Mac scans the room, and I do the same. Besides Tristan, Brian, and me, there are still several other staffers lingering and most of them are doing a terrible job pretending they aren't interested in the conversation between Mac and Kim's chief rival.

"You tell me. I don't have any idea what this is about." He's interested, curious even, but there's caution too in the tilt of his head and lift of his chin.

Mac nods, his gaze settling on Brian. "Give us the room." And then, tipping his head toward Tristan he adds, "Would you mind keeping an eye on him for a few minutes?"

"I'll go." I start to rise, nudging Tris to come with me, but Mac shakes his head.

"Stay. You're part of this."

I guess I am, since I'm the one who actually received the message. There hasn't been any further contact so it's a pretty small part, but if he wants me to stay I will. With a warning for Tris to be on his best behavior, I settle back on the couch. The others file out of the room. Brian and Tris are the last to go, closing the door behind them.

When the three of us are alone, Hennessey crosses both arms over his chest and arches one brow. "Well?"

"We received a message from an anonymous Twitter account." Mac swipes through his phone, opening the encrypted screen shot I sent him before deleting the original picture off my phone. We weren't taking any chances that we might inadvertently be the source for a leak.

Accepting the phone from Mac, Hennessey glances at the screen, his expression inscrutable. "Ah."

Ah? That's all he has to say? This dude is cool as a cucumber and it's kind of freaking me out. I mean, I'd probably be unhinged right now if I were him.

Mac takes his response—or lack thereof—in stride though. "Gwen runs the campaign's social media presence. She's already deleted the original photo from Kim's DMs, so that's the only copy we have and I'll delete it too as soon as we're done here."

That gets Hennessey's attention and he gives Mac a sharp-eyed look. "You aren't going to use it?"

"If we can't win without dirty tricks, we don't deserve to win." Mac points to his phone. "Whatever that is or isn't, it's got nothing to do with whether you ought to be President or not."

"Then why even tell me about it?" He passes the phone back to Mac and shoves his hands in his pockets, his gaze sliding between us. Despite Mac's truthful answer, he's still suspicious. I don't really blame him.

"Because it's the right thing to do," I say, rising to join them. "I don't know who sent that to me. Maybe it's just some rando who happened to be at that party and remembered now that your name and face are everywhere. But it could be someone close to you, and if it is, that's a much bigger betrayal. You deserve to know that."

Mac nods his agreement before adding, "We also don't know if they sent it to anyone else. If one of the other candidates has it, or a reporter somehow gets ahold of it, there's no guarantee they won't use it so you may want to try and get ahead of it while you can." Cocking his head to one side, he pauses to rub his lip and consider his thoughts for a moment before adding, "You publicly supported Kim when the *Dispatch* broke that story about her abortion. We owed you this."

"You didn't, but I appreciate it. Like you, I want to win but I intend to do it the right way, so you can tell your kid he can relax. I won't be backstabbing anyone." The corners of his eyes wrinkle with faint humor but there's no doubt that photo shook him, even if he'd prefer to hide it.

"He'll be relieved to hear that," Mac says and his grin is more open, like it always is when he's thinking about Tristan.

Hennessey retrieves a card from his inside pocket and passes it to me. "My direct number. You'll let me know if you hear from them again?"

"Of course." I'm a nosy bitch who apparently can't help herself and, after tucking the card in my purse, I ask, "Do you have any idea who it might be?"

"Unfortunately, yes." He doesn't elaborate and as much as I might like to, it's impossible to pry any more than I already have without being incredibly rude. He seems to realize I'm trying to figure out a way to do it though, because he hastily adds, "Well, I'd better get moving…they'll be looking for me in makeup."

CHAPTER 6

MAC

IT'S LATE when I finally make it back to our hotel room after a dinner meeting with Kim and other senior staff that would have bored even the adorably wonky Olivia to death but there's a pleasant surprise waiting for me. My roommates have all fallen asleep watching TV. The three of them are huddled together in one bed, a half-eaten bag of microwave popcorn propped against Tristan's leg.

They look crowded and they probably aren't particularly comfortable, but after three nights of Tristan punching me in the kidney, I'm too elated by the prospect of a bed to myself to have much sympathy.

After turning off the TV and throwing the bag of popcorn away, I crawl into the other bed. By myself. It's heavenly. That is, until the sound of rustling sheets on the neighboring bed catches my attention. I squint into the dark, smiling when I recognize Gwen creeping across the narrow space that separates us.

"What are you doing?" I whisper as she lifts the blankets and slides in next to me.

"Trying to escape the two of them flopping around. It's like sleeping in the middle of a game of Twister."

"Olivia too, huh?" Apparently Tris isn't the only restless sleeper.

"God, yes. One of them is bad enough, but I'd rather be waterboarded than stuck between them for another minute." Gwen sighs and scoots closer to me, laying her head on my chest and throwing an arm over my stomach. "Plus I missed you."

"Yeah?" Even I'm not depraved enough to make a move on her when her sister and our son are less than ten feet away, but her admission is almost as good.

"Sure, you don't punch and kick me all night," Gwen huffs with quiet laughter.

"True, but there's something else I'd rather do to you all night." With one arm around her, I pull her tighter against me and slip my hand under the back of her shirt. Now that she's next to me, I can't deny myself the tactile pleasure of skin-to-skin contact, even if it is just the smooth skin of her back against my palm.

"Next trip, I'll completely forgo sleep," she teases.

Next trip? Uh, no. We go home tomorrow, and we'll be there for a week before we leave again on a short jaunt to Wyoming. But there's no point whining about that now, and I don't want to wake the peanut gallery in the next bed, so I simply say, "We'll see, but if either of them comes with us again, we're getting a suite."

"I won't argue with that." Gwen pats my stomach, and it's a surprisingly soothing gesture.

Her agreeable mood spurs me to raise another issue. "I've been thinking, maybe you and Tris should stay at my place Saturday night." She stills; I'm not sure she's even breathing. It's difficult in the dark to get a good read on her expression, but her silence and tense posture aren't encouraging, so I make my case instead of giving her the opportunity to say no. "It might be easier for Tristan if you stayed too the first time he sleeps over, and it would be a good opportunity to tell him about the baby, because we can't put that off much longer. All the unexplained puking is making him worry too much. Plus it's the night before Easter, so it will help him get even more comfortable at my place before he has to face the firing squad at dinner the next day. And since you're the one making that meal, staying over means you won't have to drag yourself out of bed quite so early to do it." All solid reasons, but the truth is, I just want them there. Both of them. But that isn't a winning argument. Not with her.

That should probably bother me more than it does, but I don't want to push her because I'm afraid she'll push back. For as much as I want more of Gwen and Tris in my life, there are things I don't want to share with them too. Or rather, things I want to protect them from. Like my dad.

"Okay." Her head bobs against my shoulder in a tentative nod.

"Yeah?" I ask, squinting into the dark. That was almost too easy.

"Yeah." She still sounds uncertain, but that's all right. She wouldn't be Gwen if she weren't wary about every new step in our evolving relationship.

Hell, I don't blame her. I don't know what we're doing either, and I don't know where it's going. The only thing I do know is where it isn't headed—down an aisle. But I love Tristan, and I care about Gwen, and on the rare occasion I manage to beat down my insecurities, I'm even vaguely excited about the new baby and the second chance I've been given. This time, I'll be there from day one. I won't allow either of us to sabotage that with our baggage.

And speaking of baggage, now seems as good a time as any to finally address the money discussion head-on. It's definitely a risk, what with Tris and Liv sleeping six feet away, but maybe their presence will encourage a calm, rational conversation. Is that manipulative? I guess maybe, but we're never going to get anywhere if all we ever do is deflect or yell.

Anticipating her reaction, I cup her cheek to prevent her escape and whisper, "We should talk about—" But the rest of the sentence dies in a hiss. She's slipped one hand inside my pajama pants, palming my cock, and I don't even know what I meant to say.

Gwen scoots closer, wrapping her fingers around my shaft and pressing her lips to my ear. Her voice is so quiet I have to strain to hear her—or maybe I'm just too distracted by her hand on my dick—

when she says, "Did you know increased libido is common during pregnancy?" That's news to me, but this hardly seems like the time or, more importantly, the place to take advantage of this information. Reading my mind, she gives my rapidly developing erection a gentle squeeze and adds, "Meet me in the bathroom?"

"Yeah." I swallow hard around the urge to kiss her, instead forcing myself to stick to my original plan. "On one condition."

"I'll be quiet." She laughs softly and starts to roll away from me, but I catch her around the waist and pull her back.

"Okay, two conditions."

Wariness creeps back into her voice. "What's the other one?"

"We talk about money first."

She doesn't miss a beat, and there's no question she's angry when she pushes away from me. "Bathroom. Now."

With a resigned sigh, I follow her, watching with raised brows as she barely manages to close the door behind us without slamming it.

She rounds on me, face red and eyes wild, her voice barely constrained. "What the fuck is wrong with you, Mac? You want to make sex conditional on me taking your money?"

What? I rock back on my heels, horrified. How could she have even thought that? "Absolutely not, and I'm pretty pissed you'd think that's what I meant."

"What was I supposed to think?" She's pacing the short length of the bathroom, refusing to look at me. "You said no sex until we've talked about money, and we both know how you want that conversation to end."

Leaning against the closed door to stay out of her way, I throw up both hands in exasperation. It's incredibly discouraging that we can't even talk about talking about money without arguing. "Two separate things, Gwen. Discuss money and then, regardless of the outcome, have sex."

She stops her pacing to give me a sidelong look. "I don't think either of us is going to feel much like fucking the other by the time that conversation is over."

"Wouldn't be the first time we've had angry sex." With a sigh, I scrub both hands over my face and add, "Look, this conversation isn't ever going to be easy, but we can't avoid it forever."

Crossing her arms over her chest, she faces me, chin raised and shoulders square. "You can't force me to take your money."

She's right, I can't. My attorney had a good, long laugh when I asked. According to her, custodial parents have the right to waive child support. If Gwen won't accept it, there isn't a goddamn thing I can do about it, except sue for custody, and the very thought of that makes me ill. I wouldn't—couldn't—ever do something so drastic. She's a good mother and hauling her into court would only make things worse. Even threatening it would be sinking lower than I could stomach.

But there are things I can do that are outside her control. The remainder of the trust fund I received from my maternal grandparents has been rolled into a trust for Tris and the new baby. It's enough to put them both through college and grad school too, if that's what they want. I've also rewritten my will. If something happens to me, every penny I have to my name will go to my kids. Sharing any of that information with Gwen would probably only upset her more, though. Especially since I made her, Willa, and Jake joint administrators if I die while the kids are still minors. I figure if it comes to that, maybe they'll have better luck convincing her to spend my money than I've had.

If I could understand why she's so insistent about this, I might be able to find a way to approach the subject that would be more acceptable for her. I don't really expect an answer, but I have to try. "Can you explain why you're so resistant to letting me help?"

She shrugs. "I don't need your help."

Yeah, that's about what I expected. "Do you understand why it's important to me that I contribute?"

"Not really, no." She screws up her face and shrugs, like she's thinking about it and just can't figure out why I care so much. "I mean, I guess maybe you don't want anyone to think you're a deadbeat or whatever, but you have to know I'd never let anyone say that about you. This is my choice. It doesn't reflect on you."

Her wording reminds me of another conversation we recently had and another choice she made, except that time she specifically included me and sought out my opinion. The inconsistency doesn't sit right with me. How could she care so much about whether I wanted her to keep the baby and yet be so dead-set against even hearing me out on this? I'd be able to make more sense of it if it were the other way around, but this? I don't get it. "Why did you care whether I wanted you to have an abortion or not?"

Gwen sucks in a loud breath, her body rigid. "What?"

This is the first time either of us has ever actually said the word out loud in relation to her pregnancy. If I'd thought through what I was saying before I said it, I probably wouldn't have used it now, but I did, and I'm not taking it back. I'm also not saying it again. "You heard me."

"I don't... I guess..." she stammers, feeling around for the answer, because she evidently doesn't know. Her shoulders slump and she closes her eyes, but when she starts again, she sounds more confident. "It was an enormous decision and I was so overwhelmed, I couldn't think straight. I didn't know what I wanted. But it's your baby too and I thought you might..." She trails off and her eyes snap open, her gaze crashing into mine.

"Say it," I demand. I'm being a dick and I know it, but she doesn't answer, and I'm not backing down. If I need to be a hardass to gain any ground, so be it. "You wanted my help. Kind of shitty of you, don't you think? You want my help when it suits you, and when it doesn't, well, too bad for me, I guess. But that isn't going to work for me. Either we're equal partners in supporting and raising these kids, or we aren't."

Gwen pulls her shoulders back, her spine ramrod straight and her chin raised in defiant challenge. "And if we aren't?"

She'd let me walk. It's a painful realization, and I feel like the breath's been knocked out of me. She'd rather I abandon them all than give in on this. It's right there, unmistakable in the stubborn set of her jaw and angry blue eyes. Someone has to draw down and, at least for now, it has to be me. Deflated, I rake one hand through my hair and ask, "Is there any compromise here? Or are you determined to maintain the status quo no matter what?"

She thinks about that for a minute, her lips pressed into a firm line, but her tone has lost some of its razor-sharp edge when she says, "What do you want?"

"Ideally, to give you a couple grand a month." She holds up one hand to stop me, but I keep right on talking. "Short of that, would you agree to putting Tris on my health insurance instead of yours?" It isn't much. We both have the same plan through the agency, and the company pays for eighty percent of the premium. The small decrease in her share of the premium and increase in mine are hardly worth mentioning, but it's *something,* and at this point I'll take what I can get.

"Okay." It's clear from the tight nod that accompanies her answer that she doesn't like it, but she's apparently willing to give in, just a little, for the sake of peace.

"And I pay any co-pays or deductibles for him," I push.

She shifts her weight from one foot to the other, but she nods again.

"Same deal with the baby once he or she gets here."

Nope, Gwen's had enough and she's shaking her head, although she doesn't sound upset when she says, "You want to be equals? You want this to be fair? Well, there's two of us, and there's going to be two of them. You can have Tris on your insurance, and I'll put the baby on mine."

Even though I know exactly how this is going to turn out, I'm constitutionally incapable of ignoring the opening she's handed me. "That's a really great idea, actually. You keep paying for everything for Tris, and I'll pay for everything for the new baby. By the time they both graduate high school, we'll be square."

She narrows her eyes and purses her lips, like she isn't sure if she's more pissed at herself for setting me up or at me for taking advantage of it, and despite the ups and downs of this conversation so far, I almost laugh. She sounds like she might be on the verge of laughing too when she finally mutters, "You're an asshole."

I can feel the corners of my mouth pulling up in a smile when I say,

"Right back at you, baby." I don't know why, because this whole conversation was a disaster, but a weight has been lifted from my shoulders. This is progress. Limited though it may be, with a little patience—admittedly not my forte—and a few more conversations, we might get there. Or at least close enough that I can live with it.

"There's still a lot of time to figure out how we'll handle the new baby," she says, I guess just to make sure I understand she hasn't agreed to anything yet.

I do get that, but she needs to understand this isn't the end of it, either. If we have to have a hundred arguments like this one, just for me to wrestle one more small concession from her, that's what's going to happen. "And until then, I'll keep chipping away at you. You know that, right? That the easiest way to get me to shut up and leave you alone about this is to agree to some kind of fair arrangement?"

"I'm starting to figure that out, yeah. Just..." She waves one hand, like she's looking for something. "Just be patient with me, please. I'm not trying to be difficult, and you're a good dad—a good man—for being so determined to do your share. But this is the hardest part for me."

"It would help if you didn't go straight to DEFCON 1 at the slightest reference to money," I suggest.

She's looking down at her feet, curling her toes against the beige tile floor, but I can see the corners of her lips curling, and she sounds amused when she says, "I'll work on that." She raises her head, glancing around the small space as if she's only just remembered where we are. "Why do we keep having all the important conversations in hotel bathrooms?"

"Don't ask me." I raise both hands, palms out, in the universal gesture of innocence. "I was perfectly willing to have this conversation in bed. I thought if you were worried about waking Olivia and Tris, you might not be as likely to yell at me."

"And then I had to go and ruin your dastardly plan by being horny." She takes a step closer to me, her lips curled in a playful smile.

"Uh, no. Being hot for my dick never ruins anything. Ever." Hooking one arm around her waist, I tug her to my chest and slip my hand under her nightshirt, cupping the curve of her ass. Twenty minutes ago, I definitely didn't expect we'd end up here, with a warm and willing Gwen in my arms, but I'm relieved we have.

"Definitely good news. You wouldn't believe the amount of batteries I went through when I was pregnant before." She leans into me, pressing her breasts between us. Even through both of our shirts, I can feel her hard nipples dragging against my chest, and my cock swells with interest. I don't know if I love her or hate her for being the only woman capable of taking me from furious to turned on in the blink of an eye.

"I wasn't sure if you were serious about that," I admit with a hoarse voice.

"Unfortunately, dead serious." I must make a face, because she hastily adds, "I mean, unfortunate then. This time…" She pauses to rock her hips, rubbing against the erection tenting the front of my pants. "Although, if I remember right, that wasn't really until later. Like the second trimester, maybe? This is probably just regular horny tonight."

"Still?" I want to be sure we're on the same page. The way she's writhing against me doesn't really leave room for a lot of doubt, though.

"Still." She smiles and leans up to bite my chin.

Gently pushing her back, I let my gaze sweep over her, taking in the generous swell of her breasts and the curve of her hips, both still covered by her nightshirt. *Christ, those pajamas.* I'm about to dirty fuck a woman in a girlish pink nightgown with a cartoon yeti and the phrase "Yeti for Bed" emblazoned across the front.

My eyes drift back up to meet hers, and I snag one finger in the collar of her shirt, pulling. "Then get this off. I want to watch your tits bounce in that mirror while I fuck you. And Gwen…" She stops, her nightshirt halfway raised, exposing her pink cotton panties, and gives me a questioning look. "Remember, you have to be quiet."

CHAPTER 7

GWEN

"Got you!"

Tristan's shrill cry draws me out of the book I've been reading on my phone, and I look up to find him dancing around Mac's living room, gleefully celebrating some unknown victory in the video game they've been playing. Mac is laughing along and shaking his head, not at all embarrassed to have been curb-stomped—Tris's word—by a ten-year-old.

"Maybe you'll beat me next time, Dad." It's clear Tristan doesn't think that's very likely.

"Maybe, but let's take a break." Mac beckons him back to the couch, patting the cushion between us. "We need to talk about something, tiger."

Oh. Though we agreed to tell Tristan about the baby tonight, we didn't really have a plan for how we'd do it. Mostly, I've been trying not to think about it, lest my nerves get the better of me, but Mac has taken matters into his own hands and apparently decided now is the time. That's probably for the best. My tendency to bury my head in the sand means if it were left up to me, we'd end up telling him some-time around when I go into labor.

Tristan's gaze flies to mine, his brown eyes widening with worry. "Is he leaving?"

My stomach clenches, and I rush to reassure him, grabbing one of his hands and gently squeezing. "No, no, nothing like that."

He glances toward his dad, the question still in his eyes. It's hard not to be a little hurt by that gesture. There was a time when my word was enough. I'm glad he's developing a relationship with his father, learning to trust him, but it's a strange adjustment, not being the sole authority in Tristan's world anymore.

"I'm never leaving you, Tris," Mac insists, the emphasis on the word "never" so heavy, even I feel reassured by it.

Tristan nods and starts toward the couch again, flopping down with all the enthusiasm a kid his age can muster for a serious conver-sation, which is apparently not much. "What, then?"

"Well…" I start feebly but I don't know what to say next. How do I tell Tristan what's happening, and how it might affect him, when I don't know myself? I mean, I *know* what's happening, but I don't know what it means for any of us. I don't know if I've made the right decision or how any of this ends. What if we all end up regret-ting it?

"Your mom and I are having another baby," Mac explains without preamble. Stunned silence follows and he waits patiently, his atten-tion focused on Tristan. A good thing too, because I'm on the verge of my own panic attack.

This was a mistake. It's too soon. We should have planned better for what we would say and how he might react. *We're doing this all wrong.*

"For real?" Tristan gives me a darting look before returning his attention to Mac.

"For real," he confirms with a nod.

Tristan hesitates for three heartbeats. I know, because I'm counting mine, thumping my anxiety in my chest. Then his eyes meet mine, his brows drawn down in a tight frown. "Why?"

"Because we want to," I answer before Mac has the chance to admit otherwise.

"But I like the way things are now." He crosses his arms over his chest and glares at us both.

Mac's eyes widen, his expression mirroring the turmoil knotting in my stomach. I knew this was a possibility. Likely, even, but I thought I was prepared for it, and I was wrong. "Tris, I know there's been a lot of change for you lately, and it's kind of scary. But we—"

Standing up, hands fisted at his sides and cheeks pink, he interrupts me to turn on his dad. "You've ruined everything. I wish I never met you."

Covering my mouth with both hands, I gasp. It isn't just a surprised exhalation. It's a real, visceral thing, painfully slicing at my insides. I should do something, say something, but he's stomping toward the stairs—and presumably the bedroom he giddily picked out this afternoon—and I'm paralyzed with grief and worry. If anyone has ruined anything, it isn't Mac. It's me.

"Tris, wait." Mac lurches to his feet, jolting me out of my stupor.

"Let him go." I lean forward, grabbing hold of Mac's forearm. "Let's give him a few minutes to calm down, and I'll go talk to him in a bit."

Mac opens his mouth to argue then sighs and closes it again, collapsing on to the couch next to me. His voice is rough when he says, "I really fucked that up."

I lean into his side, entwining my fingers with his and squeezing his hand. "No, it's my fault. I knew he might be a little jealous at first, but I didn't think he'd react like that, and I should have."

"I meant to reassure him. To tell him we love him, and even though some things will be changing, nothing will change that, but he didn't give me a chance." Mac sounds as baffled as he is hurt by Tristan's outburst and my heart squeezes with empathy. I'm certain Tris loves me, but it still hurts when he gets upset and lashes out at me. How much worse must it be for Mac when all of this is still so fresh and unfamiliar?

"Sometimes you have to front load the reassuring parts with him. He has a tendency to fly off the handle because he's—"

"Like his dad?" Mac interrupts, giving me a sidelong look.

"I was going to say young and not in control of his emotions yet."

"Well, I'm old, and I can relate." Dropping his head back against the couch, he closes his eyes, his features tense.

"I know he hurt your feelings, but he doesn't mean it."

"Maybe he does, though." The doubt in his voice is raw and hard to hear. I know exactly how he feels.

"He doesn't," I insist, tugging on his shirt sleeve until he opens his eyes and rolls his head to the side to look at me. "He's told me he hates me a thousand times. He never means it. Kids just do that. They're still learning how to process and express the things they're feeling. Think about how hard all this has been for you and me, and we're adults. He'll come around, but it's going to take a little time and reassurance."

"I hope you're right, because right now it feels like that kid ran my heart through a shredder then set the pieces on fire just in case." He laughs without humor and shakes his head, his gaze drifting back to the ceiling.

Putting one hand on his cheek, I turn his face back to mine, forcing him to look at me. "I am right. You'll see. I'll go talk to him now."

But he's shaking his head again, more firmly this time. "I think I need to do this."

My initial instinct is to insist he let me handle it. After all, I'm Mom, and I've been handling everything for Tristan's whole life. But I swallow the impulse. This is parenting, and Mac is growing into the role. It would be wrong of me to demand control, even if that's exactly what I want to do. Especially now, when he was the target of Tristan's anger. I'm not helping either of them if I refuse to let them work this out without my interference. "Are you sure?"

Mac shrugs. "Yeah. I mean, I have no idea what I'm going to say, but he's upset with me. I need to fix this."

"If you need me, I'll be right here." I can't resist making the offer. It's admirable that he's stepping up, but I don't want him to feel like he has to do it alone. I've been there and it's awful.

Mac nods and gives my hand a hard squeeze before going upstairs.

~

MAC

HESITATING in the hallway outside Tristan's closed door, I consider what I'll say to him. Whatever it is, he needs to hear it from me, not his mother, because I'm the one he lashed out at. Even I'm smart enough to know that. Besides, I need to start pulling my parental weight. Gwen shouldn't have to be the one who always deals with the tough stuff. Especially now, with another baby on the way. Lightening the load wherever else I can seems like the least I can do.

The problem is, I have no idea what Tristan needs to hear. She always seems to instinctively know what to say to him, but I'm fumbling around in the dark without so much as a weak flashlight.

I was only two when Alex was born, so I don't remember how I felt about it, but when we were older, I was terribly jealous. Our father was never particularly interested in either of us as individuals. He didn't care about our interests or accomplishments unless it benefited him. But what little effort he was willing to expend on his sons, it was all directed at Alex. And although this situation is entirely different, the root of the problem is the same.

Tristan and I have only just begun developing a relationship. After so long without a dad, it makes sense he wouldn't want to share me now. Hell, he might even wonder if I'll love the new baby more. It isn't true, of course, but I need to convince him of that.

"Hey, can I come in?" I ask, rapping on the door.

"No."

Right. Set myself up for that. But I'm the parent here, the adult, and we need to talk, whether he wants to or not. Except…

Hand on the doorknob, I pause mid-turn. I want to reassure him, and if I'm going to do that, he needs to trust me. Maybe he's just a kid but barging in when he's specifically asked me not to doesn't seem like a great start. Not if I want him to feel secure and confident in our relationship. In me.

"Okay." With a sigh, I lean against the door, my hands braced on the frame. "But I have some stuff to say, and I happen to know you don't have any headphones or anything in there, so I guess you're going to have to listen."

Silence. Being unable to see his face and his unwillingness to participate in a conversation makes this harder. It makes it scarier too, the destructive voice in my head insisting he meant what he said earlier. I can't allow myself to listen to that now.

"I never wanted kids. I guess your mom probably never told you that." *And she'd kick my ass for telling you now.* This could be a horrible miscalculation and backfire in a big way. But trust requires honesty, doesn't it? "I didn't think I'd make a very good dad. But then your mom told me about you, and we met and…you changed everything, because you're amazing. You're far too clever for your own good and you make me laugh and you've been so brave about letting me into your life. I couldn't ask for a better kid, and I can't imagine my life without you now. As much as I thought I didn't want kids before, you've shown me how stupid I was, and I'm damn proud to be your dad, Tris. I'm so sorry I haven't always been here for you, but I promise I'm here to stay now. The new baby won't change that. Nothing will."

Holding my breath, I press my forehead to the door and wait to see if he'll answer. Several long, quiet seconds pass. No luck. "There've been a lot of changes for all of us lately, and you haven't had much time to adjust to any of it. A baby will be another big one. Being jealous is pretty normal, I think, and I don't know, maybe you're even a little scared. All this change is a lot, and I—"

"I'm not scared," Tristan shouts through the door. I really am making a mess of this, but hell, at least he's talking to me now. Or yelling at me. Whatever. My mom always said beggars can't be choosers.

"Well, at least that's one of us," I mumble. The truth is, I'm fucking terrified about a lot of things, and right now, number one on that list is how badly I'm screwing up this father-son chat.

"You're scared?" Tristan's voice is so soft and muffled this time I almost miss it.

"Yeah," I admit, although I'm not sure it's the right thing to do. Does he need me to be strong right now? Am I undermining that and only making this worse?

To my surprise, the bedroom door swings open, and Tristan is standing there staring up at me with wide brown eyes, so like my own that my breath catches in my throat. It's like I've been sucked into a science fiction novel, staring at a younger version of myself, and I try to shake the unsettling sensation away so I can focus on him when he asks, "Why?"

"Can I come in?" I lift my chin toward the bed behind him. I'm not trying to dodge his question, but I do need to decide how to answer, and now that he's given me an opening, I want to take full advantage of it.

Tristan nods, but the few short seconds it takes us to cross the room and sit on the edge of the bed aren't enough for me to formulate a response. He's staring up at me, expectant but wary, and all I can do is start talking and hope for the best. "I'm afraid of a lot of things. Lately, the thing that worries me most is I'm going to let you or your mom down. The new baby too, I guess."

"Why would you worry about that?" Tristan tilts his head, his natural curiosity peeking through his suspicion. It seems like a good sign, and my racing pulse settles ever so slightly.

"Because you're an incredible kid who deserves an incredible dad, and I don't know how to be that guy. But I love you, so I have to try. I'll probably still screw up a lot—like tonight—but that just means I have to love you as hard as I can and hope that's enough to make up for the stuff I get wrong." This is the first time I've told him I love him and, like the day we met, it feels like time is standing still while I wait for his response.

"Will you love the new baby?"

I don't know what I expected him to say, but that question hadn't been on my mental list. Still, this is an easy one to answer which, after all my fumbling, is a relief. "Yeah, I will. But I… It's not like money, Tris, where there's only so much to go around. Just because I'll love the baby doesn't mean I'll love you any less. I'm not going to lie to you, though, life will be different with a baby around. Maybe you could talk to your Aunt Willie about that. I think she was about your age when you came along. But whatever else changes, it isn't going to change how much I love you."

Suggesting he talk to Willa was a stroke of genius, and I'm still busy patting myself on the back when Tristan says, "But it isn't fair. I don't want to share you. And what if it's a girl?"

With a sigh, I tackle his second worry first, because it's the easiest. It's not like I don't understand where he's coming from. Olivia alone is a force to be reckoned with, and I've been bracing all week for the hurricane sure to develop with her and my dad in the same house tomorrow. "We do have a lot of girls in our life already, don't we? But they're pretty great and we love them and, if you end up with a little sister and you give her a fair chance, I'm certain you're going to love her a lot more than you think right now."

"I guess," Tristan concedes, and although he's still skeptical, it seems like we're moving in the right direction.

"As far as sharing me, that's true, you'll have to, and it's okay to be a little upset or scared about that, but I promise I'll always make time for you. You and I have a lot of catching up to do, and we're still going to do that."

How I'm going to keep that promise is a mystery, but I am going to keep it. Between work and all the travel that entails, and Gwen, and my family drama, it's hard enough now. It will only be harder with a baby, and I'm realistic enough to know the end of Kim's campaign won't offer much respite. It's the nature of my job. There's always another campaign or an A-list celebrity with a coke problem and a self-destructive streak a mile wide who needs me to clean up their messes.

"Okay." Tristan nods, his shoulders relaxing just a little. He isn't exactly happy about getting a new sibling, but that's probably too much to hope for this soon anyway. At least he's talking to me now. As long as we have that, we can figure the rest out as we go. Or at least, I hope that's the case. It's pretty much the same approach I'm taking with his mother, with only limited success, so what the hell do I know?

"Do you have any other questions? Anything else you want to talk about?"

"I just don't understand why you want to have another baby."

How am I supposed to explain that to a ten-year-old? Especially when we didn't plan this? All the sappy shit people say in books and movies doesn't really apply to our particular situation. It's too simple, too trite. And I can't very well tell him the truth. *Son, it was an accident, but then we decided to keep the baby because...I don't know why, we just did.* Yeah, no, I can't say that. "I, uh… I mean… I think maybe you'll understand when you're older."

"I know about sex, Dad."

My brain short circuits because he's giving me a serious, somewhat disdainful look. Like I'm an idiot for thinking he didn't know when that isn't even what I was talking about. "Right, of course," I stammer before trying again. "But I wasn't talking about the how, I was talking about the why. There are a lot of different reasons adults might decide to have a baby and it's all kind of complicated. I'm not sure I know how to explain it."

"I'll ask Mom." Tristan nods decisively, certain Gwen will have the answer. She probably will.

"Speaking of your mom, why don't we go see what she's up to?"

Tristan nods, and we're halfway to the stairs when he stops abruptly and turns toward me, throwing his arms around my waist mid-stride. I nearly trip over him, and I'm definitely choking on the emotion knotting in my throat. This parenting gig is hard, and I'm not naive enough to think I solved anything tonight, but one thing is certain. The feel of his thin arms stretched around my middle and his head pressed to my stomach is so, so worth all the overwhelming heartache and confusion.

CHAPTER 8

GWEN

"Did I mention last time you stayed over how much I like having you here?" Mac mumbles into my hair, his voice rough with sleep.

"Pretty obvious." Turning my face into my pillow, I smile and push my hips back. We're spooning, his morning wood nestled against the seam of my ass, and he groans at the increased pressure. "But Tristan will be up any time now." I'm not sure what time it is. Still early, judging by the golden sunlight peeking through the blinds. Like his mother—and apparently his father—Tris sometimes lingers in bed on mornings he doesn't have anything better to do. Unfortunately for us, the basket of chocolate that awaits him downstairs qualifies as better than lounging in bed, and there will be no dawdling today.

"That actually wasn't a come-on," Mac says with mock offense, his hand skimming down my side to rest on my hip.

"Oh, please," I scoff. "You're always down to fuck. Everything is a come-on with you."

Mac's chest vibrates against my back with quiet laughter, and a warm, fizzy sensation buzzes through me. It's still hours before our families will arrive and, for the moment anyway, Tris is asleep. For once, there is time for playful cuddling while we take our time waking up. It's an easy intimacy missing on the road, sleeping in nondescript hotel rooms—all different and yet the same—in a long list of cities I've already forgotten, rushing from one meeting or rally to the next. It seems *real.*

"I feel obligated to start playing hard to get now." But even as Mac says this, his hand is creeping under the T-shirt I wore to bed.

Closing my eyes against the warm rush of anticipation, I roll onto my back. "If this is hard to get, I think I'll manage."

Mac licks his lips and leans closer, one side of his mouth kicking up in a crooked smile that makes my heart skip. "You—"

"Mom!" Tristan's shout is followed by pounding footsteps on the stairs.

We scramble to opposite sides of the bed just in time, Mac's bedroom door swinging open with enough force to bounce off the wall. Tristan skids into the room, arms flailing and cheeks pink with excitement, and I'm envious. It's been a long time since I've had that much energy straight out of bed.

"Mom, it's time for—"

"What did I say last night?" Mac interrupts, his brow creased in a deep furrow, the comforter bunched around his waist to disguise his erection. It's the sharpest I've ever seen him act toward Tristan, but our kid is unfazed. Confused but unfazed.

"A lot of stuff." Tristan's thin shoulders rise and fall in a shrug.

"About knocking?" Mac prompts with an exasperated sigh.

"Oh." Tristan's eyes light up and he turns on his heel, darting from the room and closing the door behind him. Mac's head thumps against the headboard, and he looks up at the ceiling with a dramatic sigh when Tristan smacks his fist against the door.

Pressing one hand over my mouth to hide the smile that would only encourage Tristan and irritate Mac, I say, "Come in."

For the second time this morning, Tristan bursts through the door. Mac doesn't wait for him to reach the bed before he says, "You're old enough now that you need to start respecting people's privacy. That means knocking, not just here but at your mom's place too. No more barging into her bedroom anymore, either."

My stomach drops, and I stare at Tris, silently willing him not to blow my cover. Tristan, with his face scrunched up like he's working out a PhD level calculus problem, isn't looking at me but his bewildered pause gives me an opening to distract them both. "Tris, why don't we—"

"But Mom sleeps on the couch."

Mac tips his head to one side, his gaze sliding to mine.

Shit. It was inevitable he'd eventually figure out our living situation. He's been to our apartment; he knows how many of us there are. All he needed to do was take a minute to think about it, and he would realize it doesn't add up. It'll be another thing we argue about, another arrow in his quiver full of reasons I should take his money, and I was hoping I had more time.

"Is that so?" Mac asks, his gaze never leaving mine.

"Yeah." Tristan shrugs, oblivious to the silent drama unfolding between us. With the way Mac is still staring at me, I can't tell if he's incredulous or angry and it doesn't matter. Even if it's the former, it will probably lead to the latter, and I really don't want to have this fight today.

"Go on downstairs," Mac finally says, turning back to a fidgety Tristan. "We'll be right down."

All too eager to find the chocolate I hid for him last night, Tristan is happy to comply and he rushes from the room, calling over his shoulder for us to hurry. As soon as he's gone, I start babbling. "It's just temporary. Once Liv goes to school this fall, Willa and I can share a room." Mac shakes his head and throws the blankets off, getting out of bed. Heading for the master bathroom, the muscles of his broad back flexing with each step, he doesn't respond, so I try again. "There'll be plenty of room then. Plus maybe we—"

Mac holds up one hand and clips out the words, "Later. We'll do this later." And then he disappears into the bathroom, leaving me with nothing to do but wonder just how big this fight is going to be.

∼

MAC

MY PARENTS and brother are about to meet my son, and I'm fairly sure I'd be nervous as fuck if my house hadn't been transformed into a three-ring circus in the last few hours. It's distracting, to say the least.

Gwen and Olivia have taken over my kitchen. It isn't their job to feed my family, so at first I tried to help. They strongly disagreed. Gwen said I was only in the way, and Olivia chased me around the kitchen island with a potato peeler in one hand and a wooden spoon in the other, cackling like the deranged little maniac she is, until I gave up.

Willa has taken it upon herself to keep Tristan entertained, which mostly involves sitting on the couch with him and swooning over the new comic books he got in his Easter basket. It's not entirely clear to me why Gwen gives him an Easter basket at all when they aren't religious, but then again, I'm about to host Easter dinner at my house, so I'm not in any position to judge. Probably it's just a convenient excuse to buy him some candy and a few small gifts, anyway. Despite how difficult it must have been for her, Tristan hasn't been deprived. It's admirable, really, given how much she's had to sacrifice to accomplish it. Sleeping on the couch, though? That's taking things way too far.

I've been kicking myself all morning for not realizing the situation sooner. It was bad enough before, but now that she's pregnant? It can't go on, and she must realize that. She certainly looked like she was bracing for a fight when Tristan told me. She's going to get one too, but I meant it when I said later. Dealing with my dad is enough for one day.

The doorbell rings and it must be Alex, since my parents won't arrive until after church. I encouraged him to come a little early, mostly because I thought spacing out the introductions might make the whole production a little easier for Tris.

After introducing him to Oliva and Diane, who is apparently

trying to win Gwen over by making herself useful in the kitchen, Alex and I join Willa and Tristan in the living room. Willa catches my eye, both brows raised, but I shake my head. Introductions can wait for Tristan to finish showing her his loot.

"You know," Alex says, giving me a sidelong look when Willa says something that makes Tristan giggle, "I'm almost jealous right now."

"Oh?" I ask cautiously.

"This is a lot closer to what I always imagined family holidays were supposed to be like," Alex confesses with a sweeping gesture for the laughter and happy chatter emanating from my kitchen and living room.

The whole scene is warm and inviting and nothing like holidays in our family home. Which reminds me. "Should we place bets on how scandalized Dad will be when he realizes we're eating on paper plates today?"

Alex turns toward me with a horrified expression. "We aren't."

"Oh, but we are." And I'm already enjoying the turmoil such a minor act of rebellion is inspiring. Dad's nouveau-riche pretensions always chaffed at me, but Alex is more tolerant. He doesn't care about eating on paper plates any more than I do, but he considers this sort of thing unnecessary provocation. And maybe he's right, but I don't care. These little skirmishes in the much larger war are one of the few things I actually enjoy about my relationship with my dad.

"It's no wonder you two are always at each other's throats," Alex says, shaking his head.

It isn't really about paper plates, you dipshit. But Alex is rescued from death by sarcasm when Tristan closes the comic book in his lap.

"Thanks for showing me." Willa ruffles his hair before directing his attention to me. "I think your dad has someone he'd like you to meet."

Tristan slides off the leather couch and stomps across the room, mimicking one of the characters from his new comic. When he reaches us, he's bright-eyed and smiling, the suspicion he showed in the first moments of our initial meeting absent. I suppose that's because an uncle is much lower stakes for him, and he's been expecting it. Here's hoping he can maintain that once my parents arrive.

"Tristan, this is my brother Alex." And then, because I'm more nervous than either of them, and certainly more nervous than I expected to be, I hastily add, "Your uncle."

Tristan shoves his hands in his pockets and lifts his chin in greeting. "Hi."

For a fraction of a second I'm struck by how grown-up he looks, and a strange discomfort knots my stomach. *I've missed so much.* But then Alex is crouching, effortlessly engaging Tris in conversation, and the moment passes. He's a squirming, laughing boy again, and he somehow convinces his newfound uncle to join him in a game of Uno with Willa. My brother has never been much for games. At least, he never wanted to play with me when we were kids. Too serious for video games, too competitive for board games. Apparently, Uno is his weakness. Who knew?

It's a far more cutthroat game than I remember, though. Granted, I probably haven't played in twenty-five years, but Willa and Tristan are ruthless. She isn't even cutting him any slack for being a kid, not that he really needs it. And they're both trouncing Alex, his jaw clenching every time he gets skipped or is forced to draw more cards.

In the midst of setting the table for dinner, Olivia is closest to the stairs when the doorbell rings for the second time. "I'll get it," she calls over her shoulder as she bounds down the stairs, and I'm too stunned to stop her. She's taking her role as joint hostess a little far.

There's no telling what my dad might do or say when she answers the door, so I follow after her, hoping to prevent the day starting with an embarrassing scene. I'm halfway down the stairs when Dad's booming voice filters into the house. *Too late.*

"Who are you?"

"You must be Mac's mom and dad. It's so nice to meet you. I'm Olivia." There's a short, uncomfortable pause, and then she adds, "Gwen's sister."

I've reached the bottom of the stairs, and the scene unfolding in front of me is exactly as awkward as it sounds. Olivia is standing in the open door, hand outstretched toward my folks, who are both still on the doorstep. Mom looks cautious but friendly, but Dad is scowling at Gwen's youngest sister with narrowed eyes.

"Who?" he asks again, because he is exactly that kind of dick. It's no surprise he didn't recognize Olivia's name, but he knows damn well who Gwen is. He wouldn't be my dad if he wasn't trying to make someone feel small, though.

"This is Tristan's aunt," I clarify, grabbing Liv by one arm and gently pulling her away from the door, putting myself between her and my dad.

"Oh, right." Dad shakes his head, as if he can't believe he forgot such a simple thing, before twisting the knife a little further, just because he can. "I thought maybe you'd wised up and replaced Juana."

Wised up. Because Juana is an older woman with an expanding waistline and graying hair, while Olivia is young and pretty. None of which has anything to do with how well either of them would make my dinner or organize my closet, but those are the only factors that matter to him. With a wince, I throw Olivia an apologetic look and usher my parents inside. The sooner we get this underway, the sooner it'll be over, and that can't come quickly enough.

"Is he upstairs?" Mom asks, a slight tremble in her voice. She's been excited to meet Tristan ever since we made the plans for today's gathering, but now that the moment's arrived, she's nervous too. Well, that makes two of us.

"He is. He's playing Uno with Alex and his Aunt Willa," I explain, helping her out of her coat. Mom raises both brows, her lips parting, and I can't help but smile. It seems I'm not the only one mildly surprised by Alex's sudden interest in card games, and I almost say as much. Dad doesn't give me the chance, brushing by us and shrugging out of his coat. Without missing a step, he thrusts it into Olivia's hands on his way toward the stairs.

Olivia looks down at the heavy wool coat she's suddenly found herself holding, her brows drawn together in confusion. But then her expression clears and she looks up, calling after him with a syrupy-sweet voice, "Excuse me." And when Dad turns back to look at her, his own eyes dark with disapproval, she shoves his coat back at him. He doesn't take it, and it crumples to the floor at his feet as she says, still smiling, "You're rude."

Dad stares at her as if she's an alien, Mom gasps quietly next to me, and my face feels like it's going to split open with the force of my smile. I've always wished someone else could see all the little ways my dad mistreats the people around him, because Mom and Alex certainly don't. Or if they do, they refuse to acknowledge it. It's isolating being the only one to recognize his casual abuse, and exhausting being the only one to call him on it. But as much as I've always wanted an ally, I never would have guessed when I finally got one it would be Gwen's baby sister.

Before Dad can start berating Livie for daring to stand up to him, I force my smile down and say, "Hand me your coat and apologize to Olivia."

"Will." Mom's voice is soft, pleading. She doesn't want me to turn this into another battle with Dad. But I've rarely given him a pass before, and I'm certainly not going to now. Olivia matters. She's Gwen's sister and Tristan's aunt, and even if she weren't either of those things, she's right about him. She's a more welcome guest here than he is.

He holds my gaze for several long seconds. It feels like an eternity. But just when I'm beginning to think we all really might be stuck here until the heat death of the sun, Dad bends and retrieves his coat from the floor, and that feels like victory.

GWEN

WHEN MAC and Olivia come back upstairs, his parents in tow, I resist the urge to rush over and manage the introductions. He can handle this. None of them need me hovering, and thanks to the open floor plan, I can watch it all unfold from the kitchen.

Mac introduces them both to Tristan and Senior gives our son a terse hello, but he doesn't seem particularly interested in him. I'm not sure Tristan even notices though, because Joan's gushing enthusiasm is more than enough to keep him occupied.

With the initial greetings out of the way, and Mac's mom eager to get to know Tristan, Mac suggests she join the card game. It's a good idea, really, giving her an opportunity to interact with Tris and get to know him a little while providing him with the buffer of a game so he doesn't feel overwhelmed.

Even Mac gets roped into the game, which he didn't seem to be counting on, and they all gather on the floor around the coffee table. Except for Senior, that is, who says something I don't catch to Livie before taking a seat across the room. His disinterest in his grandson and the game everyone else is playing couldn't be any clearer, but just to make sure no one misses it, he takes out his phone, focusing all his attention there instead.

Liv rejoins Diane and me in the kitchen, whistling under her breath before saying in a hushed voice, "Wow, Mac's dad is an assh—jerk." Her abrupt correction of the curse word makes me smile. "Where's the liquor in this place? The boomer sent me to fetch him a drink."

I haven't been here enough to be familiar with where Mac keeps his liquor, and I haven't come across any in my exploration of his kitchen so far. There's beer in the fridge, along with a half-full bottle of champagne that, if I had to guess, is left over from New Years and probably flat as hell by now. Beyond that, I'm clueless.

"Oh, here." Diane turns to the fridge, retrieving a bottle of Pinot Grigio. "I brought this because I thought it would be nice with the ham, but you can open it now if you like."

Livie's brows draw together and she studies the label, her voice grave when she says, "He was very clear. He wants scotch. Two fingers. Neat." Each of Senior's demands is paired with an eyeroll but when she's finished, her expression brightens. "This will be perfect."

"You're terrible," I accuse, trying not to laugh. There is no situation where Olivia's mischievous impulses need to be encouraged but, in this case, I'm not inclined to discourage her, either.

"Remind me never to get on her bad side." Diane uncorks the wine while I find a glass. As she pours, she quirks an eyebrow and gives us both a sly grin. "Good thing I brought two bottles so we can spite-serve one glass and still have enough for those of us who will appreciate it later."

Grabbing the glass off the counter, Olivia smiles impishly. "I'll be right back."

With all the confidence of a seventeen-year-old who thinks she knows everything and is afraid of nothing, Olivia sashays into the living room and hands the glass of wine to Mac's dad. He takes the glass when she presses it into his hand and opens his mouth, likely to complain. But before he can get the words out, Olivia drops into a sarcastic curtsey. Senior snaps his mouth closed and returns his attention to his phone.

It isn't until Olivia is on her way back to the kitchen that I realize Diane and I weren't her only audience. Mac too had watched the whole thing play out, and when Olivia passes the coffee table, he catches her eye, a quiet look passing between them. On Mac's part, it conveys a muddled mix of embarrassment and apology. Liv's message is much clearer. *Don't worry about it. I'm on your side.*

CHAPTER 9

GWEN

A WOMAN. That was my only criteria in choosing an obstetrician. Well, that and being in-network with my insurance. Dr. Flores seems to have been a good choice, though. In her early forties, with dark, curly hair and a warm smile, there's something about her that is over-whelmingly friendly. Comforting. And more than that, she's being incredibly patient with me.

"My son will be eleven in June, so it's been awhile since I've done this."

She looks up from her review of the packet of paperwork I filled out before the appointment with a wry expression, but her eyes are smiling. "Not much has changed about having babies in the last few thousand years. You'll be fine."

"Right, of course. I don't know what I'm worried about." Shifting on the exam table, I jam my shaking hands under my thighs in a useless attempt to hide my nerves from Dr. Flores and, more impor-tantly, Mac. He's been quieter than usual all day, first at work this morning and now leaning casually against the wall, his gaze flitting back and forth between me and the doctor.

"Everything looks good here," Dr. Flores says with a final glance at the paperwork. "Based on your last period, you should be due November twenty-fourth. Ready for the exam?"

I bob my head. *Let's get this over with.*

"I'll be doing the breast and pelvic exams first, and some men are uncomfortable with that. It's up to the two of you, but if Dad wants to step out in the hall, I can bring him back for the ultrasound at the end. I'm just going to go grab my nurse, if you two want to discuss it." With that, Dr. Flores leaves the room, gently closing the door behind her.

Mac shifts against the wall, his eyes meeting mine, one brow inching toward his hairline in question.

Holding onto the scraps of my dignity is hard enough, shivering on an exam table in a pink hospital gown. And the exams are routine, nothing I haven't been through alone each and every time before, pregnant or not. There's no need for him to stay. But as embarrassing as it might be to have him watch the doctor poke and prod me, I'm not going to kick him out. I took away all his choices when it came to Tristan; I'm not going to take away any of them now, not if I can help it.

"It's up to you," I say with a shrug.

Mac swipes his thumb across his lower lip just once, his voice deliciously rumbly when he says, "I'm good, but if you want me to go..."

"No—I don't know, maybe it's silly, but I kind of want you to stay." And I really do. Yes, this is just routine, and having an audience for a pelvic exam will be mortifying. But maybe I've gotten too used to doing everything alone. Maybe it would be nice to have someone to lean on now and then, even for the easy things.

"Then I will." With a crooked smile and sweeping gesture around the room, he adds, "I've always wondered what this is all about, anyway."

"You don't know?"

"I have a vague idea. About like what you probably have of a dude's physical."

"Uh, everyone knows about that. The doctor puts her finger in your butt then tells you to turn your head and cough."

Mac's startled bark of laughter is too loud for the small exam room. "Apparently not, because you're a little confused. Those are two separate things. The finger is checking for prostate cancer, something they don't usually do until your older, and they grab your nuts and tell you to cough to check for a hernia."

"Oh." Heat blooms on my cheeks, but I'm saved from having to say anything else when Dr. Flores and her nurse return.

"You staying, Dad?" the doctor asks. He nods and, though she doesn't say it, I get the distinct impression she approves of that decision. Then to me, she says, "Go ahead and lay down and get comfortable, and we'll get this started."

The breast exam is awkward, but it could be much worse. Mac stays out of the way, and more importantly, out of my line of sight and doesn't say a word so I can almost pretend he isn't there. But a new worry crops up when Dr. Flores begins the pelvic exam.

What if my pregnancy changes the way Mac sees me? If he's thought at all about how it changed my body the first time, it was probably with some distance and detachment. He wasn't there. He didn't see and experience those changes firsthand. It will be different this time, and anxiety curls in my stomach. There are probably entire psychology textbooks written about men who don't view their partners the same way after they've had a baby. Once the reality of this sets in, will he still want me? And am I only hastening that inevitable outcome by allowing him to see this?

The potential answers to those questions bother me more than what Dr. Flores is doing, and that fact only makes me more uneasy. Mac has committed himself to our children, but he hasn't made me any promises. I haven't wanted him to. Sleeping with Mac was a casual, no-strings-attached affair. That's exactly what I wanted, or at least I thought it was. Now, the idea of him calling it quits because he's developed some misguided Madonna-whore complex or decides I've gotten too fat is devastating. As much as I wanted to believe our relationship is strictly sex, it isn't. Or at least it isn't only that. Not now.

When did that change? How did my feelings for Mac get so complicated, and why did I allow it to happen?

"Great, all done," Dr. Flores says, sitting back on her stool. It's a good thing too, because with a few more minutes, I'd have worked myself into a full-on panic attack. Over Mac. *What the fuck is wrong with me?*

"I'll just go get Coleen," the nurse says, excusing herself from the room.

"Coleen is my ultrasound tech. You ready for the fun part?"

My heart kicks in my chest, a well of old and new emotions opening. The familiar excitement of seeing my baby for the first time is tangled with a sense of relief that is entirely new. My life is different now, more stable, and whatever happens with Mac, I'm more prepared to be a mother this time. I'm free to be excited without every moment being tinged with worry about how I'm going to make it all work. That makes my joy bigger and fuller than it was when I was pregnant with Tris. It's overwhelming.

It isn't long before Coleen comes in and I'm squinting at the monitor, anxious to get that first peek. But as soon as the image resolves on the screen, my stomach drops. I'm not a doctor or a medical professional of any kind. My only experience with ultrasounds is from my first pregnancy, more than a decade ago. But even with nothing but those murky memories for comparison, I know this ultrasound is different. The quiet look that passes between Dr. Flores and Coleen only confirms my suspicions, and even Mac must sense the wrongness of the moment, because the heavy weight of his hand falls on my shoulder, his fingers squeezing.

MAC

"Is everything okay?" My question feels loud and intrusive in the hushed quiet of the room, emphasizing just how out of place I am here. But whether I belong or not, I have to ask. It's only been a few seconds since the black-and-white image appeared on the screen and I don't know what any of it means, but Gwen's brow is pinched, her body tense, and every tick of the clock feels like a thousand years. Something I don't understand is happening.

"Oh, yes," Dr. Flores exclaims, her serious expression morphing into a warm, reassuring smile as she turns away from the monitor to face us. "Everything looks exactly as it should at this stage, but you're having twins."

"What?" Gwen shouts, and the rest of us flinch, even Dr. Flores, who's probably delivered this news a bunch of times. I understand Gwen's reaction, though, because I'm racking my brain, trying to remember if there is some other meaning of twins that I've temporarily forgotten. Some definition that doesn't mean two babies. *Twins. Holy shit.*

"You're having twins," the doctor repeats with a soothing voice and a patient look that makes me thinks she's used to having to repeat herself in situations like this.

"See?" Coleen says, pointing at a roughly bean-shaped area on the screen. "That's one." Her finger slides across the monitor, indicating a second spot that's eerily similar to the first. "And that's the other."

"Oh my God." Gwen's quiet exclamation is followed by a strange half-gasp, half-hiccup sound, but I can hardly hear her over the thudding of my own heartbeat.

Dr. Flores rushes to reassure us, but I can't understand what she's saying. I seem to have gotten stuck on that one word. Twins. Unable to process that, everything that comes after it is a blur of meaningless medical terms and hollow encouragement. I'm like a broken robot in some second-rate science fiction movie. *Does not compute.*

Not even the sound of the heartbeat—heartbeats—jolts me out of my stupor. If anything, it makes it worse. I asked Gwen when this would feel real, and now, hearing first one steady thud and then the other, it has become very fucking real and far more terrifying than I ever imagined possible.

By the time we're walking back to my car, Gwen's next appointment with Dr. Flores scheduled for next month and a referral for a specialist in hand, I'm still struggling to make sense of what just happened, and Gwen has noticed. Giving me a sidelong look, she asks, "Are you okay?"

"Are you?" I'm not trying to avoid answering her. It's a sincere question, and far more important than if I'm all right. This must have been just as shocking for her and, at least until they're born, it will impact her far more than it will me. Who cares if I'm all right?

Gwen stops abruptly, and when I turn to face her, there are tears welling in her eyes.

Concern for her overrides my own confused panic and in two long strides I'm in front of her, pulling her into my arms and stroking her back. "It's okay. This is going to be okay," I say into her hair. I don't know if that's actually true or not, but I will do everything in my power to make it true.

"Will it, though?" She pauses to wipe her face and avoids meeting my eyes when she starts speaking again. "This doesn't change anything for me. I want these babies. But I understand if you want out."

There it is. My escape hatch. I don't know what makes me angrier. That she offered it to me or that for one, awful fraction of a second, I think about taking it. How can I go from promising her it's going to work out—and vowing to myself I'll make that happen—to contemplating bolting in a matter of seconds?

Unreliable. It's Dad's voice, whispering in my head, telling me I'm worthless. That I should run. That they'll be better off without me. It makes me even angrier. This moment should be about me and Gwen and our kids and what's best for all of us. My dad and the insecurities he's spent decades instilling in me have no place intruding here. Gwen and Tristan and now the twins, they're more important than he's ever been.

Cupping her cheeks in both hands, I tilt her head back, forcing her to look at me. Hoping she'll see the certainty in my eyes. "I'm not going anywhere. I promise."

Her lower lip trembles, both eyebrows rising, and her voice hitches. "You're sure?"

"Positive."

"Do you want to have sex?"

"Right now?" I ask, furrowing my brow. But I'm already scanning the parking lot, considering our options, because the answer is yes. It's always yes, at least when it comes to Gwen. Granted, we're both upset, so her timing isn't great, but maybe that will make her feel better. It did the day she realized she was pregnant. Why not now?

"No, I mean, later. Or ever." Her cheeks are turning a deep shade of red, and she shakes her head, taking a step away from me before I can respond. "Never mind. It was a stupid question. I don't know why I asked."

I think she does know, she's just embarrassed, and I think maybe I know too. When Jess was pregnant with Amy, she started dating a new guy fairly early on, before she was showing and I have vivid memories of her crying on my shoulder, worrying about whether he would lose interest when her baby bump became more apparent. Her insecurity was painful to witness, especially when there wasn't much I could do but listen, and I definitely don't want Gwen to feel the way Jess had back then.

The undefined nature of our relationship probably only amplifies her insecurities. We've both avoided labels and discussions about what exactly we're doing together or where we want this to go. I don't know why she hasn't mentioned it, but for my part it's because I don't know. I keep hoping that if I take one day at a time, the answer will eventually become clear. No luck so far, and I can understand why my *laissez-faire* approach isn't working for her. Especially now.

"I am not going to stop thinking you're the sexiest woman I've ever met just because you're pregnant, if that's what you're asking." Taking a step toward her, closing the gap she created, I pull her against me and kiss her before she has the chance to object.

It was meant to be a sweet, reassuring gesture but, as is often the case between us, it flares hot. Gwen is greedy, biting my lips and moaning into my mouth. The middle of her OB's parking lot is definitely not the place for this, but reassuring her feels more important than scandalizing a few medical professionals and their patients, so I don't push her away. When we do finally break apart, we're both panting and my voice is hoarse. "Does that answer your question?"

Gwen nods and touches her lips with her fingers, but I can still see the hesitation in her expression when she says, "I'm going to get fat."

"You are. So fat. Because you're pregnant. With twins, apparently." There's no point in sugar-coating it when we both know it's true. It's the next part she really needs to hear, and I hope she'll take it to heart. "But months from now, when you're so uncomfortable having sex is the last thing on your mind, you'll still have to chase me off with a baseball bat."

That earns me a small smile and a quiet laugh, but then she says, "That's sweet of you to say, but you can't know that."

"Can't I?" Pausing, I consider my words carefully. The last thing I want to do is reopen old wounds and upset her further, but there's only one way I know to explain it. "I have wanted you every day since the first day I saw you. Even after you disappeared without a trace. Even after you showed up again, pretending you had no idea who I was. Even after I discovered you'd had our son and never told me. Things aren't easy with us, they aren't simple, but in spite of all of that, I have always wanted you. So yeah, after everything else, I think I can be pretty damn sure baby weight isn't going to be the thing that finally changes it."

What still remains unsaid between us feels like it has grown exponentially in the time it took me to say that. Because while that speech was very pretty, if I do say so myself, and absolutely heart-felt, it was also entirely about sex. That doesn't make it any less true, and it was her concern about how I would react to her changing body that prompted it in the first place, but it seems to have under-lined the other, stickier parts of our relationship. Or non-relation-ship. Or whatever the hell you call it when two people keep fucking and having kids without talking about things like feelings or the future.

Judging by her conflicted expression, Gwen feels it too, but she's apparently not ready to try and put it into words either, because she only smiles and says, "Thanks, Mac."

"Anytime." Taking her hand, I give it a gentle tug, pulling her toward the car. "We need to get back to the office before someone starts wondering where we disappeared to, and there's something else I want to talk to you about on the way."

Gwen gives me a puzzled look but lets me lead her. It would be easy to find a reason to chicken out. This has been a rough, emotional day for both of us already, so it may not be the best time for the subject I'm about to raise. But it has to be done. I've been thinking about it for a while now, and I've become practically obsessed since Tristan announced she sleeps on the couch. That was bad enough before, but now that I know she's not just pregnant but pregnant with twins...it can't wait.

Once we're both buckled in and I've backed out of the parking space, I say, "I've been thinking, maybe you and Tris should move in with me."

"No." Gwen's answer is abrupt and decisive, all of her earlier hesitancy gone. That would be a relief, except now she's pissed and glaring at me like I suggested she move in with Hannibal Lecter, which is a pretty stiff blow to my confidence.

With a sigh, I grip the steering wheel a little tighter. "Just hear me out, okay?" She nods tightly and turns away from me, staring out the window. "It would be cheaper than maintaining two separate households." Prying one hand off the steering wheel, I count the reasons off on my fingers. "It would get you off the couch. And it would allow me to spend more time with you and Tris and the...babies." I almost said "baby." This whole twin thing is going to take some getting used to.

Gwen is unimpressed. "Even if I wanted to, and I don't, I can't abandon Willa and Olivia like that."

I can admit I didn't consider her sisters. I've had a lot on my mind lately, you know? But that's easy enough to overcome. "Then they can come too. I'm not trying to cause more problems for you, I've trying to solve them, and I have space for everyone."

"There's nothing to solve. Livie will be leaving for school at the end of August, and then we'll have plenty of room."

My frustration surges, and I have to take several deep breaths so I don't shout at her. "So you're just going to keep sleeping on the couch until you're seven months pregnant with twins and Olivia leaves for school?"

"Six months," Gwen quietly corrects me, and that stuns me into brief, confused silence. *Does she really think a few weeks makes it any better?*

"Okay, six months. And what happens after the twins are born? I bet Willa will love sharing a room with two crying newborns." It's impossible to keep the sarcasm out of my voice, and Gwen rolls her eyes in response. "You need to move, Gwen, and the way I see it, you've got two choices. Move in with me or let me start paying child support so you can afford a bigger place of your own." Even if she does move in with me, this isn't the end of the child support discussion, but baby steps. She's so resistant to accepting my help, I can't throw too much at her all at once, or she'll just dig in harder. I'm already pushing more than I'd like so soon after she conceded to switching Tris's insurance, but it can't be helped.

"You're being unreasonable."

"Am I, though?" We're at a stop light, a couple of blocks from the office. We need to wrap this up. "Just think about it, okay? And we can talk about this more later."

"Fine."

"Fine," I repeat with a stiff nod. I never expected that getting what I wanted would be easy or instantaneous. But I've laid the groundwork, and that'll have to be good enough for today.

CHAPTER 10

GWEN

As with everything about Mac and me, his birthday is complicated. I wanted to do something for him, because it's my firm belief that everyone should feel special on their birthday. It's the one day of the year that should feel entirely your own.

But what does a baby mama get her baby daddy for his birthday? How do I convey that he's important to me, that I care about him and want to celebrate this day with him, without giving him the impression that I want more than what we have? Especially since I do want more than he is apparently willing—or able—to give.

In the end, I decided I was making it harder than it needed to be. Just because we have years of baggage doesn't mean I have to unpack it all now. That made deciding what to give Mac for his birthday obvious. Something he would love and didn't stray beyond the established boundaries of our non-relationship.

We were out late last night, watching the primary returns for Connecticut, Delaware, Maryland, Pennsylvania and Rhode Island with the rest of the team. It went well for Kim. Even better than expected, because she'd won all five, and the most recent polls had favored Hennessey in Connecticut and Pennsylvania. The champagne had already been flowing, but that pleasant surprise led to everyone drinking more than they normally would have.

Everyone except me, that is. I kept a full glass in hand, surreptitiously trading it with Mac's half empty drink now and then. Our subterfuge seemed to work, and no one noticed I wasn't actually drinking. Hashtag teamwork. But Operation Hide Gwen's Pregnancy did have one casualty. My partner in crime, obligated to drink both his share of the bubbly and mine, was blistering drunk by the time we stumbled back to our hotel room.

As a result, Mac is still sleeping soundly next to me. I slept later than I intended as well. I've been doing a lot of that lately, even sleeping through my alarm a few times. Fortunately, when that's happened, we've been on the road and Mac was there to wake me so I wasn't late for any work events.

Dr. Flores warned me that my symptoms might be more intense with twins, but I'm not sure they have been. It's been so long my memories of pregnancy are hazy, and it's not like I don't have plenty of other reasons to be tired all the time. Between work, Tristan, my sisters, and Mac, I'm burning the candle at both ends. It's no wonder I'm exhausted.

Fortunately, we have an easy morning today, our first campaign obligation a round table with local educators and parents at noon, so there's still time for the private birthday celebration I planned. Rolling on to my side and pushing up on one elbow, I slide my other hand across Mac's stomach. His muscles jump under my fingers, and I glance up, checking to see if he's still sleeping. He isn't.

"What are you doing?" he asks, his voice still thick with sleep.

"Wishing you a happy birthday," I answer with a smile.

"It's just another day." It's such an aloof response, but the way his breath hitches when I wrap my fingers around his half-hard cock gives him away.

"I know. You think every day is all about you, but this one really is." I slowly stroke him with a grip looser than he prefers. He spends so much time tormenting me with pleasure, now it's my turn.

"Don't be a tease, then. Get on with it," Mac grumbles.

Ducking out of the way when he reaches for me, I throw the covers back and scoot around to kneel between his spread legs. He's fully hard now, and I tighten my grip, my fingers sliding over his length with smooth, firm strokes. "Don't rush me."

Mac fists his hands in the sheets but, to my surprise, he doesn't argue. There's something tantalizing about his acquiescence. Usually he is very much the one in charge when we hit the sheets, and I've always preferred it that way. Not today, though. Today, Mac is at my mercy and I feel powerful, my pulse thrumming with excitement. Is this what it always feels like for him? If so, I might have to do this more often.

Leaning over him, my hair falling forward to shield my face from his view, I take him into my mouth. I woke him with slow strokes and soft kisses, but now that I have his throbbing length between my lips, I have a new plan. It's possible the moment has gone to my head, but I have only one goal. How fast can I make him come?

Judging by his surprised grunt, Mac wasn't expecting me to have quite so much zeal for sucking his cock right from the start. He probably thought there'd be a slow build—that's usually more my style— but it doesn't take him long to get with the program. And when I take him deeper than I ever have before, until the broad head of his erection is pushing against my soft palate, nearly triggering my gag reflex, his back bows.

"Jesus fucking Christ." Mac's voice is so rough and sexy it sends a shiver down my spine, and I suck him deep again, stroking his shaft with my tongue as I go, just to see what he might say next. It's difficult and super messy—I never imagined I could drool so much—but so, so worth it. That's the thing about Mac. He's usually in control but he never abuses it, never pushes me to my limits, and today I want to find out just how much we both can take.

Not much more, it would seem. Mac lets go of the sheets to grab my head, his strong fingers tangling in my hair. But even as he gently tries to disengage my mouth from his dick, he hooks one leg over my hips, pinning me to the mattress. *Mixed messages.*

With the next bob of my head I hum, and the soft vibration has an enormous effect on him, because he groans and bucks his hips, pushing so deep my eyes water. He's resorted to pulling my hair too and my scalp is tingling, but still I don't stop. Why would I, when this is quite possibly the hottest moment of my life? And that's saying something. I've had a lot of hot moments with Mac.

I didn't count on him wresting back control, though. A miscalculation on my part. He's bigger and stronger than I am and overpowers me so effortlessly I don't really realize it's happening until it's already over. I'm still on top, but now we're chest to chest, his mouth slamming into mine at the same time his cock fills me. It's a free-for-all, both of us kissing and nipping and grabbing while we fuck. My orgasm arrives out of nowhere, overwhelming me with sharp pleasure, like a dessert that's too rich but you just can't stop eating.

Mac tightens one arm around my back, crushing my breasts against his chest, and grabs a handful of my ass. The sound he makes when he comes is so feral, I shudder, another burst of pleasure roaring to life in my center.

We're both still panting and trembling in the aftermath when he draws my mouth back to his. But this time it's a tender kiss, soft and sweet and searching. It's his way of checking in, of asking if I'm okay. I'm better than okay and I hope my answering kiss conveys that, but it's possible I overdo it just a little.

Breaking away, Mac slaps my bottom and gives me an admonishing look, his voice still raspy with sleep and sex when he says, "Enough. I'm not ready to go again."

Liar. Part of him, anyway, is very much ready to go again. I know, because I can feel it against my stomach. But since we're both still trying to catch our breath, and my heart feels like it's about to jump out of my chest, it's possible neither of our cardiovascular systems are up for a repeat performance just yet. And, as long as I'm being honest here, I could probably do with a nap before we have to meet the team and start our day.

Rolling—or more accurately, sliding—off of Mac, I land twisted at the waist, with my shoulders both on the mattress and one leg draped over him. He's apparently displeased by my departure, such as it is, because he pushes up on one elbow and says, "What are you doing?"

"Taking a nap." The last word is garbled by a yawn. When that's passed, I add, "Wake me up when you're ready for more or it's time to go to work."

With a laugh, Mac collapses back against the pillows, one big hand landing on my stomach as he says, "You're starting to show."

I am, although I was hoping he hadn't noticed. At only ten weeks, it seems early, but I suppose it's to be expected with a second pregnancy, and especially with twins. But Mac noticing—and worse, mentioning it—makes me uncomfortable, so I deflect. "I'm pretty sure that's just all the bacon-wrapped dates I ate last night. Those things were amazing." They really were. The caterer Cece hired for the watch party really brought their A-game.

"We're going to have to tell people soon. Not just because of this." Mac's fingers flex over my burgeoning baby bump. "Dr. Flores said you'll need to see the specialist every two weeks, plus her once a month. I don't see how we juggle all those appointments and the campaign without cluing people in."

It's a fair point. But not yet. My first appointment with the specialist is later this week, and I figure we'll know more after that. Besides, there's no way I'm telling anyone until after twelve weeks, just to be safe, and given the weirdness of my relationship with Mac, I'm not sure how to explain the situation to people. Everyone will know this was an accident, and given our history, that's hard to admit. I'm just not prepared to face their judgment yet.

"Soon," I tell him, hoping he'll let such an ambiguous answer slide.

Fortunately, he does.

～

MAC

GWEN and I are the last to make it to the lobby, where the rest of the team has gathered to head off for Kim's round table. Considering how our morning has gone, it's a miracle we made it at all. In our post-sex lethargy, we both overslept. Round two of my birthday present—which involved me blowing my load all over Gwen's gorgeous tits—delayed us further, and round three—Gwen riding my face in the shower—sealed our fate. And although we aren't technically late, I'm usually one of the first on the scene, so our straggling arrival doesn't go unnoticed.

"Happy birthday." Alex smirks at me, clearly expressing that he thinks my birthday has probably already been happy enough.

"Thanks." Rocking back on my heels, I give him a satisfied smile of my own because he's right, it has, and I don't care if he knows it.

Alex laughs, asking, "Have you heard the news?"

Nope. These few hours this morning with Gwen are the most unplugged I've been in months, if not longer. No TV or radio or internet, and Gwen apparently set my phone to silent before she woke me. Other than the few seconds it took to turn the ringer back on, I haven't even looked at it yet. If I had to guess, I probably have a few birthday texts and voicemails waiting from my mom and Jake. Maybe a few of my other friends too. Outside of that, I have no idea what's going on in the world. "No, what?"

"Carpenter dropped out. It's just Kim and Hennessey now."

"What? That's great. We need to—"

"Already done," my brother interrupts.

"But you don't—"

"I do, and it's done."

"But—"

"Let it go, Mac. Brian and I took care of it."

"Would you stop fucking interrupting me and listen?" I demand, my temper finally getting the best of me. Still amused and irritatingly full of himself, Alex nods and, after taking a deep breath, I say, "Start from the beginning."

"Carpenter held a press conference at nine o'clock this morning and dropped out of the race. Brian and I prepared a statement thanking her for her service to the country and a competitive but fair campaign, expressed Kim's willingness to meet with her to discuss her innovative policy ideas, and welcoming her supporters into the fold if they wished to join us. Kim reviewed the statement, and we released it to the press by a quarter after nine." Alex shoves his hands in his pockets. The expectant way he's looking at me, like a kid who just finished reading his book report to the class and is waiting for the teacher's verdict, makes me uneasy.

No, that isn't right. I feel guilty. He's done exactly the right thing, as I should have known he would. I'm not his parent or his boss. We're equals in the company, and he doesn't need my approval, even if this campaign is a special project for me. "That's great," I say, if only to get him to stop looking at me like that. And then, because I evidently just can't help myself, I add, "But you should have told me."

Alex's eyes cut to Gwen, in conversation with Cece a few feet away. When his gaze returns to mine, he arches one brow and says, "I was informed in no uncertain terms that you were not to be disturbed this morning for anything short of a literal nuclear war, and even in that case, I should strongly consider whether you really needed to know."

His response is both unexpected and hilarious, and a surge of laughter escapes me before I can tamp it down. The Gwen I met in a crowded nightclub a dozen years ago never would have been so assertive. But these days, she's a force to be reckoned with when she wants to be. Like when she doesn't want to talk about child support or living arrangements. Or, apparently, when she doesn't want her morning dicking interrupted. That she made enough of an impression on Alex that she won out over me when he weighed her potential anger against mine? It's goddamn priceless, and I'm still laughing when I say, "Good call."

"Really?" he asks, and I'd swear he's holding his breath.

"Yeah, really. I wouldn't want to get on Ms. Pierce's bad side, either." And then, because there's something about this moment that strikes me as sad, I clap his shoulder and say, "Besides, you had it covered. You didn't need me."

Alex's answering smile, both genuine and a little sheepish, confirms that was exactly the right thing to say.

CHAPTER 11

GWEN

"Come on, baby, we're going to be late," Mac calls from the bottom of the stairs.

Barely giving his dad time to finish, Tristan's higher-pitched voice filters up next. "Don't make me come up there!"

That, at least, coaxes a genuine, albeit nervous, laugh from me, and I glance at the clock on Mac's dresser.

12:17 p.m. The red digital numbers stare back at me, and my stomach roils with another wave of nausea. I don't know what I'm so worked up about today or why Mac is in such a hurry. We're meeting his family and my sisters at a restaurant downtown for Mother's Day at one o'clock. We have plenty of time, and this will be a nice, easy lunch. There's no reason to worry. It's probably just my out-of-control hormones and lingering morning sickness making me so anxious.

"Almost ready," I holler, hoping to buy myself a few more minutes. Mac and Tristan's voices drift upstairs, but I can't make out what they're saying, so I'm guessing it worked.

Turning toward the mirror, I smooth my pastel blue-and-green maxi dress over my middle. Funny the difference a few days can make, because there's no blaming this on bacon-wrapped dates anymore. For the moment, I can still hide it with blousy tops and flowing dresses, like the one I chose today, but my pants are already uncomfortably tight. At this rate, I'll be in maternity clothes—or at least pants—before I know it.

"Can you feel the baby move?"

Tristan's question startles me, because I didn't hear him come up, and that's immediately followed by a twinge of guilt. After the way he reacted when we told him I was pregnant, we've held off on telling him he'll be getting two new siblings instead of just one. Honestly, I'm not sure Mac will let me get away with it, but I'd prefer not to tell anyone we're having twins until they get here. That probably isn't practical, at least with our immediate family and friends, but I remember the way people touched me all the time when I was pregnant with Tristan. It will be so much worse if they know it's twins, and there's a lot that could happen between now and their arrival.

Shaking out my dress to camouflage my bump again, I face Tristan. "Not yet. Why?"

Tristan shrugs. "It seems like it would be weird having someone else inside you."

"It is weird, but it's kind of cool too. Have I ever told you about the first time I felt you move?" I smile when Tristan shakes his head. "Well, come sit with me, and I'll tell you all about it."

Mac is going to be so pissed, but what's he going to do? It's Mother's Day and if I want to be late for lunch because I'd rather cuddle my half-grown son and force him to listen to my maudlin stories, I will.

Besides, it serves him right. He invited Tris and I to spend the night last night under the guise of making it easier for him to help Tris spoil me for Mother's Day. And they *did* treat me to a phenomenal plate of pancakes in bed and a bouquet of flowers, but I know Mac's game. This is all part of his campaign to convince me to move in with him and I'm not going to lie, it's working. Well, sort of. If I weren't so worried about becoming dependent on him, I'd have probably already agreed.

We settle on the bed with our backs against the headboard, and I drape one arm over Tristan's shoulders before I begin. "I was about five months pregnant and—"

"How pregnant are you now?"

Under other circumstances, I might chastise him for interrupting, but this is the most interest he's shown in my pregnancy and I'm not about to discourage that. "Almost three months, so it'll be a while yet before I can feel anything and even longer before you and your dad can."

Tristan's eyes widen. "I'll be able to feel it?"

"Sure, if you want to, and eventually you'll be able to see it too." That might have been too much new information all at once, because he's looking at my stomach like it's possessed by aliens. Probably best not to let him think about that for long. "Anyway, I was having a terrible time with your aunts. You know, it hadn't been that long since our mom left, and Liv was understandably clingy. She needed so much attention back then."

Tristan rolls his eyes, banging his head against the headboard when he looks up at me. "She still needs too much attention."

"She would probably say the same about you." He screws up his face but doesn't say anything else, so I continue. "And Willa was acting out and getting in a lot of trouble at school. I was so stressed and worried, and one night, after I'd put the girls to bed, I was lying in bed crying and feeling sorry for myself when I felt this strange little flutter in my stomach. At first I wasn't sure what it was, but then after I calmed down, it happened again. And then it kept happening and I started crying again, except this time it was happy tears because I knew that was you."

"That's it?" He looks crestfallen. Did he expect superhero-movie levels of action here or what?

"Yeah, that's it. Maybe it doesn't seem that way to you, but it was very exciting at the time." Ridiculously, I'm feeling defensive because my almost eleven-year-old isn't impressed.

"Will you be excited when this baby moves?" He points at my stomach without extending his arm, like he's afraid something is going to jump out and grab him if he gets too close.

"Yes, very. And I know you're still getting used to the idea, but I hope eventually you'll be excited too."

"About that," Mac interjects, and I yelp, startled for the second time this morning. *This cannot be good for my heart.* I need to have a talk with the both of them about sneaking up on me.

"About what?" Tristan asks, looking between Mac and me.

My heart rate has returned to normal, or as normal as it can be with Mac leaning against the door frame, arms crossed over his chest. He really is too handsome for his own good, and I'm so busy ogling him it takes me a minute to realize he's talking. Damn hormones, making me objectify a perfectly innocent man just trying to have a conversation.

"Gwen, are you listening to me?" The spike of irritation in his tone is what finally gets my attention. Pressing my lips together to hide my smile, I shake my head. Mac heaves a heavy sigh and starts again. "Tristan is going to slip up sooner or later and spill the beans. You—"

"I will not!" Tristan sits up straighter, squaring his shoulders and glaring at his dad.

"Dude." Mac chuckles and pushes off the door, coming toward the bed. "I've almost slipped about a million times. Keeping secrets is hard work, and we have to be realistic about this. People—and by people I especially mean your aunts—are going to be pissed if they find out you knew first." That isn't exactly true, since Olivia more or less guessed the truth long before we told Tris, and Willa will definitely understand. Mac is well aware of all of that. But his over-exaggeration seems to mollify our son, so I'm not going to get nit-picky.

I have other, bigger things to worry about anyway, because it isn't hard to guess where Mac is going with this. Usually when we disagree, I try to shut him down from the start. That only seems to frustrate us both. So this time I'm going to try something new. I'll quietly listen while he states his case, *and then* I'll shut him down.

"You were saying?" I prompt. He's standing at the edge of the bed, looking down at Tris and me, and his gaze has gone so soft I think maybe he's forgotten what he wants to say.

Mac jerks his head back like I've surprised him, but he recovers quickly. For the third time, he starts over, this time with a concession for Tristan. "The point is, eventually one of us will slip, and you aren't going to be able to hide that much longer."

From the finger he points at my belly, it's clear what *that* is, and as much as I hate to admit it, he isn't wrong. With Tristan tucked into my side, the loose fabric of my dress has drawn tight across my midsection, and it's obvious. Still, if I'm careful, I can hide it for a few weeks longer.

But Mac isn't finished. "I agreed with waiting until you were twelve weeks. All the books say that's best too. But you're literally two days away from that now, and everyone is going to be together already today. It would be a good time to tell them."

Books? "What books?"

Pinching the bridge of his nose, Mac sighs. "That's your takeaway?"

I'll admit I may not be focusing on the most important thing he said, but I had no idea he's been reading up on pregnancy. "What books?" I ask again.

"You aren't going to let this go, are you?"

I shake my head and glance at the clock. "No, and we really are running late now, so you'd better hurry."

"You are the devil," Mac mutters, but then he answers my question. "I don't remember the titles, but the clerk at the bookstore recommended them. Now can we talk about—"

"Wait," I say, holding up one hand. I'm still not ready to move on just yet. "You actually went to the bookstore? You didn't just go on the internet and search 'what do I, a clueless person with a penis, need to know about pregnancy?'"

"Gwen." Mac's clearly had enough of this derailment.

"Fine," I give in, sliding off the bed. And, out of consideration for the gray hairs Mac will someday probably name after me, I bring the conversation back around to what he wants to talk about. "I'm not ready yet."

"I knew you'd say that," Mac says with a resigned sigh. But he follows that with a nod and looks at Tristan. "We're going to have to keep our secret a little longer, tiger."

"No problem." Tristan mimes zipping his lips and throwing away the key. Then he hops off the bed and straightens his shoulders. He seems so happy, almost proud, to be included in our family secret, which means he probably won't blow it. And maybe, just maybe, he's coming around to the idea of being a big brother.

~

MAC

WE'RE LATE TO LUNCH. It's a developing trend that I don't love, especially because I don't understand the reason. A year from now, when we're trying to wrangle two infants in addition to ourselves and Tristan? Yeah, that would make sense. But now? Why?

It wasn't like this before she got pregnant, and one of the books I picked up the other day said pregnancy can cause lapses in memory and attention. There's even a name for it. *Baby Brain.* It's the only explanation I can think of, but when I mentioned it to Gwen on the ride over, she frowned and told me not to be *that guy.* And when I asked what the hell that meant, Tristan piped up from the backseat to inform me that I was mansplaining. I don't know what stung my pride more, that he was right or that my kid had to point it out to me.

"There you are!" Olivia stands up from the table and throws herself into Gwen's arms as we approach. "Happy Mother's Day!"

Willa, always the more subdued sister, rises to greet her sister too. Tapping Tristan's shoulder to get his attention, I circle the table with him close on my heels. Diane and Alex are seated across from each other, inexplicably talking about sailing, and my mom is at the head of the table, watching happily as Tristan and I approach. But there's no sign of Dad. He's probably in the restroom, or out on the patio hitting on some poor waitress, but there's a small chance he isn't here at all and I cling to the possibility.

"Happy Mother's Day, Mom," I greet her as she rises from her chair.

Since a crowded restaurant in the heart of D.C. definitely counts as a public setting, I'm expecting a restrained greeting, and that's exactly what I get—an arm's-length hug and an air kiss in the general vicinity of my left ear. But when she turns her attention to Tristan, who gives her a big smile and calls her grandma, she goes bananas.

"Thank you, darling. I'm so glad to see you today." She ruffles his hair and bends over to kiss his cheek. A legit kiss. And then she keeps right on chattering, inviting him to sit next to her and asking about his friends and school and manga.

Who is this woman? How does my mother—Joan Hastings MacKenzie—even know what manga is? Let alone that Tristan loves it? He's been emailing with her a little since Easter, but I had no idea they'd been talking enough for her to know all that. Since Mom is flat-out ignoring me, all her attention focused on Tris, and our server is hovering nearby, presumably eager to take our orders, I leave them to it and find my seat between Gwen and Alex.

Disengaging from his conversation with Diane, Alex leans toward me, his voice low. "Where's Dad?"

"Don't know. The restroom, I assume," I answer absently without looking up from my menu. I have more important things to think about right now. Like how pissed will Gwen be if I order the ceviche, and is it worth it? *Probably not.*

"No, I was the first one here. He didn't come with Mom."

That gets my attention and I scan the table, noticing the empty seat at the far end. There isn't even a place setting. "What did she say?"

"Nothing, and I didn't ask. I mean, it's her day, you know? If they're fighting or something, I didn't want to ruin it by making her talk about it."

"He's probably working," I suggest. Unless he bailed because they're fighting—something that has literally never happened before

—that's almost certainly what he told Mom. Whether it's true or he's simply using it for cover so he can spend the day with some other woman could go either way.

"Probably." Alex relaxes, leaning away from me again to fidget with his fork. "I'm hearing rumors that Whitaker's campaign is going all in. At this point, it's almost impossible for him to rack up enough delegates to win outright."

"I'm hearing the same things. Unless the President backs down, the Republicans are headed for a contested convention."

"We can really capitalize on that. Assuming Hennessey doesn't try to pull the same thing." Alex frowns and drums his fingers on the table. "Do you think he will?"

It's been a month since Gwen and I told him about the photo. Since then, we haven't spoken again but the Twitter account that sent the image has been deleted so I'm assuming he's discovered the culprit and shut that shit down.

It is perhaps uncharacteristically optimistic of me, but my instincts tell me we can trust him. He said he wanted a clean win and for now, I'm willing to take him at his word. "No, I don't."

"Are you two talking about work?" Olivia pipes in from across the table.

"Sorry." Alex dips his head in apology.

"You should be," she complains. "I seriously love listening to you guys talk about the campaign, but today is supposed to be about Gwen and Mrs. MacKenzie."

While my mom leans in front of Tristan to pat Livie's hand and tell her she should call her Joan or Grandma—*and seriously, who the fuck is this woman?*—I turn to Gwen, intending to make my apology to her instead of her bossy younger sister. But when she looks up at me, her lips are pressed into a thin line and her eyes are watery. "Hey, what's wrong?"

"Nothing. It's just my s-s-stupid hormones. I've been a wreck all day t-today." She's definitely crying now, stuttering and sniffling, and I almost believe her. On-again, off-again morning sickness, paired with her rapidly fluctuating emotions, has made for a wild couple of weeks. But then her gaze cuts to Tristan and my mom, laughing with Olivia about something, and I figure out the problem. I should have realized it sooner and guilt picks at me.

"Shit, I'm sorry. Mom asked him to sit with her, and I didn't even think about it. I'll switch places with him, okay?"

"What? No!" Gwen grabs my forearm and ducks her head to unobtrusively wipe her tears. "He doesn't have to sit by me. The three of us having pancakes in bed together was way better than a stupid restaurant lunch. But…" She hesitates for just a second before finishing. "It makes me happy to see him hitting it off so well with your mom. He's never had a grandma before, and this is good for him."

"It's good for her too," I agree, glancing down the table at them again. And actually, it's good for all of us. But as my gaze returns to Dad's empty chair, I'm reminded just how complicated family can be. I can only hope my family problems don't multiply at the same exponential rate my family is growing.

CHAPTER 12

GWEN

THE TRICK to pretending you're not pregnant, when you're very obviously beginning to appear pregnant, is to be so scary that everyone's afraid to ask. I've spent a lot of time the last week or so glaring people into silence when they stare a little too long. Random people on the street, the people who come to Kim's various campaign events, coworkers, friends and family. Cece.

God, Cece is the worst. I love her dearly and, when we're traveling, I've come to rely on her nearly as much as Mac does. But the girl has no filter and, worse, she isn't easy to intimidate. Complicating matters, she's the one who coordinates all our travel with Kim's personal assistant. Since that means she needs access to my calendar, I've blocked off all my doctor appointments—and holy crap, there are so many appointments and scans and tests in my life right now—and labeled them as "unavailable" without any additional details. So, of course, I have to also maintain a separate calendar that only Mac and I have access to, that lists which appointment is with which doctor.

Heaven forbid I show up at Dr. Flores office when I'm supposed to be at the specialists or vice versa.

"Have you seen Mac or Kim?"

Speak of the devil. Cece is doing an impressive job jogging down the hallway toward me in her four-inch heels, but I still have the urge to cover my eyes in case she wipes out.

Fluffing my billowy tunic shirt, I glance down to make sure my belly isn't too obvious before she gets close enough to notice. No dice. It's because I'm sitting down. That must be the problem. It makes my clothes lay funny, emphasizing instead of hiding my bulging middle. It's ridiculous, really. Pushing to my feet just as she reaches me, I point down the hall. "They went that way."

Cece groans. "Why is this place so big? I'm never going to find them in time."

It's big because it's a hospital. One of the premier hospitals in the country, in fact. They run an extremely successful clinic for low-income families, providing access to top-rate healthcare at a reasonable cost. Hoping to incorporate some of their more innovative ideas into her national healthcare plan, Kim wanted to meet with the doctors and administrators who run it.

"In time for what?"

"I'm not one hundred percent sure, but I think Hennessey is about to drop out of the race. He's got a press conference scheduled in fifteen minutes, and he wants to talk to Kim first. Alex went one way to look for them and I went the other, but this place is a maze and—"

"Alex found us," Mac interrupts, rounding the corner with Kim and his brother close on his heels.

"Where's everyone else?" Cece asks when Brian and the rest of the campaign staff don't materialize with them.

"Finishing the tour." Kim gives Cece a wide smile before adding, "And taking really good notes, if they know what's good for them."

Mac grins and steps aside, opening Dr. Shaw's office door. He was leading the tour of the facilities, and I assume told Kim she could use his office to make a private call.

To Hennessey.

Because he's about to drop out.

My eyes meet Mac's as he holds the door for Kim, and a current of energy zings between us. This is it. We're halfway to a future where Kim is President of the United States and I might burst with happiness. Mac seems to feel how big this moment is too, because he winks at me—a gesture I've learned he only deploys when he's in the very best of moods—before shutting himself in the office with Kim.

When I turn back to Alex and Cece, he's intently studying an OSHA poster about workplace safety, and she's examining her nails as if the glossy red polish were the most interesting thing she's ever seen. It's strange, overly nonchalant behavior from both of them, especially in a moment as big as this one, and I'm reminded of something Cece said when she found me.

Alex went one way to look for them, and I went the other. But the last time I saw them, they were with the rest of our group. How did they get separated from the others, and why?

"Where were you two?" I ask, zeroing in on Alex. He's the weak link here and he apparently knows it, because he shoves his hands in his pockets and stalks away without a word, like I hadn't just spoken to him. *Rude.*

Whatever they were up to, it isn't very gallant of him to abandon Cece to her fate like that, but who am I kidding? She can handle herself, and she proves it when she ignores my question to ask one of her own. "What were you doing sitting here by yourself? Mac put you in timeout?"

Hardly. If anything, I put myself in timeout. Dr. Shaw talked fast and walked even faster and, early though it may be, I have two babies squishing my insides. I haven't thrown up in four days—a new record —but after ten minutes hoofing it after Dr. Shaw, I was nauseated, and the last thing I want is to start puking again. But I'm not about to admit any of that to her.

"I'm just a little tired today." It's not untrue. Last night was another late one, first watching the primary returns in Arkansas, Kentucky and Oregon, and then celebrating Kim's wins, which made Hennessey's surrender all but inevitable.

Cece isn't satisfied with my answer but she also apparently isn't inclined to push. Either that, or the excitement of Kim's success overcomes her, because the conversation shifts to planning a celebratory dinner for Kim after her rally tonight, and that's just fine with me.

❧

MAC

KIM HANGS UP HER PHONE, taking the time to calmly slip it in her pocket. But when she finally looks at me, her face is flushed with excitement. With a whoop that's probably heard throughout the hospital, she launches herself at me, pulling me into a hug. She's breathless when she says, "We did it!"

"You did it," I correct her with a gentle squeeze.

She squeals again and takes a step back, her joy so boundless she stamps her feet on the linoleum floor to burn off some of the excess energy coursing through her. But she's still restless with it, swaying on her feet and hugging herself when she says, "Be honest with me, Mac. Did you ever think we'd make it this far?"

"Well, if it's honesty you want, when I was a kid I thought you were a dictator." She definitely knew how to be a hardass when necessary back then. And she still does; it's just not aimed at me all that often anymore. "But you'll make a fine President as long as you don't go power mad."

Kim laughs, then cautions, "Let's not get ahead of ourselves. We still have a general election to win." Pacing around the small office, pushing the chairs out of her way as she goes, she says, "There's so much to do. I want Cece to take over as point person with the convention planning committee. And it's probably time I accept the Secret Service protection everyone's been nagging me about for months."

Her grudging tone on that last point makes me smile, but it's a relief she's finally prioritizing her safety. We've been lucky—so far there haven't been any serious threats or issues the private security team traveling with her couldn't handle. But she's been eligible for Secret Service Protection for a while now, and it was frustrating all of us that she refused to take it. "I'll call Homeland Security today."

"I should've known you'd be all over that one," Kim jokes, but her expression sobers and she stops pacing. "There's something else I want to talk to you about."

"What's that?" I ask, apprehension making the small hairs on the back of my neck stand on end. Kim is usually straight to the point, so it's unlike her to announce she wants to talk about something instead of just…talking about it. Which means I'm probably not going to like what comes next.

"I'd like you to consider coming to work for the campaign full time."

Oh. Well, at least she isn't firing me. Yet, anyway, because I have to say no. "I can't."

Unfazed by my answer, she comes to stand in front of me. "Yes, you can. I know you're thinking about the agency, but your dad ran that place alone for decades until you boys were old enough to join him. There's no reason Alex can't do the same. And maybe your relationship with both of them will improve if you get out of the family business and spread your wings a little."

Kim knows exactly how to tempt me. I never wanted to work for my dad. He offered me a place within his business because my mother made him. I accepted it, in part because I knew he didn't want me to. And I foolishly thought I might be able to exercise some control over his behavior while also protecting my mom and brother from learning the ugly truth about him. I'd failed at the former and succeeded at the later, for what little good it's done. So yes, getting out of the family business appeals to me. But there are other things to consider.

"You have no idea how much I appreciate the offer, Kim. But I can't." Working for the campaign full-time would mean even more travel, and with Gwen's pregnancy, that's impossible. Hell, I'm not sure how long we'll be able manage as things are, let alone if I change jobs.

In addition to the standard schedule of appointments with Dr. Flores, Gwen needs to see the high-risk specialist, Dr. Williams, every two weeks. So far, he's been optimistic and says everything is going exactly as it should. But he's had some hard facts for us too. Like even in the best-case scenario, Gwen shouldn't travel after twenty-eight weeks, and more than half of all twin pregnancies are delivered before thirty-seven weeks. If she does make it to thirty-seven weeks, Dr. Williams will want to induce her, because apparently, in the risk/reward analysis, that's the ideal time for delivery, both for Gwen's health and the twins. Which means something's going to have to give, because Gwen will be twenty-eight weeks on September first. And thirty-seven weeks? That's November third. *Election Day.*

"You don't have to decide today. Take a few days, think it over."

Blowing out a harsh breath, I shove my hands in my pockets and look at the ceiling. *Sorry, baby. I have to tell her.* "A few days isn't going to matter. Gwen's pregnant."

Kim isn't shocked by my announcement, and she's smiling when she says, "She told me. Or I guess I might have pried it out of her. But I would hope you know me well enough to know how strongly I believe that family always comes first. For heaven's sake, we just released a policy paper last week detailing my plan for a year of paid parental leave. I would never begrudge you whatever time you need for her and the baby."

"I do know that, but this isn't that simple." When Kim scoffs, I give her the rest. "We're having twins. Which, weirdly, means more than double the doctor appointments and that they're probably going to come before the election."

"Oh, Mac." Her eyes light up and she pulls me into yet another hug. "I'm so happy for you."

It's my turn to scoff. Now that I've had some time for the idea to settle and we have enough ultrasound pictures to wallpaper one of the bedrooms in my townhouse, I am oddly happy about Gwen's pregnancy. Sometimes I'm even excited. But so much worry and stress come with it that it feels strange to be congratulated. "Thank you. And I assume you can see now why I can't accept your offer?"

"I don't, actually. I'm not asking for you to put my campaign first. I'd never ask that, and I will do whatever you need to help you balance it all."

She still has her arms around my middle, but I throw my hands up in frustration anyway. "If I accept your offer, what the hell am I supposed to do when I wake up on November fourth and, win or lose, I'm unemployed?" I'm not exactly hard-up for money, and Gwen may still be refusing to take a damn penny from me, but there's something about having twins on the way that makes my chest feel tight at the prospect of being jobless.

"You stupid boy." Kim reaches up, pinching my cheek like she used to do when I was a child and she was my babysitter. "If I'm going to the White House, I intend to take you with me. You'd make a dashing Press Secretary, don't you think?"

Oh. I take a stumbling step backward and, judging by her triumphant smile, Kim is immensely pleased to have shocked me. She wants me to be her Press Secretary if she becomes President? I never saw that coming.

"I trust you more than anyone else on my team, Mac. You're the only one I can count on to always be honest with me, even when you know I won't like it. So do me a favor and take some time to think about it. Talk it over with Gwen. And then if you still think you can't do it, I'll accept that."

Shame slithers through me, knotting in my stomach. Her faith in me is misplaced. I haven't been honest with her in more than a decade. I've kept secrets from her and, over the years, I've flat-out lied to her in order to maintain them. And though I hated every minute of it, I did it because I always believed it was for the best, not just for her but for everyone involved. *If only I were still so certain.*

CHAPTER 13

MAC

"So, it looks like I missed that Facebook announcement," I deadpan.

I expected Jake's wife Heidi to win the baby debate. He's always been a pushover, after all, but thought it would take her a little longer to do it. She and Gwen are on the other side of my terrace, happily chatting while Tristan, Meredith, and Autumn play nearby. Tristan was not thrilled to be saddled with entertaining a four- and five-year-old, but Meredith in particular seems fascinated by him in that way little ones often look up to bigger kids, and she's slowly winning him over. Levi, barely more than a year old, is sitting on his mother's lap, such as it is, given that Heidi is more than a little bit pregnant.

"Same, man, same." Jake shifts his gaze to look at me, a smile tugging at his lips. "And you fibbed when you told me you weren't sleeping together before she told you about Tris."

"I didn't, actually. When is Heidi due?"

"October ninth. Gwen?"

Ah, yeah, that explains it. Heidi's baby bump is definitely more noticeable, but Gwen doesn't look as far behind as she should. You know, if she weren't having twins.

"October ninth? Really? Isn't Autumn's birthday in October?"

"You know it is. Are you going to answer my question?"

So much for changing the subject. "Can't. Sorry."

"Can't?" Jake glances at Gwen, his brow furrowing, and then back to me.

"Can't," I confirm with a nod. "I've learned in the last few months that Gwen has the incredible ability to simply...deny reality when she's under pressure."

"Like pretending she didn't know you?"

"Exactly."

"And now we're all supposed to pretend we can't tell she's pregnant?"

"No comment. But I'm reliably informed that an official announcement will be forthcoming once everyone arrives today." And thank God for that. The situation has gotten way out of hand, and the looks everyone keeps giving me—like they aren't sure if they should congratulate me or feel sorry for me—are starting to get under my skin.

Earlier this week, a woman on the rope line before one of Kim's rallies asked Gwen when she was due. Gwen, being the most stubborn person I've ever met, pretended she couldn't hear over the crowd and kept right on moving. It made an impression, though, because back in our hotel room that night, she was the one to raise the subject of finally sharing our news.

Today was the perfect opportunity. Jake and his family always come back to D.C. to visit his folks on Memorial Day weekend. Over the years, we've developed the habit of getting together at my place on the holiday. Jake's parents usually come, at least for a little while, and his sister and her family if they're in town. Sometimes Alex or Jess or some of our friends from school stop by too. With a little guest list maintenance, it was simple enough to ensure everyone we needed to tell was here, a necessity, because Gwen insists she's only doing this once.

"I'll do my best to feign surprise." Jake snorts, still watching Gwen and Heidi. They've scooted their chairs closer together, their heads bent close in conversation. It's nice to see them getting along so well. Jake and his family are an important part of my life, and it would suck if Gwen didn't get along with his wife.

It isn't long before my rooftop is teeming with people. Kim and Arnie have arrived after the National Memorial Day Parade across the river. Cece and a few other coworkers and campaign staff are here. My mom is here, suspiciously without Dad again. If I hadn't seen him on one of the twenty-four-hour news channels yesterday bloviating about "Traditional Family Values," I might start to wonder if Mom hadn't finally done him in and hidden his body in the freezer.

Even Sean Hennessey showed up, at Kim's request. She recently read a book about the sometimes difficult relationships Presidents have sometimes had with their Vice Presidents and how that complicated achieving their shared goals. As a result, she isn't interested in choosing her running mate with the usual series of interviews and background checks. Or at least, not only that way. She wants to make sure whoever she ultimately picks fits in with her and her team. Inviting Sean today is a test of sorts, because whether he realizes it or not, he's the front runner in her mind. Mine too, for that matter.

Alex and Jess are the only stragglers, and once they arrive, Gwen and I can make our announcement. Hopefully they'll hurry, because based on the way my mom is looking at Gwen and Heidi, we don't have long.

～

GWEN

"I COULD HAVE GOTTEN that for you," Olivia chastises while I fill a glass with ice. For reasons I don't understand—which is often the case with Liv, if I'm being honest—she's designated herself hostess for the day. It's a little weird, since this is Mac's party, at his own house, with his friends and family, but he doesn't seem to mind. Probably because it saves him running up and down all those stairs every time someone arrives or needs a refill.

Stupid stairs. I'm already dreading the trip back up to the rooftop.

"And let you hog all the air conditioning? No way."

"Okay, but—" Whatever Olivia was about to say is interrupted by voices coming up the stairs, and she changes tack, instead murmuring, "Who would just let themselves in?"

Answering the question before I can, Jess crests the landing, her daughter close behind her. Earlier, when Mac told him Jess' daughter was his age, Tristan seemed indifferent, but after the last hour entertaining kids half his age, I'm guessing he'll be a lot more interested now.

"Hi, Jess," I call to her.

Jess smiles and waves, guiding her daughter toward the kitchen. "Hey! It's good to see you again."

"You too." Gesturing to Livie, I step around the counter to introduce them. "This is my sister, Olivia. Liv, this is Kim's daughter, Jess."

Jess's eyes drop to my middle, and I hold my breath, waiting to see if she'll say anything. Not that it matters, since we're breaking the news today anyway, but God…this is so awkward. *Why did I insist on waiting this long?*

Evidently deciding against mentioning the elephant in the room, Jess nudges her daughter in front of her and says, "This is my daughter, Amelia."

"Amelia! What a pretty name," Liv gushes.

"I prefer Amy," she says, sounding so grown. She's a pretty girl with dark, loosely curling hair and big brown eyes that would melt any adult's heart.

Not mine, though, because I know those eyes, and my heart has become a frozen slab in my chest. It's stopped beating, I've stopped breathing, and I clutch desperately at the edge of the counter to keep myself from falling as the room spins out around me.

"I never meant for her to be called that, but Mac started it before she was born, and it stuck," Jess is explaining, but I'm not listening.

Not really. Except I can hear the affectionate exasperation in her voice when she says Mac's name, and I think I might be dying.

This can't be happening.

I once asked Kim about Amy's father, and she dodged the question. Now I know why, and I wish I didn't. The resemblance is too strong, not just to him but to Tristan. Their families are so close, everyone must know, even if no one speaks the words out loud. Everyone but me, because I'd never met her until now, and Mac didn't tell me.

"Are you okay?" Olivia asks softly, one hand on my elbow to steady me.

"Yeah, fine," I mumble, pulling my arm away. If I'm lucky, the ground is going to open up and swallow me, and I don't want to take her with me.

"Okay. Ready to go back upstairs? Now that Jess is here, Mac will be champing at the bit to spill the beans," Olivia asks, and I catch Jess looking at my belly again, a small smile curving her lips.

"You aren't even supposed to know," I complain, but I let her guide me toward the stairs, Jess and Amy following.

The last thing I want to do is announce my pregnancy now. Just a few minutes ago, I was so happy. So excited. Not really about telling everyone, because that just feels awkward and weird even in the best of circumstances. But I was excited, if nervous, about being pregnant. About sharing it with Mac this time. About Mac's flourishing relationship with Tristan. And now it feels like it's all crumbling around me.

"She's like a sister to me." And I believed him. Not just because I wanted to but because it seemed that way the one time I saw them together. The banter and teasing, it felt like a sibling relationship. But I was so, so wrong.

Stepping out onto the terrace, Mac catches my eye and waves me over to where he's standing with Alex and Jake. And I go to him, pasting a smile on my face and pretending my heart doesn't feel hollow.

~

MAC

A CHORUS of congratulations and enough backslaps to require I see a chiropractor tomorrow follow our announcement. Next to me, Gwen accepts it all stoically, but something is wrong. Her movements are stiff and jerky, almost like a marionette, only the person pulling her strings doesn't understand the way her body is put together, the way she's meant to move. And the smile she keeps giving everyone is the same plastic smile from her job interview, the one I haven't seen in months. She was nervous about sharing our news, but whatever is wrong now, it's more than that, and worry crawls down my spine.

"Are you feeling okay?" I whisper when there's a brief pause in the parade of well-wishers.

Without looking at me, Gwen nods, and then my mom is pulling her into a hug before I can press the issue.

"November twenty-fourth? That's the week of Thanksgiving, isn't it?" Mom asks when she releases Gwen.

If I weren't so preoccupied with worry, it would be amusing the way nearly every adult on the terrace looks at their watch or their phone, but it's Alex who confirms the date. "The Tuesday before Thanksgiving."

"A Thanksgiving baby would be perfect, wouldn't it?" Mom turns, looking for Tristan and beckoning him closer for a hug.

"It could be earlier or later. Tristan was late," Gwen says, tempering expectations.

"Could be," Mom chirps, wrapping Tris in her arms. She squeezes him so tight he gives me a bug-eyed look over her shoulder. "I'm the luckiest grandma in the world to have you, and now we get a new baby too! Are you excited, Tris?"

Tristan scrunches up his face and lifts one shoulder in a shrug. "I guess?"

"That's okay." Mom laughs and pats his cheek. "You'll see, you're going to be a very good big brother, just like your dad, and having a little brother or sister will be great fun. Look at your dad and Uncle Alex."

Yeah, look at us. We're not the example she apparently thinks, although I guess I'm glad she doesn't realize the distance between us. We rarely even talk if it isn't about work. Granted, things have been a little better recently, but my relationship with Alex is not what I would wish for my children. I'd much rather Tristan and his new siblings share the kind of closeness Gwen has with her sisters.

The rest of the afternoon passes in a blur, and it's difficult to focus on the cheery conversation happening all around me because Gwen is still off. I don't know if she isn't feeling well or if there's something bothering her. Every time I try to ask, she gives me a tight-lipped smile and insists she's fine, but she clearly isn't.

"I think I'm going to go home with Tristan and the girls tonight," she says when we've closed the door behind the last of the departing guests.

We have an early flight tomorrow, so the plan was for her to spend the night with me, while Tristan went home with his aunts. With the way she's been acting, I'm not entirely surprised by her change of plans, but that doesn't mean I have to like it. And since we're alone on the terrace while her sisters are inside helping Tris gather his things, I'm not going to let her go without an explanation if I can help it. "Will you tell me what's wrong?"

"How many times do I have to tell you I'm fine?" she snaps. Then, after a deep breath, she blows her hair out of her face and says, "I'm just tired, that's all."

"Did someone say something to upset you?" I press, because yeah, I'm sure she is tired—hell, I'm tired, and I'm not the one who's pregnant—but that felt like a dodge.

Gwen pauses in reaching for an empty glass on the table and looks up at me, her lower lashes wet with unshed tears. Her voice is thick and quiet when she asks, "Why didn't you tell me?"

"Tell you what?" Frowning, I rake one hand through my hair. *What should I have told her?*

"About Amy."

"What did Jess say to you?" I demand too quickly, and Gwen flinches.

"Nothing. She didn't have to."

"Then I don't understand—"

Gwen interrupts me, turning toward the skyline as she asks, "When is her birthday?"

"Amy's?" I ask, confused by what feels like a random, unimportant question. Gwen nods stiffly, so I try to answer. "April ninth, 2009, I think. No, maybe the eighth, but I'm pretty sure it's the ninth."

"You don't know for sure?" Gwen shakes her head and laughs bitterly, still not looking at me. "So she was conceived the summer you and I were together in Ann Arbor."

"Yeah, I guess." Amy's only two months older than Tris, so she must have been. I found out Jess was pregnant when I came home for Thanksgiving that year, but I've never really thought about when, specifically she got pregnant. The timing and circumstances of Amy's conception are something I try to avoid thinking about in any detail at all costs.

"You guess." She sounds incredulous and when she turns around to face me again, her eyes are blazing. "Why didn't you tell me you have another kid?"

I jerk back, startled by the accusation and the hurt and fury tangled in her voice. But my surprise is quickly replaced by my own anger, my skin prickling with it. I should have anticipated this and prepared Gwen for meeting Amy. No one else has ever had the guts to ask me directly, but most of them probably assume the same thing she just did, and I should have expected that Gwen, of all people, would see the resemblance. I was stupid not to have realized what might happen. But I'm not just angry with myself, I'm angry with her too. Why is it always so fucking easy for her to believe the worst about me?

"Amy isn't mine." It's the truth, but she isn't going to believe me, and I'm already anticipating how the rest of this conversation will play out. This is the end of whatever it is we've been doing together.

"No? I suppose you're going to try and tell me she's Alex's?" She throws up her hands in disbelief.

"No." It comes out terser than I intended. I'm not going to lie to her, but I don't know how to fix this without telling her the truth, and I don't know if I can do that, either. For one thing, it isn't my truth to tell, not really. And for another, I've kept the secret so long I don't know how to tell it around the shame and embarrassment roiling in my gut.

"Then what? You came home at least once that summer. I remember, because I wondered where home was, and Lindsey called me a mopey bitch the whole time you were gone. Am I supposed to pretend that's just a big coincidence? And I'm not fucking blind. She has Tristan's eyes. Your eyes, Mac. If she isn't yours and she isn't Alex's, where the hell did she get those?"

The righteous indignation in Gwen's voice breaks something inside me, and the truth pours out of me before I can stop it. "The same fucking place I got them, Gwen. She's my half sister, not my kid."

CHAPTER 14

GWEN

His sister? I sit down hard in the nearest chair, one hand covering my mouth. My voice is quiet, muffled by my fingers, when I say, "But that would mean—"

Pacing toward the edge of the terrace, Mac interrupts me with a single terse word, as if he can't bear for me to finish that sentence. "Yes."

"I don't…" *Know what to say.* But even saying that seems impossible, and the words get stuck in my throat. Jess and Mac's dad? My God.

"Don't believe me?" His back is to me, his shoulders square and his head high as he looks out over the urban sprawl, but he sounds defeated. "That's fine. Why would you? The boy you knew back then —hell, the man I was until a few months ago—there weren't many women I wasn't interested in fucking. And I've always been careless with you, haven't I? So it's not such a leap to think I might have gotten someone else pregnant too." His shoulders rise and fall with a deep breath and he leans forward, resting his forearms on the railing. "I realize at the moment I'm not in a particularly good position to be asking you for favors but, if you can, I'd appreciate it if you wouldn't mention any of this to Alex or Kim or my mom."

"They don't know?"

Mac shakes his head.

Scrubbing both hands over my face, I lean back in my chair and try to understand what just happened. I mean, it's simple, isn't it? But in some ways, this raises more questions than it answers, and I'm not sure I have any right to ask them. If what he's just told me is true, it doesn't really have anything to do with me. Him either, for that matter, except that he's carried this secret around for all this time. I'm no stranger to the way keeping secrets can beat a person down and it only makes me feel worse for assuming what I did.

Because the thing is, I do believe him. He's too obviously wounded for this to be anything but the truth and, as vile as it is, it isn't difficult to imagine his father doing this. Well, sort of. Both Cece and Mac have alluded to his philandering. But with Jess? She's the daughter of one of his wife's closest friends and like a sister to his own sons. He's more than twice her age, for heaven's sake.

"Dad!" Tristan shouts as he bursts through the door.

Mac turns to face him, his eyes still strained but a small smile tugging at his lips. "What's up, tiger?"

"Aunt Willa said to tell you she put all the leftovers away, and Aunt Liv loaded the dishwasher but she didn't start it because..." Tristan stops in front of his dad, eyes narrowed with concentration. But then he shrugs and admits, "I don't remember why she didn't run it, but we're getting ready to go now."

"Tell them they didn't have to do all that and I owe them big."

"Okay. Will you call me tomorrow?"

"Tomorrow and every day until we get back," Mac promises.

Tipping his head down, Tris looks up at Mac from the corner of his eye and gives him a sly smile. "It would be a lot easier if I had my own phone." He's been bugging me about getting a phone for a long time now. With his birthday fast approaching, he's really ramped up his efforts and zeroed in on his father, who he seems to think is his best bet. He's probably right.

"Uh-huh, I'm sure it would be." Mac chuckles and gives him a hug. "Be good for your aunts."

"I'm always good," Tristan insists, although we all know that isn't true, and when Mac releases him, he skips across the terrace to give me a hug too. Then with a shouted "I love you" that seems to be directed at both of us, he's gone, the door thumping closed behind him.

"I thought you were going with them?" Mac asks, his expression wary as he walks toward me.

"I changed my mind." And then when he's dropped into the chair next to me, I reach over and take his hand, lacing my fingers with his. "I believe you. I just wish you'd told me before."

"I know, and I'm sorry." Mac sighs, his gaze fixed on our joined hands. Stroking my palm with his thumb, he says, "This is probably going to sound crazy, but I forget sometimes how much she looks like a MacKenzie. When Jess told everyone she was pregnant, she said she didn't know who the father was, and even back then, before Amy was born, I think some people thought it might be me because Jess and I had always been so tight. After she was born, and especially when Amy got older and started to look more and more like one of us..." He pauses, pointing at his own chest. "Well, I think that convinced most everyone, and I let them go on thinking that because it was easier. But no one has ever actually asked me and I didn't think...I just didn't think about how it would look to you."

Because I shouldn't have thought it. Yes, the resemblance is obvious, but why did I assume Mac was her father? I mean, I'm not going to beat myself up for not considering Senior as a possibility. He's gross, but I had no way of knowing he's that gross. But Alex? Why didn't I consider him? And why did I fly off the handle instead of just asking Mac like a reasonable person? But I know the answer to those questions too, even if I've been trying to ignore it for a long time now.

I love him, and I'm terrified that he doesn't feel the same way.

Oh, God. I love him. This is the first time I've allowed myself to acknowledge it, but I'm still not prepared to deal with my feelings or what they mean. I need to focus on something else. Like, oh, the conversation we're actually having. That would be good. Ignoring the sound of my own blood whooshing in my ears, I try to keep my voice steady and ask, "How did you find out the truth if Jess claimed not to know?"

"My dad told me." Mac doesn't seem surprised by my shocked gasp and he tips his head back against his chair, staring up at the darkening evening sky. "I didn't even know she was pregnant. She'd been avoiding my calls for months at that point. Ever since she...ever since they got together, but I didn't know that at the time and I was pissed at her. You know, you'd taken off and I was a wreck about it, and she wouldn't answer her damn phone or return my calls. I was so fucking self-absorbed it never even occurred to me maybe she was going through some shit too. And then I came home for Thanksgiving and my dad sat me down and...it was almost like he was bragging about fucking this girl who was younger than I was, like he thought that would impress me or something. And he said she'd gotten pregnant and she was being unreasonable about it. Since we were close, he wanted me to talk to her. To convince her to have an abortion."

My stomach cramps, and I knot my hands in my lap, hurt and angry on Jess's behalf. And Mac's too. How could his father put him in that position? How could he ask such a thing? How could he know so little about his own son that he would think Mac might do something like that? Even I knew better. When I found out I was pregnant with Tris, I didn't tell him because I thought he wouldn't care. I thought he'd abandon us. But never, never in a million years, would I have thought he might try to bully me into having an abortion. And he wouldn't have done it to Jess, either. "What did you do?" I ask, my voice cracking.

"Nothing. I mean, when she finally quit ignoring me, I told her I knew my dad was the father and she...she looked so relieved that someone shared her secret. By then, she knew it was a girl and she'd already named her Amelia, and I thought that sounded like an old lady, like my grandma or something, so I started calling her Amy." A small smile flits across his face at the memory but then it's gone, his expression darkening again. "It was so obvious what she wanted to do, so I never even raised the subject with her, and Dad has never forgiven me."

It's almost incomprehensible to me that someone could be so cruel, but my experiences with my own mother taught me otherwise. No one should know what it feels like to be anything but loved and adored by their parents, and I hate that Mac and I share this understanding. But it is difficult to imagine how someone as awful as his father could convince someone as sweet and kind as Jess to have an affair with him. Unless...

"Mac," I start, my voice wobbling. "Did your dad... I mean, him and Jess...was that..." It's impossible to finish the question. I'm not even certain I want to know the answer.

He gives me a troubled frown. "He didn't rape her, if that's what you're trying to ask. At least not in any legal sense of the word, but he definitely took advantage of her. She was twenty years old and naïve, and he was so much older and...charming. He could be charming when he wanted to be."

"He still can be," I say, remembering my first meeting with Senior and the way he flattered me. Even in his mid-sixties, he's still an attractive man. Big and broad, like both his sons, the gray hair at his temples giving him an air of dignified nobility. As if even age couldn't diminish a man as powerful as him. It isn't hard to imagine the way he would have seemed to Jess more than a decade ago.

"When I was a little boy, my mom used to tell me I was just like him. That I could charm anyone into doing whatever I wanted, and I thought...I don't know. It sounds stupid now, but I was so proud when she'd say that and I thought if only he could see that, how much alike we were, he might love me." His voice is flat, like he can't feel all those long-ago hurts anymore. My heart aches for him, because I know better, and his voice roughens when he adds, "But being like him hasn't seemed like a good thing in a long time."

"You're nothing like him," I insist, as certain of that as I've ever been of anything, but he doesn't seem convinced. I can't stand that he'd think he's anything like his dad, and on impulse I get up and go to him, ignoring the surprised sound he makes when I sit in his lap.

"What are you doing?" he asks, but he's laid one hand on my knee, applying gentle pressure to help me sit crossways in the unforgiving patio chair.

But I ignore that too, instead laying my head against his chest so I don't have to look at him. "When my dad was alive, he used to tell me how pretty I was all the time. He'd say I was the prettiest girl he'd ever laid eyes on, and—"

Mac interrupts, his voice gruff. "He was right."

"Well, I'm glad you think so anyway," I say, fighting a smile and the warm, bubbly feeling in my chest. Now is not the time to let myself get distracted by flattery. "But my mom disagreed. Or, well, I don't know, I guess she didn't. But she acted like being pretty was a bad thing. If I misbehaved or she didn't think I was trying hard enough in school, she'd tell me it was a good thing I'd be able to get by on my looks when I was older. And then when I was older, and especially when I started dating, she'd say I was too pretty for my own good. That it was just going to get me in trouble."

"And then it did." Mac sighs and leans his cheek against the top of my head, his thumb stroking the inside of my knee beneath my sundress.

"No. You were the first person who helped me see I wasn't the things she said I was. I wouldn't trade that for anything. I wouldn't trade—" *You for anything.* But I swallow that confession, because it comes too close to admitting my feelings. "Anyway, my point is, neither of us is what our parents said we were. We made different choices and became different people. You're so much better than your father. Who cares if you're the most charming motherfucker I've ever met? You're a good man, a good father, and that's what matters."

"Well, I'm glad you think so anyway." There's a hint of humor in his voice as he parrots my own words back to me. "You seem to be more evolved than I am, though. Better at dealing with all the bullshit."

Or just better at hiding it. But saying that might open a whole other can of worms I can't deal with tonight, on top of everything else. So I say something else, which I think is partly true anyway. "Maybe it's because all that stuff with my mom is good and truly in my past, you know? She left, and I don't have to deal with it anymore. Not like you do, seeing him all the time while keeping this enormous secret from everyone else you love. It's still part of your life."

"That's probably it."

"How come you've never told anyone?"

He shrugs and my head rises and falls with the lift of his shoulders. "Never seemed like my story to tell. Mom already knows he's a cheater. I can remember hearing them argue about it when I was younger than Tris. So what's the point? And as far as I know, Alex has no idea about any of it, and I figure he's better off that way. But Kim..." He tenses, and I know not telling her bothers him more. "Jess didn't want me to tell her, so I haven't."

Talk about being stuck in the middle, between mother and daughter, both of whom he loves and respects. It must feel awful, but I can understand why he honored Jess's request, and I get why he hasn't told his mom too. But Alex, that feels different. I can't imagine keeping that kind of secret from Willa and Liv. "You should tell your brother."

He doesn't hesitate, and his voice is hard when he says, "No."

"But—"

"But what? You think I haven't considered telling him? I have, a thousand times. But what good would it do? If he hasn't figured out on his own that our dad is a shitbag, he's better off not knowing. I mean Jesus, Gwen, I wish I didn't know. I'm sure as hell not going to make him feel this way too."

"Okay." I'm not sure I agree, but what else can I say? It's his family, his decision, and I have to accept that even if I think he's wrong. But there's one other thing I need to say before I can let the subject drop. Tipping my head back to look up at him in the gathering dark, I swallow hard. "I'm sorry I made the assumptions I did today. It was wrong of me, and I should have talked to you."

"Nah, it's okay. What else could you have thought? As sleazy as my dad is, most people wouldn't think he'd do something that sordid. And Alex?" He actually laughs and shakes his head. "He's practically a monk as far as I can tell. Who would ever suspect him?"

"Poor Cece."

Mac grins. "Yeah, I'm afraid she's destined for disappointment."

With one hand on his shoulder for balance, I straighten in his lap and palm his cheek with my other hand. His five o'clock shadow is rough beneath my fingers, and I spend a few seconds caressing his cheek, enjoying the sensation, before looking him in the eye. "Let's just agree we both should have handled today differently." He nods, his gaze drifting to my lips, watching them move as I continue. "And no more secrets, Mac. Not between us."

"No more secrets." Mac dips his head, his lips brushing mine. I think he meant it to be a soft kiss, a promise of sorts, but it doesn't go quite as planned.

Maybe it's just the physical expression of our overtaxed emotions, but it ignites like a match to gasoline. His mouth slants over mine with bruising pressure, and it reminds me of when we were younger. I used to think Mac and I were most honest with each other when we were touching. It feels that way again now, with his tongue sliding against mine and his hand pushing under my skirt to gently spread my legs. Like our bodies can admit how much we need each other, even if neither of us can say it. Except then he does.

"I need you, Gwen. I need you so fucking much." And even though he's already hooked one finger inside my panties to rub my clit, it doesn't feel like he's talking about my body or sex. Or not just that.

"I need you too." I'm not sure he understands me, because he's pushed two fingers inside of me and my whole being—my voice, my body, my heart—shudders. A certain giddy relief comes with the realization that while we've both made stupid choices and acted foolishly a time or two, we can still come together like this. No matter how I tried to convince myself otherwise, it's never been just sex between us.

Not even that first night. He was twenty-three and I was eighteen and we met in a crowded dance club and had what was for me a wildly uncharacteristic one-night stand in his car. But even then I knew there was something different about him. Something special. And as much as I couldn't resist him, it scared the hell out of me.

It still does.

It would be easy to blame the sudden swell of my emotions and the tears pricking the corners of my eyes on my wildly fluctuating hormones. Easy, but wrong, and it's unnecessary anyway, because Mac seems to sense that the moment has become too much for me. Too heavy with feelings I don't know how to share.

Withdrawing his hand, he helps shift me in his lap until I'm straddling him, the hard bulge behind his zipper pressing against my center. One hand clasps my hip and the other lands on the back of my neck, drawing my mouth back to his. Disregarding all the overwhelming things he makes me feel, I focus on the way he touches me, the way his lips move against mine, the feel of his erection and the rough friction of his jeans when I grind against him. I can worry about my feelings—and his—later. Some other time. For now, I just need to revel in the one uncomplicated thing we've always been able to share.

CHAPTER 15

MAC

Compared to the airports in DC, which are always teeming with people, Pensacola International Airport is all but deserted early on a Tuesday morning. Other than the cheerful employees, yet to be worn down by the demands of the day, and a short line of travelers waiting to get through the security checkpoint, there are only a few other people loitering around, and they are keeping their distance from us.

I don't blame them. Gwen's in the kind of mood that suggests we would all be better off giving her a wide berth today. I get it, though. It's Tristan's birthday and for the first time, she isn't spending it with him. Or rather, she doesn't *think* she is.

"Why did we have to do this?" she whines, glaring first at me and then at the paper cup in her hand. She insisted on getting a coffee on the way to the airport and promptly turned a shocking shade of green after the first sip. But she's still carrying it around because...hell if I know, and I'm not about to ask. Just like I didn't say a goddamn word about the caffeine. Ever since she found out she's pregnant, she's given it up, but she's feeling sorry for herself today and I don't blame her for wanting to splurge a little. I'd definitely prefer she not vomit, though.

"I don't know," I lie with only the faintest twinge of guilt. "Kim said someone needed to pick Tammy up at the airport. I didn't ask why, because I didn't think it would be a big deal." This is the fourth time I've said more or less the same thing since I told Gwen we were picking Kim's best friend up today. I do feel a little bad about it, but this is a different kind of lie. More of a fib, really. The kind that's sometimes required to pull off a surprise. Short-term and in service of something the person being deceived will appreciate when they realize the truth. Hopefully, anyway.

My phone vibrates in my hand, and I angle the screen away from Gwen so she won't be able to see it.

WILLA: *LANDED and off the plane. See you in a sec!*

ANTICIPATION SWELLS IN MY CHEST, and I give Gwen a sidelong look. "We have a few more minutes before Tammy's plane lands. Do you want to call Tris and wish him a happy birthday now?"

Gwen's expression brightens instantly, but there's a sad gleam in her eyes that I recognize. It's the same look she's gotten every time she thinks about being away from him today. She wanted to call him before we left the hotel, but she would have worried when no one answered. I couldn't stand the idea of her starting the day that way. Especially not when I planned this to be a special day for all of us. If I hadn't been able to distract her with my rambling half-fabricated worries about the campaign, I'd have broken down and spoiled my own surprise just to keep her from worrying unnecessarily.

"He should be eating breakfast about now." She pulls out her phone and turns her back to me and the sliding glass doors that separate us from the secure side of the airport. I can't see her expression when the call connects, but Tristan must have been the one to answer, because Gwen immediately launches into song. "Happy Birthday to you…"

She reaches the third verse before her voice cracks on the word "happy." Biting the inside of my cheek, I ignore the impulse to interrupt her and blurt out the truth, ruining the surprise moments before its culmination. *I've lasted this long. Just a little longer.*

When she's finished singing, she asks, "What's all that background noise?" There's a short pause and whatever Tris said must have satisfied her, because she changes the subject. "Remember to take your cupcakes to school today. Liv will be mad she went to all that trouble to make your favorites if you forget them."

Too busy focusing all my attention on the security doors, I'm only half listening to her side of the conversation, but Tristan must have told her Liv didn't make his cupcakes. Her voice takes on an irritated note and she simultaneously apologizes to him and promises to have a talk with his aunt.

Tristan doesn't care about the cupcakes, though. I can tell because I can see him now, bounding toward the sliding doors a few steps ahead of Willa. Holding the phone to one ear and smiling, he waves excitedly when he sees us.

I step closer to Gwen, tapping her on the shoulder to get her attention. She turns, her lips pinched in an annoyed frown, but I'm pretty sure she'll forgive me for interrupting once she realizes why.

"Look." I tilt my head toward Willa and Tristan.

She rolls her eyes but spins again, this time toward the security doors. Willa and Tris are only about ten yards from us now—it's impossible to miss them in the deserted airport, and I hold my breath, waiting for Gwen's reaction. She looks at Tristan, then the phone still clutched in her hand, and back to our son one more time. Then all at once, she's laughing and crying, arms spread wide and rushing forward to meet him. Tristan barely has time to pass Willa's phone back to her before Gwen envelops him in a crushing hug, her cup still clutched in one hand and sloshing now-lukewarm coffee on the floor.

"Mom," Tristan wheezes with that lilt that means she's embarrassing him. But he doesn't squirm or otherwise try to escape, instead accepting her enthusiastic welcome with resigned grace. It reminds me of the way I endure my own mother's sometimes over-the-top affection, and that would be enough to make me smile if I weren't already smiling so big my face feels like it might crack.

Still sniffling, Gwen pulls back a little and pinches his cheek. "You're terrible at keeping secrets. How did you manage to pull this off?"

He shrugs, and it's Willa who answers. "I didn't tell him until after you guys talked to him last night. We weren't taking any chances that he might accidentally blow it."

"Good call," she admits with a watery laugh. Hugging Tristan tight again, she looks back and forth between me and her sister. "I can't believe you guys did this."

All I can do is shrug like an idiot, because my vocal chords don't seem to be working. It isn't just Gwen's reaction that has me a little choked up either, although I am definitely pleased she likes her surprise. But the truth is, my motives weren't entirely selfless in planning this. I've never shared his birthday with him before, and there's no way in hell I was going to miss it now.

"Don't look at me." Willa shakes her head and points at me. "It was his idea, and he took care of all the planning. I'm just here to babysit the hooligan on the plane."

"Hey!" Tristan nudges Willa's hip, glaring at her. "I'm not a hooligan, and I'm eleven now. I don't need a babysitter."

"Technically, you won't be eleven until 4:27 this afternoon," Gwen says, setting the record straight, and Willa is nodding right along with her.

He turns to me, brown eyes wide and pitiful. "They never even let me open my presents until after dinner."

I'm apparently meant to believe that's akin to child abuse, but he's out of luck. "Sorry, tiger, but I agree with them. You're still ten for another eight hours or so."

Disappointed with my answer, Tris screws up his face, obviously expecting the worst. "And presents?"

"We'll see," I reply, ignoring the narrow-eyed look Gwen is giving me.

With all our travel, we agreed it was time to give in to his persistent begging and get him a phone of his own. Since she didn't know we'd be seeing him today, we planned to give it to him this weekend when we're home again.

It's a big enough gift that it made sense it ought to be from both of us. We even thought giving him a joint gift, like normal parents in a normal family, might help soothe some of his lingering insecurities over Gwen's pregnancy.

What we hadn't been able to agree on was who would pay for what. No surprise there. Gwen suggested—and by suggested, I mean unilaterally decided—that we would split the cost of the phone fifty-fifty and the line would be added to her monthly plan. Although that might not be unreasonable in other circumstances, it didn't work for me, and I didn't agree. Rather than argue, we left the discussion unfinished, and I assume she was counting on an audience in the cell phone store to keep me in line when the moment of truth arrived.

She's right, I wouldn't have caused a scene in public, but that didn't mean I would meekly go along with her plan, either. She isn't the only one who can be bullheaded, after all. And since I knew we'd be seeing Tris on his actual birthday, I took matters into my own hands. I bought the phone, added it to my plan and, after she fell asleep last night, I wrapped it, my hand shaking a little as I scrawled *From Mom and Dad* on the tag.

"Mac—"

"Later," I interrupt, ignoring the warning in her voice. She's a smart woman and I'm sure she suspects what I've done but this isn't the time or place for that argument. Turning to Willa and Tris, I ask, "You guys want to go get some breakfast?"

That's all it takes to set Tristan off on a soliloquy about waffles, effectively preventing Gwen from pressing the issue. With any luck, I'll be able to hold her off until after we get Willa and Tris back on a plane tonight. Here's hoping, anyway.

~

GWEN

WITH BREAKFAST FINISHED, Mac revealed we're spending the day at the beach. Tristan squealed, beside himself with excitement, because he's never been to the ocean before. Willa, who in this one area bears a striking resemblance to Cece, packed approximately ten gallons of sunscreen and their swimsuits in the carry-on bag they brought with them. Knowing I wouldn't have packed it for a work a trip, she'd even thought ahead and brought my suit too.

"You going to take that off or what?" Willa digs her toes in the sand, gesturing to the sundress I have on over my suit. Since it's a bikini, it still fits. Sort of. My boobs are trying to bust out of the top and the high-rise bottoms don't exactly lay right, but all the important bits are covered.

"Eventually, but I don't want to burn my bump." I'm not entirely kidding. On arrival, we all slathered on sunscreen, but I burn easily and I'm not taking any chances. The last thing I want to do is add a sunburn to the growing list of body aches that already plague me.

"Ha, ha." Willa rolls her eyes and gives me a gentle elbow in the side, but her tone is serious when she says, "So what's going on anyway?"

"What do you mean?"

She waves one arm toward the water where Mac and Tris are engaged in a splash fight. "With you and your baby daddy."

I groan and throw myself back on the blanket we've spread in the sand. Even with my sunglasses perched on my nose, the sun is too bright, and I close my eyes against it.

"Don't want to talk about it, huh?" Willa lays down next to me and nudges me again with her arm.

"There's nothing to talk about."

"Well, I have something to talk about then."

She doesn't go on though, so I turn my head and open my eyes, shading them with one hand. There's hesitation and uncertainty written all over her face. I have no idea what she wants to talk about, but knowing her, it will be easier without me staring at her. Propping myself up on my elbows, I dig my toes into the hot sand and focus on Mac and Tris playing in the surf. "What's that?"

"Don't be mad, okay?"

Still not looking at her, and definitely not making any promises I might not be able to keep, I say, "Spit it out, Willie."

She does, almost literally, cramming the entire sentence into one enormous compound word. "Well-it's-just-that-Diane-and-I-are-kind-of-talking-about-moving-in-together."

"Huh?" But mentally I'm adding spaces between all the words, and they're beginning to make more sense. *She's moving in with Diane?* "Oh. This is kind of fast, isn't it?"

Now she's the one looking everywhere but at me, and her voice is stiff. Awkward. "I mean, we haven't picked a date or anything, but you know…soon-ish, I guess. I thought I should let you know we're thinking about it though, because if we do, I won't able to help you as much anymore. I didn't want to leave you in a lurch or anything."

"Don't worry about that. We'll be fine." I'm not going to lie, Willie has been an enormous help over the years. First, supervising Liv and Tris and shuttling them between activities so I could work and go to school. And more recently, after she finished school and got a job at the hospital, financially too. But it wasn't fair to her that she spent so much of her teenage years looking after her younger sister and nephew, and now that she's grown, I'm not going to get in the way of her living her own life, even if that does make things more difficult for me.

Besides, some of the financial pressure is easing now that I've gotten a good job in my field. I'll still have to take out loans for Liv's school, just like I did for Willie, but I make enough that I don't have to worry about keeping a roof over our heads or food on the table anymore, even if Willie does move out.

Willa is unconvinced. "Are you sure?"

"Absolutely. I mean, I worry you might be rushing things, but that's just the mom in me—I can't help it. If this is what you want, if you're happy, then I'm on board." Setting aside the worry isn't quite that easy, but I like Diane and I trust Willie's judgment. She's always been the most sensible of the Pierce girls, never impulsive like Livie or struck stupid by dick like me. Or, I guess, pussy in her case. The point is, she has a good head on her shoulders, and I'm not going to start doubting her now. Still, I wouldn't be a mom if I didn't add, "And my door will always be open if you ever need to come back for any reason. Not that I think you will, but just in case."

Her cheeks color, and for a split second she almost looks like the shy little girl she was when our mother left. But then she squints toward the water and lifts her chin in Mac's direction. "When Livie told me you were pregnant again, I kind of thought you might move in with him."

"She wasn't supposed to say anything." I swore the brat to secrecy after the spring break trip, but obviously it didn't do much good.

"Because that's the important part of what I just said." Willie laughs and kicks sand at my legs. "Besides, I'd have figured it out on my own long before you finally 'fessed up. I don't remember you getting this big this fast with Tris."

It's on the tip of my tongue to tell her I'm having twins. It would almost certainly be an effective way to dodge the other subject she's raised. But no. There's so much that could go wrong, and I'm not prepared for all the extra attention everyone is sure to give me once that secret is out. So instead I say, "It's like that sometimes with second pregnancies. Everything is already all stretched out, I guess."

"Yeah. You know, I really liked my rotation in obstetrics. Maybe after I get a little more experience under my belt, I'll switch things up a little and go back."

"You should. Or pediatrics. You really liked that too when you were in school," I remind her.

"Maybe." Laughing, she leans closer and bumps my shoulder. "But you aren't changing the subject that easily."

"I'm not moving in with Mac," I insist in a tone that hopefully suggests she should drop this.

Willa is undaunted. "You think he'd balk?"

"No, he asked a while ago." I would have preferred not having to admit that, but I can't lie to my sister. And now she's never going to let it go.

Willa turns toward me, her eyes wide. "And you said no?"

"Of course."

Willa sighs, knotting her hands in her lap. "Because of me and Liv."

"No. I mean, I did mention I couldn't desert you guys, but he said you could come too."

"His place is pretty nice. If living with him is on the table, maybe I don't want to move out. Do you think he'd mind if Diane came too?" Willa laughs, and her relief is obvious. She's always so quick to blame herself for the things I've had to give up in order to raise her and Liv when none of it is her fault. At least this time she seems to believe it.

"No one is moving in with him."

"Why not?" It's like she's eight again, when "why not" was her response to literally everything. It's even more irritating now.

"I just... You know, it isn't like that with us. When he asked, it wasn't even about him wanting us to live together. He listed all the practical reasons why we should. Like, that it would be cheaper than living apart and that he'd be able to see the kids more, which is all true, but...I don't know. It didn't feel right."

"He's kind of a dumbass, isn't he?" Willa shakes her head and laughs, making it clear that "dumbass" was meant with affection. "But I get it. He knew you were going to fight him, so he was trying to convince you with logic when what he should have been doing is telling you how much he can't live without you."

"Except he doesn't feel that way. And even if he did, I still would have said no. This thing with us, whatever it is, isn't going to last forever, and it'll only make things harder if we live together."

"How can you be so sure of that?"

"Because nothing lasts forever."

"Maybe." Willa pauses, giving that some thought. "Or maybe you're just scared and letting that sabotage your future. You should think about it, because if that's the case, it really isn't fair to any of you."

CHAPTER 16

MAC

"So, can I have my presents now?" Tristan asks, his gaze trained on the two wrapped packages sitting in the center of the table. I'm fairly sure he hasn't taken his eyes off them since we sat down for dinner.

I'm not sure how I got put in charge of making this decision, but Gwen and Willa both just look at me so I shrug. "Sure, why not?"

In his enthusiasm, Tristan throws himself across the table, nearly knocking over his glass of water, and Willa snatches the gifts away at the last second, eliciting a high-pitched whine from the birthday boy. "Oh, come on!"

Snickering, she passes him the larger of the two gifts, which is her own.

He shreds the green-and-blue striped paper without so much as glancing at the tag, although he does seem to know who it's from. "You got me a cookbook for kids?"

Willa nods, ignoring his scowl. "Yeah. You're always complaining about my cooking. I thought that might be something fun we could do together."

"I guess." He sounds even more skeptical than he looks, but he's flipping through pages, at least making an effort to appear interested. That isn't good enough for Gwen though, because she nudges his arm and softly hisses his name. It's all the reminder required to prompt a more grateful thank you for his aunt.

Passing him the second gift, Willa explains, "Liv wanted to give you her present in person, so you have to wait until we get home for that one."

Tristan nods without complaint, probably having already expected as much, and pauses to read the tag this time, underlining the words with his finger. "From Mom and Dad." His brows draw together, his lips moving as he reads it one more time silently. His voice is heavy with disappointment when he finally says, "I thought you'd both get me something."

Greedy little punk. "We did. We got you one thing, together."

Gwen clears her throat, clearly disagreeing with my use of the word "together," but she doesn't otherwise react. It's Willa who says, "And I'll bet this is bigger than if they'd gotten you two separate gifts."

That seems to encourage him, his eyes brightening with interest. "Is it?"

"You're acting like a spoiled brat. Do you want the present or not?" Gwen's no-nonsense tone is sufficiently stern, and Tris tears the package open so quickly I wonder why I bothered to wrap it. I don't have long to consider that question, though. As soon as he realizes he's finally gotten his phone, he squeals loud enough to draw the attention of several of the surrounding tables. "I got a phone!" Before anyone can respond to that, he's out of his chair and throwing himself into his mother's arms. "Thankyouthankyouthankyou!"

"You're welcome." Whatever animus Gwen has for me about the phone, it's undetectable in her tone now. Smoothing his hair back, she kisses his forehead, but he's already on the move again, dancing to my side for a quick thank-you hug. But he's too excited to linger and before long, he's back in his own chair, absorbed in his phone.

~

GWEN

It's always hard saying goodbye to Tris, but for some reason, leaving him and Willa at the airport tonight was harder than usual. It was such a wonderful, happy day. Even my irritation over Mac's stunt with the stupid phone can't overshadow it, and I remind myself I shouldn't be too upset with him. Spending Tris's birthday with him was an unexpected and wonderful surprise, and I only have Mac to thank for that. Well, Willie too, but it's clear he's the one who came up with the plan and put it in action.

But I can't lie. I *was* upset at the airport this morning when I first realized what he must have done. My gut instinct was to confront him, to shut him down, just like I always have, but that isn't fair to either of us. I love him and if I want him to love me back, I have to get over this and learn to compromise. To be real partners. Because ultimately, that's what I want, and no matter how difficult it is for me to deal with, he's right about this.

There's no doubt he's expecting another argument too, because as soon as our hotel room door has closed behind us, he says, "All right. Say it." And the resigned tone of his voice only makes me feel worse.

Dropping my purse on the desk, I force my voice to remain casual. "So what do I owe you? I'm not sure what half would be with tax and the accessories?"

"What?" He's standing at the edge of the bed, emptying his pockets onto the nightstand, and stops abruptly, turning toward me with both brows raised.

"Well, we were going to split it, right?"

Mac nods, apparently too dumfounded to speak, but after a moment he recovers enough to say, "I don't remember exactly. It was a little more than a thousand dollars but I'm willing to call it even if you give me five hundred. Otherwise I'll have to find the receipt. I think they emailed it to me."

My natural impulse is to demand he find the receipt because yes, I absolutely want to pay exactly half, to the penny. But I manage to ignore that because I have to be better. I have to do better. So instead I say, "Sure, that's fine."

One corner of his mouth kicks up, and he shoves both hands in his pockets. "I can accept PayPal, Venmo, or Apple Pay. If you want to write a check, I'll have to see your driver's license first."

"Okay, I'll catch you in the morning." And with that, we're both laughing. It's a giddy, weird moment, like neither of us can quite believe we've managed to have this conversation without fighting. Changing my destructive mental habits is hard work and kind of sucks but it isn't difficult to see how this is so much better.

But there is one other issue about the phone. I've decided not to mention it because it shouldn't matter, but Mac raises it anyway. "He's on my plan. Is that going to be a problem?"

"No. I mean, my lizard brain is saying yes but it's, like, ten bucks. I'm trying really hard to be a normal, reasonable person about this."

"You're doing a great job." The smile he gives me with that bit of praise makes it clear he appreciates my effort, even if he's never really understood why it was such a challenging issue for me.

After brushing my teeth and washing my face, I slather lotion on my sunburned nose and cheeks. I was so careful with the sunscreen, but apparently not careful enough. At least it isn't too bad, and my face took the brunt of the damage, if you don't count the new freckles that have appeared on my shoulders.

By the time I emerge from the bathroom, Mac's already in bed. He's on his back, one arm behind his head and one knee bent, the sheet draped across his middle. He looks straight out of one of those sultry cologne ads you see in fashion magazines. I always assumed one could only achieve that level of sex appeal with a bevy of professional stylists, flattering lighting and, in most cases, probably Photoshop.

"What are you looking at?"

Oops. Guess I should have been more subtle about my staring, but since I've been caught, I might as well be honest. "You."

He grins, throwing the sheet off and fisting his cock. He gives it a long, slow stroke and says, "Get over here and you can do more than look."

It's impossible not to get distracted by the view. His broad shoulders and narrow waist, the ridges of his abs tapering into a V, like an arrow telling me exactly where to go. Pressure settles in my core, heavy and aching, and I squeeze my thighs together.

"Gwen." He's still smiling, but his voice has an exasperated edge.

What the hell is wrong with me? Why am I so preoccupied drooling over the eye candy instead of taking advantage of the eye candy? Mac seems to be wondering the same thing, and he's given up waiting on me.

Getting out of bed, he crosses the room and comes toward me. He doesn't stop until I'm against the desk, its beveled edge digging into the backs of my thighs, his hands on my hips, tugging my sundress up. "You're wearing a lot of dresses lately. I like it."

"That's because they're the only thing that still fits," I admit with a grumpy frown. This is not a sexy conversation. I've already had to replace most of my work clothes. The pencil skirts and fitted slacks I previously favored just don't fit anymore. For more casual wear, I can still get away with some of my looser-fitting dresses and I've been making the most of them, but I don't like being reminded of my rapidly expanding girth.

Gathering the skirt around my waist, he helps me up to sit on the desk then parts my legs with one hand. "I know, but I like it."

"Easy access?" I joke, my voice tight. It's so hard to concentrate, especially when he starts to stroke the damp fabric between my thighs. It's like being lost, worrying about the way I look and what he thinks of my changing body while simultaneously I'm on the verge of begging him to kiss me or touch me or fuck me. Something. Anything. I'm nervous and needy and a little bit scared, and he's the only one who can help me, so I clutch his shoulders with both hands.

"No." He pauses, catching his bottom lip between his teeth and then letting it go, his lips tipping up in a mischievous grin. "Well, yes. But not just that."

That forces a breathy laugh from me. "Then why?"

One hand splayed on the small of my back, he rubs me through my panties. It isn't enough, not nearly, but it feels so good, and I list forward until I can press my face against his chest. Mac kisses the top of my head then answers the question, the words a warm puff of air against my temple. "It turns out, being pregnant makes you hotter."

I want to tell him not to lie to me. That he's going to get laid either way, but the bullshit will only piss me off, because I know that's what it is. But he hooks my panties to the side, slipping one finger inside me, and the only sound that comes out of me is a low moan that's pathetically close to a whine.

"Christ, that bikini you wore today almost killed me. All I could think about was getting my face between your legs."

"Oh, God."

"Would you like that, baby? Do you want me to suck your pussy?"

"Y-Y-Yes."

Mac lets go of me, withdrawing his finger and taking a step back. Lifting my dress over my head and dropping it on the floor, he turns his attention to my panties, helping me shimmy out of them while I unfasten my bra. By the time I've discarded it on the desk next to me, he's kneeling in front of me, spreading me open with two fingers and gripping his cock with his other hand.

The first swipe of his tongue makes me gasp and lean back, bracing myself on one hand. He groans in answer, lapping at me eagerly. But it isn't enough, not for me, and I grab the back of his head, my fingers sinking into his thick, dark hair, and hold him against me in silent plea.

He takes the hint, his tongue plunging inside me and his thumb plucking my clit. It's exactly what I need, and my hips jerk, the pleasure that was simmering in my pelvis gathering into something more powerful. More imminent. But Mac keeps me there, hovering in the in-between, until I can't bear it and I'm pulling his hair and urgently rocking against his mouth, desperately seeking the orgasm I need more than air.

That's what Mac was evidently waiting for, for my need to reach that frantic, wild peak, because he says, "That's it, baby. Ride my face and come for me."

And then he changes tactics, his lips latching onto my clit and sucking hard as he pushes two fingers inside me, curling them to hit the perfect spot. The pressure that's been gathering inside me tightens then flares, my inner muscles clenching and my skin tingling as my release blazes through me.

Abruptly, Mac stands and steps between my legs. Still quivering through the aftershocks of my orgasm, I'm boneless and panting, but it doesn't matter. He guides my hands behind me, urging me to lean back on them, then hooks one of my knees around his hip and leans forward, bracing himself against the desk as he rocks into me.

There's no teasing or lingering in the in-between now. This is a frenzied race for the finish, the sound of the desk crashing into the wall marking our tempo. His mouth finds mine, our tongues tangling, and I can taste myself on his lips. It's heady, intoxicating, and my breasts ache, my nipples burning with the need for friction. I need to feel them crushed between us, rubbing against the hard planes off his chest. I need to be closer.

Careful not to disrupt our balance, my ass teetering on the edge of the desk, I put my arms around his neck, clinging to him. Mac doesn't falter, banding one arm tightly around my back to hold me close, the muscles in his other arm flexing as he leans into it, supporting us both.

"Fucking hell, Gwen, I..." His deep, rumbly voice is broken by his labored breathing, but even so, it's so rough with emotion it's palpable. A real, tactile thing I can feel as surely as I can his touch, and my oversensitive skin blooms with goosebumps.

"What?" I ask, tugging on the hairs at his nape. Whatever he'd been about to say, I want to hear it.

Mac shakes his head, pressing his face into my hair, his lips tickling my ear. "Just don't ever run away again, Gwen. Please don't run."

His vulnerability takes me by surprise, my already racing heart slipping into overdrive. Torn between offering him reassurance and begging for forgiveness for the way I hurt him, I don't know what to say. The words and thoughts are all jumbled together, twisted up with the volatile sensations of my looming orgasm, and I can't sort through them to assemble a coherent thought. So instead I say his name and hope that in that one word, he can hear all the things I want to say and can't.

~

MAC

Christ, I'm an idiot.

I almost told Gwen I love her. Almost admitted that I lied the day of her job interview, because I never stopped loving her. Then—as if it couldn't get worse—I practically begged her to stay with me. What a fucking sad sack I am. And now, back in bed, both of us sleepy and sated, she's snuggled into my side, her head on my shoulder, and the words are still there, hovering on the tip of my tongue.

I love you.

I've always loved you.

I need you.

I want us to be a family. All three of us.

Shit. Five of us.

Five?

Oh, God, what the fuck are we doing?

"Mac? You still awake?"

"Hmm?" I don't trust myself to speak for fear of what I might say.

"Thank you for making today happen." Pushing up on one elbow, she rests her hand on my chest and stretches to kiss my cheek. Given what we just did on the desk—which seems to have picked up a permanent wobble—such a chaste gesture would be funny if it weren't so damn sweet.

And since when have I liked sweet anyway?

Her cheeks are still pink from exertion—and maybe a little sunburn—and her full lips are turned up in a tender smile, her tousled golden hair framing her face, her soft blue eyes holding mine, and it's too much. Too confusing.

The sex I understand. That's never been a problem between us. It's the earnest, sentimental looks that do me in, because they make me think she could love me and I've wanted that since before I was willing to 'fess up to my own feelings, even to myself.

Clearing my throat, I collar the back of her neck with my hand, gently pushing her back down and tucking her head under my chin. Once she's settled, I stare up at the ceiling and say, "I knew it was important to you. That you didn't want to miss it. But it was selfish too. It's the first birthday I've ever spent with him, you know? So don't go giving me too much credit."

It seemed like a good, soft way to try and re-establish some parameters in our strange non-relationship relationship. Judging by the way her lips curl against my chest, it didn't work though, and I can hear the smile in her voice when she says, "I know, but I guess I just wanted you to know how much it meant to me."

I want to tell her it a meant a lot to me too. Spending Tristan's birthday with him but also the real effort she put into meeting me halfway on his phone. It was obvious she struggled, but in a way, that only makes me appreciate it more.

The thing is, with all the adversity she's overcome in the last decade, I don't know if she could've done it without that stubborn determination. Raising her sisters and Tris, going to school and working full-time, it all seems impossibly hard to me, but she got up every day and made shit fucking happen. I admire the hell out of her for it and it probably shouldn't be any big surprise if, after all of that, it's difficult for her to learn to lean on someone else for a change.

So I haven't begrudged her the struggle. To some degree, I understand that, even if she has been unwilling or unable to articulate it in any detail. No, the thing I resented was her unwillingness to even try until now. It gives me hope for some kind of future together, if that's what we both want.

But I don't know how to say any of that without blurting out the one thing I'm too big a coward to say. So instead I kiss her and tell her to go to sleep. And long after she has, I'm still staring into the dark, wondering if we really could make this work for real. Forever.

CHAPTER 17

GWEN

Bus tours are a common and popular campaign tool, but if I ever find out who first came up with the idea, I'll kill them. Or I guess, since they're probably already dead—no thanks to me—I'll think a lot of really mean things about them. Whatever.

It's not that I object to the concept so much, and in some ways I can see the appeal. For one thing, it's easier to work between stops, and Kim can invite individuals or small groups of journalists to ride on her bus, giving them more one-on-one time with her and a peek behind the scenes. The bedroom at the back of the bus is another plus. It's certainly convenient when the pregnant lady needs a nap.

But there are downsides too. Like the lack of privacy. We're still stopping at hotels each night, but it's impossible to get a moment to yourself when we're all crammed on a bus. And, if I'm being totally honest, it's kind of boring. While the others pour over polls and strategize for the general election, I'm left occasionally checking in with social media and staring out the window watching the miles fly by. I've managed to read a little, but now that the morning sickness seems to be well and truly over, I haven't wanted to tempt the vomit gods and risk a case of motion sickness, which has occasionally been a problem for me in the past.

I don't know what it's like on Kim's bus or the bus full of reporters behind us, but on this bus, my fellow travelers are like a bunch of third graders on a field trip, and I'm their buzz kill chaperone.

When a paper airplane comes sailing through the air, I'm already looking for the culprit before it makes contact with the back of Alex's head. The guilty party, whoever they are, has a good poker face, because all the suspects, which includes Cece and several other staffers who are huddled at the front of the bus allegedly working on planning the convention, appear oblivious.

Alex is across the aisle from me, sitting at the table with Mac, who asserted oldest-sibling privilege to claim the front-facing seat. Which means Alex has his back to the culprits and couldn't have seen who launched the projectile. Nonetheless, he seems to think he knows exactly who to blame. Hooking one arm over the back of his seat, he twists around to yell, "I know that was you, Cece!"

The accused doesn't look up from the papers spread in her lap. "Kind of busy here. What are you talking about?"

It's a pretty convincing response. She certainly appears to be engrossed in something else. Alex isn't buying it, though. Snatching the airplane off the floor, he unfolds the paper, carefully flattening it on the table with his palm. Judging by his triumphant shout, I half expect it to contain a signed confession. "It's a menu for a fucking caterer in Miami!"

Okay, not a signed confession, but it might as well be. Cece is in charge of all things related to the convention, which is being held in Miami this year. Though several others are helping her, no one else would dare to dispose of her reference materials.

Mac seems to agree. Slouched in his seat with his arms stretched across the back, he's watching the scene unfold with amusement.

Ignoring Cece's next round of denials, Alex turns to glare at his brother. "This isn't funny, and you aren't helping. You're her boss, for God's sake. Maybe you could tell her to knock it off?"

Mac rubs his lip in contemplation before asking, "Why do you take it so personally? Yesterday she played keep-away with what Gwen thought was the last popsicle. She's just having fun, and she does it to everyone."

"Uh, no. That," I say, waving one arm at the crumpled paper in front of Alex, "is all in good fun. The popsicle thing was bullshit." Granted, it hadn't actually been the last popsicle, but my cravings are no joke, and it's ninety degrees outside. If there really weren't more, Cece wouldn't still be breathing.

Although, now that I think about it, I could go for a popsicle.

Demonstrating his recently acquired talent for clairvoyance, Mac slides out of the booth and crosses the aisle to the small refrigerator freezer combo and retrieves a popsicle. The very presence of a freezer is, I have to grudgingly admit, a point in the pro column for bus tours.

Alex rolls his eyes at his brother's back, irritated by his obvious hypocrisy. "Like you're so easygoing about it when she targets you. Have you already forgotten what she did when you told her Gwen's pregnant?"

Overall, Alex isn't wrong, but he's chosen a poor example to advance his argument. A week after our announcement, Cece approached Mac with a stack of research and informational pamphlets on vasectomies, including a list of local urologists, ranked by average user review across three different review platforms, and a printout from Mac's medical insurance detailing the relevant copays and deductibles.

It was her way of teasing him, since he was previously so vocal about never wanting kids but, unbeknownst to her, he was already considering it. I don't know if he'll decide to go through with it or not but honestly, in light of our track record, who could blame him if he does? Hell, if I end up needing a c-section, I just might have Dr. Flores tie my tubes while she's in there. We obviously can't be *too* careful.

Mac grins and sits down next to me on the couch, pointing the popsicle at his brother and stretching out his long legs to rest his shiny brown oxfords on the edge of Alex's seat. "That was actually very helpful."

"That isn't the point," Alex insists, frustrated Mac isn't taking him seriously. "This is work, not a playground, and her behavior is unprofessional."

With a shrug, Mac unwraps what turns out to be a yellow—*ugh, lemon*—popsicle. "Lighten up. This is a grueling fucking job, in case you haven't noticed, and you can't blame people if a little fooling around makes it easier to cope."

"Of course you'd say that," Alex says, his gaze flicking to me.

Oh, shit.

Mac's expression darkens and he pauses, one hand extended to offer me the popsicle, his suddenly very serious gaze fastened on Alex. "You are way out of fucking line."

The temperature on the bus—or at least our little section of it—has cooled considerably. If I had to guess, I'd say it's probably reached equilibrium with the freezer, and I shift uncomfortably in my seat. I don't want them to fight, and I especially don't want them fighting because of me. In a frantic attempt to defuse the situation before it can further escalate, I gently push Mac's hand with the proffered popsicle away. "I want a blue one."

There's a tense moment where the brothers' eyes remain locked, and I hold my breath until Mac sighs and turns to me, one corner of his mouth kicking up. "We're stopping in less than twenty minutes. You really want to get off this bus and face Kim's supporters, not to mention the press, looking like you just polished Papa Smurf's pole?"

Snatching the popsicle from him, I shove it in my mouth and start searching for my personal cell phone. I can feel it vibrating, but it isn't in my lap with my work phone like I thought. By the time I find it wedged between my thigh and the couch cushion, it's stopped vibrating, the notification pop-up advising me I have one missed call from Joan MacKenzie.

Since school let out, Tristan's been spending a couple of days a week with his grandma—carefully scheduled for times when Mac's dad is on the road with Whittaker's campaign. I'm not sure if she's realized we're doing that on purpose or not, but I'm relieved we've been able to work out a way for Tris to spend time with her when the old creep won't be around. And it's been nice, allowing the two of them to bond and freeing up my sisters from having to watch him all the time. But Joan has never called me. We've texted a few times, mostly when she's had questions about his interests or preferences, but she arranges their visits through Mac.

With a worried frown, I tilt the screen toward him and take the popsicle out of my mouth. "Your mother just tried to call me."

"She has Tris today." His brow creases, and he gives me a sidelong look.

I nod. "Mac, she's never, ever called me before. What if—" I'm interrupted by the arrival of a text message. In our worry, we're both so eager to read it we bump heads.

Joan MacKenzie: *Hi! Sorry if I interrupted something important. I know how busy you kids are! I was just thinking, when you're home sometime, we ought to go shopping. Maternity clothes, baby clothes, fun stuff for the nursery. I know all the best shops!*

Alex must have picked up on our momentary panic, because his voice is tinged with concern, their disagreement forgotten. "Everything all right?"

"Yeah, Mom wants to take Gwen shopping," Mac explains.

"For the baby, right?" Alex guesses.

"She says she knows all the best shops." If I sound mystified, it's because I am. Her youngest child is thirty-three years old. It's hard to imagine she has her thumb on the pulse of the maternity and infant scene.

"That...doesn't really surprise me," Mac admits.

"I've sort of always imagined her keeping a future grandbabies scrapbook," Alex agrees. "Like the girls in all the romcoms do with their wedding fantasies."

"Real girls do that too." I know, because there are three scrapbooks exactly like that in my apartment, although mine has gotten pretty dusty in the last few years. Hopefully, Willa and Olivia will have better luck.

Alex perks up and shoves Mac's feet off the bench so he can turn sideways and lean toward me, elbows on his knees and chin on his fists. "Do you have a wedding scrapbook, Gwen?"

He's smart enough to see an indirect answer as deflection, but what other choice do I have? Next to me, Mac is already uncomfortable, squirming in his seat like Tristan on the rare occasion he has to wear dress clothes. He'd probably break out in hives and start puking if I told the truth. *Deflection it is, then.* "I didn't say that."

Preventing Alex from pressing me further, Mac jumps in to redirect the conversation. "You should go. You were just complaining the other morning about needing more maternity clothes."

Sucking on my popsicle, I consider the possibility. I definitely need to expand my wardrobe, but I'm not so sure I want his mom tagging along. It would be different, I think, if we were a normal couple and Joan was my mother-in-law. Or even my boyfriend's mom. But we're living in this undefined space that makes everything more complicated, more awkward, and I'd feel like a fraud hanging out with her. Besides, I can't imagine Joan and I have much in common. What would we even talk about? "I don't know. I mean, I hardly know your mom."

"I know, baby, but see, this is how you get to know people. You spend time with them."

"Could you be more patronizing?"

Unrepentant, Mac shrugs and smiles.

"He definitely could be, yes," Alex volunteers, and some of the tension that always seems to be simmering between the brothers creeps back into his voice. But then he laughs and says, "I agree with him, though. You should go. Once you have that baby, you won't be able to get rid of her, so you might as well get used to having her around now."

It probably says a lot about the kind of person I am that I preferred it when they were fighting with each other over them ganging up on me. But Alex has a point, a better one than he even realizes. Once the twins come, I'll have enough on my plate without adding building a relationship with my baby daddy's mama to the list. Better to get that out of the way now.

CHAPTER 18

GWEN

JOAN MACKENZIE IS STANDING on the sidewalk in front of The Bump Boutique in Old Town Alexandria, waiting for me when I round the corner. With her trendy white capri pants and sleek emerald blouse she's the embodiment of a D.C. society matron, and it's intimidating as hell. I mean, what kind of person has the guts to wear white pants? Certainly not me. The one time I tried, Tristan smeared ketchup all over them.

She greets me with a hug and a vivacious, "Hello, darling!"

The way she says "darling" almost sounds like the stereotypical rich lady in the old black-and-white movies. *Dah-ling.* It's a good distraction from her effusive—and entirely unexpected—embrace, and I have to stifle a giggle. "Um, hi."

Joan frowns and, one hand on my arm, leads me toward the shop. "Don't tell me Will made you take the Metro."

"He would have dropped me off, but it was in the wrong direction, and he still has to pick Alex up. I was afraid they'd miss the boat if he brought me too, so I insisted," I explain.

I'm not the only one experiencing a little forced bonding today. It's Father's Day and, as Mac's present from Tristan, I got them tickets to the Washington Nationals game today. It was the perfect gift, one I was certain they would both enjoy, but I bought a third ticket too. For Alex. Mac was less enthused about that.

"Oh, they're taking the baseball boat? How fun!"

"Yeah, I'm a little jealous, to be honest." The water taxi normally runs between National Harbor, Alexandria, the Wharf and Georgetown, but on game days there's also a ferry to Nationals Park. Today is one of those rare summer days where it's bright and sunny without being oppressively hot and humid. The perfect kind of day for a boat ride up the Potomac.

She claps her hands and steps ahead of me to hold the door. "Say no more. There are several shops on my list in Georgetown. We can take the water taxi too!"

Oh, God. She has a list.

Stepping inside the shop, it's immediately clear I can't afford to buy a pair of socks from The Bump Boutique, let alone actual clothes. The word "boutique" in the name should have been my first clue. It's probably futile, but I hope every shop on her list isn't like this one.

"Welcome!" The approaching sales clerk sweeps her arm wide. "I'm Chloe. How can I help you ladies today?"

"Oh, I—"

Joan steps forward, offering Chloe her hand. "I'm Joan, and this is my friend Gwen. She's due in November and she's a career woman, so she's looking for casual and professional attire." Turning to me, she gives me a questioning look. "Probably a couple of cocktail dresses too. For the fundraisers and whatnot, don't you think?"

The immediate relief I felt at the way she handled the introductions is overshadowed by the expectant way they're both looking at me now. "Um, I don't—"

This time it's Chloe who interrupts with a gesture to the gray-and-navy striped T-shirt dress I'm wearing. "It looks like you've done a little shopping."

"It's from Target," I admit unnecessarily, my cheeks burning. I am so far out of my depth here it's crazy. Like Julia Roberts in *Pretty Woman* levels of crazy. Which, I guess, makes Joan my Richard Gere, smoothing the way for me in a world where I definitely don't belong. *This is so fucking weird.*

Chloe nods and smiles, her tone nothing short of gushing. "Oh, yeah, when I was pregnant, my favorite pair of jeans was from Target. They were so soft. But we have some things I think you'll love too. Let's get you set up with a dressing room, and I'll bring you a few things to try."

It's hard to say what surprises me more, Chloe's appreciation of Target or the dressing room. No, I take that back. It's definitely the dressing room. It isn't like any I've ever been in before. Instead of a cramped, closet-sized space with a mirror, it's a spacious room similar to what you find in bridal shops. With a comfortable-looking couch and two wingback chairs, there's seating for at least five, and the three-way mirror surrounds a raised platform for optimal preening. Off to one side, there's even a playpen and a basket of toys in case the mother-to-be has to bring her older children with her, I guess.

What there isn't is a separate changing room, a subject Joan raises as soon as Chloe has left us alone. "I'll step out in the hall when you need to change."

Ordinarily I'm not particularly modest. I once shared a fitting room with three complete strangers when a popular department store was going out of business and the line wrapped around the inside of the store. Being pregnant has made me slightly more insecure, but Joan's had two babies—she knows what it's like. "No, I'm okay." And then, as an afterthought, because everything isn't actually about me, I add, "Unless you'd rather?"

"I'm fine." That settled, she gets comfortable in one of the wingback chairs. But when she looks up at me again, she has a slightly horrified expression on her face. "You don't have any lovebites, do you?"

Lovebites? I stare at her in confused silence for several seconds before it finally dawns on me what she means, and then I start laughing. Not just a little, either. It's the kind of laughter that makes my ribs hurt and I worry I might pee a little. It's too absurd, not only because Mac's blue-blooded mother asked the question but also because, now that I think about it, I do in fact have a hickey. "As long as I don't have to take my bra off, we're good." Joan blinks at me and that only makes me laugh harder, but I manage to wheeze, "I'm sorry, I shouldn't have said that."

Joan continues to stare at me, and I'm aware this is an awful turn of events. She's going to hate me. Still, I can't stop laughing. She'll probably tell Mac I'm a deranged tart. Or hussy. She's definitely too uptight to call me a slut. Maybe a strumpet or jezebel, though?

"It's my fault—I did ask. It's just that…" But the rest of the sentence is lost to her own bubbling laughter.

"What?" I ask, still giggling but curious.

"Well, this is a little awkward, isn't it?" She waits for my nod then continues. "I don't want it to be, but I know how Will is…how things must be for you with him."

My mood sobering, I'm slow to respond. "I'm not sure what you mean."

She considers her words carefully. "He was always so adamant about never marrying or having a family, and despite the circum-stances he's still rather…cavalier about the nature of his relationship with you. I imagine that's difficult for you and might make spending time with his family a little uncomfortable. I don't want it to be like that with us, though. Whatever is or isn't between you and Will isn't my business. But you're the mother of my grandchildren and, at the very least, I'd like it if we could be friends, which is what I was thinking when I invited you to do this with me. And I was thinking of you as a friend when I said I wouldn't be bothered staying in the room, but then I remembered you're really my son's…" She flounders, clearly unsure how to finish that thought.

I don't really have any useful suggestions for her and the conversa-tion is getting pretty deep, so instead I go for humor, hoping to lighten the mood a little. "He calls me his baby mama."

Joan is aghast. "Good lord, but he is a hot mess, isn't he? Well, I suppose I only have his father and myself to blame for that."

"Hot mess" seems like such an unusual turn of phrase coming from her that it takes me a minute to process the rest of her comment. There's something resigned and a little bit sad lurking in her expression, and I rush to reassure her. "He's not all bad or else I wouldn't…" *Don't say love him. Don't say it.* "I wouldn't keep having babies with him. And you know, he's a great dad."

Chloe chooses that moment to return, a pile of clothes slung over one arm. Joan smiles at her and waves toward the rack by the mirror. "Just leave those, please, and we'll let you know if we need you."

When the clerk has departed again, I walk over to the rack to check out what she's left for me. I make the mistake of looking at the price tag for one of the blouses and nearly go into cardiac arrest. Two hundred thirty-seven dollars. *Two hundred thirty-seven fucking dollars.* For a blouse. That I'll only be able to wear until November. It's obscene.

"Everything all right?" Joan asks.

"Yeah, it's great. There's just so much." There's no way I can tell her I can't afford this stuff, and she's obviously been looking forward to this. I don't want to disappoint her, so there's nothing else to do but play dress-up. I'll be her very own Pregnant Barbie. And at the end I'll pick out one dress or blouse, put it on my credit card, and come back tomorrow before my appointment with Dr. Flores to return it. Easy peasy.

"Try that brown dress first. It will look amazing with your complexion." She pauses while I tug the dress off the hanger then continues in an offhand manner, "And no peeking at the price tags, darling. Today is my treat."

What the fuck is it with these people? At least now I know where Mac gets it. "That's very generous of you, but I—"

Joan interrupts me with a firm shake of her head. "I told you I'd like for us to be friends, but the truth is I'm hoping we can be more than that, whether Will ever gets his head out of his ass or not. I don't have any daughters, and the way things are looking, I may not ever have daughter-in-laws, either." Joan studies my face then frowns. "I'm not doing a very good job of this, am I? The point is, I know I'm not your mother and I'm not trying to be. But it would mean the world to me if you would indulge me now and then and allow me to share things like this with you and the children."

It's difficult to respond, because I'm not even sure how I feel about what she's just said. It's overwhelming. This woman, who I've only met a handful of times and has every reason to hate me for abandoning her son and keeping her grandson a secret, has in a few short minutes today been kinder and warmer to me than my own mother ever was. Which is probably why I say, "I don't have a mom."

Joan gets up and comes to stand in front of me, taking one of my trembling hands in hers. "Tristan mentioned something about not having another grandma. I don't want to pry, but if that's ever something you need to talk about, I'm happy to listen."

Biting my lip to keep it from quivering, I wipe away the tears that seem to have appeared out of nowhere. Everything with my mother happened so long ago, and most of the time I think I've put it behind me, that it doesn't affect me anymore, but this is not one of those times. I have the most ridiculous urge to crawl into Joan's lap and cry. Obviously I can't do that, so instead I manage to choke out, "Thank you."

"Anytime, dear." She gives me a brisk hug then takes my face in both hands, wiping my tears and kissing my forehead. "Now, will you let me spoil you a little today?"

"Yeah, I can do that," I agree with a watery laugh. But Lord help me if Mac finds out I allowed his mother to do this.

"Good." She tugs on the dress I'm still holding. "Now let's see this before poor Chloe starts to wonder what happened to us in here."

∽

MAC

. . .

"I haven't been to a baseball game in…" Pondering how to finish that sentence, Alex frowns and looks down at Tristan as if he might know the answer.

"Ever?" I suggest.

"I went to some of your games," Alex replies, defensive.

Right, sure. Watching a bunch of high schoolers play ball is definitely the same as going to a major league game. Is it really any wonder I find it so hard to connect with my brother?

"You played baseball?" Tristan is sitting between us and he looks up at me now, wide-eyed and a little offended, like I've been keeping some life-changing secret from him.

"Just in high school."

Apparently when you're eleven, even high school seems like the big leagues, because Tristan is undeterred. "What position?"

"Left field," Alex answers, and my eyebrows creep up. He's never shown much interest in sports and we weren't any closer back then than we are now, so I'm surprised he knows. Frankly, that was a long time ago, so I'm even more surprised he remembers.

Turning to Alex, Tristan cants his head to one side, his voice grave. "What do you think about designated hitters?"

Oh, shit's about to get real now. The designated hitter rule was the subject of the first argument Tristan and I ever had. The kid is surprisingly passionate about it. Wrong, but passionate, and I have to admire that. But Alex has evidently already reached the limit of his baseball education, and his eyes dart to mine. I shake my head and grimace.

"Terrible," Alex says with more confidence than he ought to have. By now, he should know better than to trust me.

"Why?" Tristan demands, sitting up straighter in his seat and squaring his shoulders.

Alex immediately realizes his mistake and gives me an accusatory look before stammering, "It just doesn't seem fair."

"There's nothing unfair about it," Tristan insists. That is, I've learned, the entirety of his argument. He's grown up watching and loving an American League team, so that's just the way it ought to be in his mind.

In an attempt to buy time, Alex takes a long drink of beer but when he lowers the plastic cup, it's clear he's still at a loss.

Taking pity on him, I make the case for him. The same one I make every time Tris and I argue about this. "If you can't play offense and defense, you aren't really a baseball player. And you know as well as I do, the Tigers might have won the World Series in 2013 if the Sox hadn't been able to keep Big Papi around all those years as a designated hitter." Noticing Alex's blank look, I clarify for his benefit, "David Ortiz." It doesn't seem to help. "How many young guys never got a chance because players like Ortiz and Victor Martinez were taking up space on the roster?"

Tristan rolls his eyes. "Ortiz and Martinez were great hitters. They weren't just taking up space."

"Maybe," I concede. "But maybe some young player could have played first base *and* been a beast at the plate if he'd only had the chance."

"You know what that sounds like to me?" Alex asks, nudging my son's shoulder. Tristan gives him a questioning look and he continues, "A guy who's still butthurt he never got scouted."

Ouch. I mean, probably true, but still. And it only adds insult to injury when Tristan laughs and offers his uncle a fist bump. I suppose I had it coming but even so, I'm glad the first batter has stepped up to the plate, commanding Tristan's attention.

At the bottom of the sixth, Tristan has to go to the bathroom. He claims he can go by himself, but that's a hard no. Besides, I could use another beer. His own cup empty, Alex comes too.

Fresh beers in hand, we're both waiting outside the bathroom for Tris when Alex looks over at me and says, "It's too bad Dad is working this weekend. He'd have enjoyed this."

We've been having a good time and I don't want to ruin it by getting into the same old fight about our dad, but sometimes it's hard to understand how he can be so oblivious. "You're assuming he would have been invited even if he were in town."

Alex is unimpressed. "Gwen would have included him. It's Father's Day, for heaven's sake."

"You're wrong." And then, because I just can't help it, I add, "She actually has my back."

The implication is clear, and Alex doesn't miss it. But instead of getting angry or defensive, he says, "Then you should marry her." I'm too stunned to respond and I must look it, because he explains, "I'm serious. I've known you my whole life, and I don't get it. If she does, you shouldn't let her get away."

"Dad!" Tristan shouts, skipping out of the bathroom. "Can I have another hot dog?"

Glad for the distraction but uninterested in cleaning up puke later, I'm skeptical. "You've already had two."

Tristan looks me straight in the eye and deadpans, "The baby likes them."

We stare at each other in silence for a second then both burst out laughing. It's his mother's favorite phrase lately. When I walked in on her eating her second turkey sandwich in an hour. When there was only one piece of pizza left and all three of us wanted it. When she ate an entire box of popsicles in one evening. It's her answer for everything, and it's a winner. I mean, really. What kind of monster is going to take the last cookie when a woman pregnant with twins gives them sad eyes and says the baby wants it?

"I promise I won't puke," Tris vows when we've gotten our laughter under control.

I reluctantly agree, and he bounds ahead of us on the way to the concession stand.

"He's a great kid," Alex says, smiling when Tris digs the money I gave him earlier out of his pocket and gets in line.

Of course I think so, but it's nice to hear someone else say it. "Thanks."

"Are you scared? I mean, about having another?"

"You have no idea." There's no point lying about it. Hell, just answering his question is enough to make me queasy.

In the beginning, I wasn't all that upset about her pregnancy, because it was too abstract and a little surreal. But with each passing week—and each new milestone—that's changing, and my worries mount. I never knew how much there is that can go wrong with a pregnancy and especially with twins. What if something happens to one or both of the babies? Or Gwen? It seems like Tristan is coming around to the idea of being a big brother, but what if he isn't? What if he resents us for having them? What if I'm a terrible father? I mean, I think I do okay with Tris, but he's half grown. Newborns are an entirely different thing, and I might suck.

But all of that is normal, I think. Most parents must ask themselves those questions. It's that insidious voice whispering in my head that really makes me feel sick.

What if Gwen takes the kids and leaves again? It would be the cruelest practical joke the universe could play on me. All those years, so certain I didn't want kids, only to learn I have one and discover I love him more than I could have ever dreamed, just to have it ripped away from me. I wouldn't survive it. But even worse than that, sometimes it says, *you should have run.* That's my biggest fear. That things will get hard and I won't be able to hack it. Or worse, I won't even try.

"Can I tell you something? A secret, I mean." I wait for Alex's nod but I'm still not satisfied. "I'm serious. You can't tell anyone, and you definitely can't tell Cece."

"Why would I tell her anything?" Alex scoffs, and I sigh. That's a can of worms for another day.

"Tristan doesn't even know, and I don't think Gwen's told her sisters."

"But Gwen knows?"

Against my will, I can feel my mouth curving into a smile. "Yeah."

"Well, are you going to spit it out?"

"Finding out she was pregnant was scary enough, but now...well, it's just that...it's twins." Alex's eyes widen and he opens his mouth like he's going to say something but now that I've told him, I can't seem to stop talking. With one eye on Tristan to make sure he's still in line for his hot dog, I start rattling off all the terrifying things I've learned.

I'm halfway through a recitation of everything I've read on the internet about preeclampsia when I pause to take a breath, and Alex seizes the opportunity to interrupt. "Everything is fine so far, right? With Gwen and both babies?"

"Yes, but—"

Alex puts his hand on my shoulder and squeezes. Hard. "What do her doctors say?"

"That she's doing great. Her OB says everything's textbook so far and the high-risk specialist agreed, but sixty percent of—" Another shoulder squeeze, even harder than the last. This time I shrug him off. "Christ, stop it. That hurts. Have a little fucking respect. I'm the older brother here."

"Yeah, but I'm bigger and not the one freaking out about a bunch of stuff that might never happen."

"And if it does?" I ask, because really, that's all that matters. If something awful happens, what will I do?

"Then you'll deal with it." Alex shrugs. "Worrying isn't going to help. All you can do is hope for the best and support Gwen however you can, which, I assume, you're already doing, and that's why you're dumping all this on me instead of stressing her out with it."

He's right, of course, but our conversation is forced to an abrupt end by Tristan's return. In the thirty yards between the concession stand and where Alex and I stood waiting, he's already eaten half of it, and I resign myself to the likelihood I'll soon have a kid with a belly-ache to deal with.

When we resume our seats, Tristan is absorbed by the game. We could talk about what we planned to get him for Christmas and he wouldn't notice. Alex seems to agree, because after a quick glance at Tris to make sure he isn't paying attention, he says, "I'm sorry, by the way, for the thing I said on the bus the other day. You were right, I was out of bounds and I never should have said it. You're obviously more committed to..." another glance at Tristan while he fumbles for a vague way to make his meaning clear, "...the situation...than I realized, and it was wrong of me to assume I knew anything about it from the outside."

It's hard not to stare, because it's possibly the most genuine apology he's ever given me. I already have my arm around the back of Tristan's seat, so I raise my hand, clamping it on Alex's shoulder to give it a gentler squeeze than those he gave me. And it's probably because I've had a little too much beer that my voice sounds gruff when I say, "That means a lot to me, man. Thanks."

CHAPTER 19

GWEN

"I just can't get over how soft those yoga pants are," Joan says with a dreamy voice. Sticking her hand in the bag on her lap for what must be the hundredth time since we boarded the water taxi back to Alexandria, she fondles the pants in question and sighs happily.

Bumping her shoulder, I laugh. "Yeah, well, I can't believe you bought a pair of maternity pants for yourself."

She straightens her shoulders and looks down her patrician nose at me. "If you keep your mouth shut, missy, no one will ever know they're maternity pants. I just got them to wear around the house anyway."

It's fun to tease her but she's right, they are preposterously soft. I'd have probably still bought a pair even if I wasn't pregnant. Leaning over to retrieve my own bag from the floor so I can do a little fondling of my own, a fluttering sensation in my belly stops me midway. Half bent over, one hand covering the place I felt it, I freeze in place, waiting to see if it will happen again.

"Is everything all right?"

Too afraid to speak, because I don't want to get distracted and miss it, I nod. I shouldn't have worried, though. A few seconds later it happens again, and this time it feels slightly stronger. Unmistakable. I sit back in my seat and turn to Mac's mother, euphoric. "I just felt one of the babies move for the first time!"

Joan's brows draw together and she blinks at me, her lips pursed. It isn't the reaction I expected. Not even close. Granted, nobody but me can feel it, but this seems like the sort of thing grandmas should be excited about, and disappointment balloons in my chest. Why isn't she?

She puts one hand on my wrist and her voice croaks. "Did you just say one of the babies?"

Oops. Slapping one hand over my mouth, I bob my head up and down, confirming what she must already know. I inadvertently revealed too much but I can't find the energy to be upset with myself, especially when she breaks into a radiant smile, her eyes watering, and we spend the next several minutes sniffling and laughing and hugging. "I'm sorry we didn't tell you sooner, but we're just trying to be cautious," I explain when we finally break apart.

"Of course, I understand, and if there's anything I can do to help, you let me know." Wiping her eyes again, she sounds wistful. "And to think, not that long ago I worried I might never get to be a proper grandmother. Now I have Tristan, and soon there'll be two new babies to spoil."

A proper grandmother, as if she was already an improper one. Suddenly it feels like Amy is sitting right there on the bench between us because there isn't a doubt in my mind Joan believes Mac is Amy's father. Our eyes meet and Joan pales, her lips pressing into a firm line. She didn't mean to say it and I can see the question in her eyes—it's there loud as if she shouted it. She's wondering if I know.

The truth crowds into my throat but I force the words back down. It isn't my place. This is Mac's secret. Mac's mother. Mac's life. So instead I smile and pretend it never happened. "I'm glad to hear you say that. The whole idea of having twins is pretty intimidating, and I'm sure I'll need lots of help along the way."

She's relieved I've carried on as if her slip went right over my head, but her laugh is still a little strained. "Oh, I bet. My boys are only two years apart, and I thought I was a martyr for that."

"I mean, you definitely had your hands full with those two. They're still a lot, especially when they're together." It's a joke, or at least that's how I meant it, but Joan sighs and rubs one hand over her heart, like thinking about this physically hurts her.

"He'd probably never admit it, but Alex idolizes his big brother. Always has. But Will's never had time for him or... I don't know. Maybe he just didn't know what to do with a little brother. I always wished they had a different kind of relationship, like the one Vicky and I have, and I've tried to foster that but it's never seemed to work. Maybe it's just more complicated for brothers than it is for sisters." She shrugs and gives me a helpless look, but I can tell she doesn't really believe that.

I sympathize with her position, wanting to help them build a better, stronger relationship and not knowing how. At least from the outside, it's plain to see they both want something from the other that neither is able to offer. It would help if Mac would share his secrets. Then they'd be on level footing, better able to understand where the other is coming from, but the one time we talked about it, Mac made it clear he'll never do that. In the absence of that, it's hard to see how they might make lasting progress no matter what their mother or I might do. Accepting you can't help your loved ones is another matter entirely, though.

"Well, enough of that." She forces a smile and shudders, like she's shaking off her sad thoughts. "We've had a good day today, haven't we? We've had fun. We'll have to do it again when it's time to decorate the nursery. Have you thought about a theme? Maybe baby zoo animals or boats. Oh, a nautical theme would be so fun!"

It's my turn to blink at her in confusion. A nursery? With a theme? Not subjects I've given any thought, primarily because there won't be a nursery. Tristan didn't have one. When he was an infant, he shared a room with me. There wasn't space for anything else. I'm not sure how things will work out this time, especially with Olivia leaving for school in August and Willa considering moving in with Diane, but a dedicated nursery isn't on the table. Unless...

The faint quiver in my abdomen catches my attention again, and I reflexively lay one hand over it, wishing Mac were here so I could tell him. Anticipating his reaction is equal parts exciting and terrifying. Will he be happy? Or will this be the milestone that finally makes this real for him, triggering the freakout I've been expecting but has yet to come?

He's been such a steady rock for me, soothing my fears and catering to even my smallest, silliest desires. I couldn't possibly have asked for a better partner, and it makes me even more regretful for keeping Tristan from him all those years. I robbed him of so many experiences the first time, and now, even though he wouldn't have been able to feel it anyway, he's missed what feels like a big moment with the twins.

Short of chaining him to my side, it's impossible for him to be present for everything, of course. But I'm making it harder for him, and for what? My stubborn need for independence and a fearful desire to protect myself from being hurt? Is it really worth it, though, when I want to share these moments with him?

No, if I'm honest with myself, it isn't just the milestones of my pregnancy or family time with Tris that I want to share with Mac. The truth is, I want to share all my moments with him, even if I am just setting myself up for heartbreak in the end.

MAC

LOTS OF SUNSHINE, three hot dogs, and a competitive ballgame have worn Tristan out. Right through the ninth inning and the boat ride back to Alexandria, he was raring to go. Babbling endlessly about Soto's homer and the look on my face when Alex spilled his beer on me. But once we were in the car to take his uncle home, it was like someone removed his batteries. He just sort of crumpled in the back-seat, head against the window and snoring softly. By the time we got back to my place, he was still out cold and, sucker that I am, I carried him upstairs without waking him and left him on the couch.

I've been around long enough now to know that, three hot dogs or not, he'll inevitably be hungry when he wakes up, and I'm unsure if Gwen and my mom are eating dinner together. Judging by the time, probably, but hangry Gwen has never been funny and hangry preg-nant Gwen is nearing national emergency levels of catastrophe, so I'm not taking any chances. I'm in the kitchen chopping vegetables for omelets—eggs being the one and only thing Tris will concede I make better than his mom—when I hear the front door.

"In the kitchen, baby," I call out to Gwen, not at all worried about waking Tristan. He's already been asleep for more than an hour, and we'll all be sorry come bedtime if he oversleeps.

I can hear her coming up the stairs, but she doesn't actually speak until she's behind me. I took my damp shirt off as soon as I got home, and she wraps her arms around my waist, pressing her face to my bare back. "Right where you belong. In the kitchen, barefoot and not pregnant."

With a surprised huff of laughter, I glance over my shoulder at her. She looks tired, but her blue eyes are sparkling with mischief. "That last part is your job. How'd it go with Mom?"

"We had a really good time. Tris?"

"Sacked out on the couch. We had a great time too, and you were mostly right about inviting Alex." I've turned back to the counter and resumed chopping the onion but it's hard to concentrate, because Gwen has slid her hands into the front pockets of my jeans.

"Mostly?"

"He's still annoying."

Gwen's chest vibrates against my back with laughter, but her voice is husky when she asks, "How long has Tris been out?" Still in my pocket, she slides one hand over to grip my cock, and I drop my knife on the counter with a clatter. "Think we've got time for a quickie?"

"Yeah, I think so." It doesn't take much to get me going, not where she's concerned, and I'm already hard. Gwen gives my dick a firm squeeze, and I groan.

"Half bath?" She withdraws her hands from my pockets and takes a step back, giving me room to turn around.

The half bath is the only room on this floor we can get a modicum of privacy, and we've made use of it a few times before. But it's been a long day, and tonight I'm too tired to put that much effort into keeping quiet. Grabbing her hand, I start toward the stairs. "Bedroom."

"But the stairs," she whines, and I have to laugh. If she didn't live on the fourth floor in a building without an elevator, I might believe the stairs are the whole reason she won't move in with me.

"Come here." Pulling her up against me, I grab her bottom with both hands, lifting. Gwen presses her face to my neck to muffle her laughter and wraps her arms and legs around me. "I've already carried the boy up one flight today. I might as well carry you up another."

"Good thing I know all the best ways to show my appreciation." She punctuates that declaration with an open-mouthed kiss on my neck.

We've reached the top of the stairs and in three long strides we're in my room. I don't know what she has in mind, but as soon as I've kicked the door closed behind us, I set her on her feet at the edge of the bed. Unbuckling my belt with one hand, I put the other on her hip and turn her toward it. "Lift up your dress for me."

Bending over the bed and bracing one hand on the mattress, she reaches behind her to pull up her skirt. She's wearing white panties and she tugs those down too. "Hurry, Mac."

Fuck. I was planning to kneel behind her and lick her sweet pussy first, but I can't ignore the urgent tone of her voice or the view she's giving me. With her dress flipped up and her panties around her thighs, my dick aches to be inside her, and I shove my jeans and underwear over my hips, just as eager as she is. One hand on the small of her back, I thrust into her and grab her hip with my other hand, steadying her. She pushes back to meet me with a low, shuddering moan, her ass slamming into my pelvis.

I can't think straight. Hell, I can't think at all. Everything is Gwen. The feel of our bodies moving together. The urgent, breathless sounds of her pleasure. The way she reaches back to grab my hand on her hip, as if she's desperate for that little bit of extra contact. *Gwen.*

It's hard and rough, both of us reaching a scorching climax that leaves us trembling, but it's impossible to be disappointed that it's over so quickly. There's a time and place for hours of foreplay and drawn-out lovemaking, but after being apart all day, I just needed the connection. It's gratifying to know she feels the same way, especially when she rearranges her clothes and crawls up on my bed.

Lying on her side, she gives me a sated and satisfied smile, her voice still husky when she says, "You should be ashamed of yourself, treating a pregnant lady that way."

It admittedly took me a while to get with the program as her pregnancy advanced. The more obvious it became, the more awkward I felt about anything but the most sedate sex. I got over it quickly, though. I had to, because Gwen's appetites for just about everything— food, sleep, dick—were insatiable, and she didn't have a lot of patience for my reticence. That doesn't mean she won't still tease me about it, though.

"Me?" I pause in buckling my belt to give her my best innocent look. The kind that says I'm the victim here, not her. "I was just trying to make a nutritious meal for my family, and you attacked me."

My joke doesn't land the way I intended. She winces on the word "family" and pats the mattress next to her. "Come here. I want to talk to you about something."

Even in my post-orgasmic haze, those words are enough to set warning bells clanging in the back of my mind. But other than that so-quick-I-almost-missed-it flinch, she looks too relaxed, too happy, for this to be anything alarming. Or at least, that's what I'm telling myself as I stretch out on my back next to her. "What's up?"

She scoots closer until the dips and swells of her body are pressed against my side. Meeting my gaze, she licks her lips nervously. "I want to move in with you. I mean, if you still want me to. Us to. Me and Tristan. Maybe my sisters. I don't know, I'll have to talk to them and see what they want to do. God, there's so many of us. I'm sorry."

My first response isn't relief or happiness as I might have expected. It's suspicion. "What's brought this on?"

Her eyes widen and she starts to pull away from me. "You've changed your mind."

I put one arm around her to prevent her escape. "Nope, but I want to know why you have."

Since they first stayed over at Easter, they've gradually begun sleeping at my place more frequently. It's gotten to the point now that when Gwen and I aren't traveling, they stay over more often than not. They both have clothes here. Tristan has toys and books and God knows what else in his room upstairs, and Gwen has left a shocking number of bottles of shampoo and lotion in my master bathroom.

If she needs to get her mail at a different address and sleep on a couch in an overcrowded apartment four or five nights a month to satisfy her need for independence—or whatever it is that's driving this —I can live with that for now. Why rock the boat when I'm more or less getting what I want already? But she was so adamant about not moving in, about not even talking about it, that I feel like I need to know why she's made such a sudden about-face. *What's changed?*

"Don't be mad I didn't lead with this, okay?"

"Gwen."

She lifts up on one elbow and points to her belly. "I felt one of the babies move today. It was like a little tickle right here."

"Yeah?" Everything else forgotten, my smile is so big my face feels like it might crack and I palm her stomach, knowing I won't be able to feel anything but unable to stop myself.

She nods excitedly, resting her hand on top of mine. "I can't wait for you to be able to feel them."

"Me too, baby."

I lean over and give her a quick kiss and when I've settled back against my pillow, she says, "That's why I changed my mind. You missed everything with Tris, and that was my fault. I don't want you to miss anything this time." That strikes me as not the right reason, although I'm not sure I can articulate why. Before I can try, she adds, "I want to share all of it with you. I want you to be Tris and the twins' dad all the time. I want us all to be together."

Well, that's better. My first instinct is to kiss her, so I do. My mouth gentle on hers, this isn't about sex. This is about showing her exactly what I want. Her in my bed every night and at my breakfast table every morning, our too-smart-for-his-own-good son and impending twins included. And yes, even her sisters if that's what it takes. It's about telling her I love her without saying the words, because I did that once and she threw them back at me.

Gwen hums with contentment, and I lean back so I can look at her. "There's something I need to tell you too."

"What?"

"I sort of told Alex about the twins. Do you mind?"

Gwen shakes her head and a small, tired laugh escapes her. "No. I accidentally told your mom."

"We should probably consider telling everyone soon." My gaze drifts to our joined hands resting on her stomach, and I consider my words carefully before adding, "Last week, Molly Gutierrez asked me if we were certain of our dates." Molly is the state director for Kim's South Carolina campaign. A friendly woman in her fifties—and the mother of twins—she smiled knowingly when I said yes, we were sure.

"Dad! I'm hungry!" Tristan's bellow is loud enough to make Gwen and I both wince. If I had to guess, he's halfway up the stairs between the second and third floor. It's his go-to maneuver when he's looking for one of us—stand in the exact center of my townhouse and yell at the top of his lungs.

"In my room." After a quick glance to make sure we're both decent, I add, "Come on up."

"Are you sure you want us to move in?" Gwen asks, her lips twitching.

"I'm sure, but I might see about getting an intercom installed."

She's still laughing a moment later when Tris knocks on the closed door. After being invited inside, he throws it open and repeats his complaint. "I'm hungry." Then, noticing his mom on the bed next to me, he adds a surprised, "Oh, you're home."

Home. We haven't even told him our plans yet, and he's calling my place home. Something warm and shimmering unfurls in my chest, and a lump forms in my throat.

"Your dad will make us some eggs in a few minutes." Gwen scoots away from me and gestures to the space she's created between us. "We want to talk to you about something first."

I didn't really think we'd tell him tonight. After all, she's only just agreed to move in, and there are still a lot of details to work out. Like rent. I just fucking know she's going to want to pay rent. It'll be a cold day in hell before I agree to that, especially when she won't take my money. But if she's eager to tell him they're moving in, that's fine by me. If nothing else, it makes it that much less likely she'll change her mind again.

Tristan, on the other hand, looks wary. Probably he's thinking about the last time we had one of these family chats and what a disaster that was. "But I'm hungry."

It's unbelievable how much that kid can eat. Well, almost. I still have vague memories of the constant gnawing hunger that accompanied growth spurts when I was his age and well into my teens. "Dude, you ate three hot dogs today. I don't think you're going to waste away in the next twenty minutes."

Recognizing defeat, Tristan clambers onto the bed. Sitting between us, he crosses his legs and puts his elbows on his knees. "What?"

Without preamble, Gwen says, "Your dad and I are talking about you and I moving in here. What would you think about that?"

It's moments like this one that I realize what a rank amateur I still am at this whole parenting gig. Unlike when we told him Gwen was pregnant—a situation he had no control over—she's framed this to make him feel like he has a choice. She's made him part of the decision instead of this being something he just has to accept. That seems far more likely to win his approval.

"What about Aunt Willa and Aunt Olivia? Would they stay at our old apartment?"

Gwen is surprised by his question and I am too, although perhaps we shouldn't be. He might like giving them a hard time, but his aunts have been constant fixtures in his life, and he loves them.

"We'll talk to them, just like we're talking to you," I explain. "They can keep your mom's old apartment if they want, or they can move in here too."

His brow creases with worry and he picks at the hem of his shorts, not looking at us. "What if they don't want anyone to move anywhere?"

"That's not up to them." She scoots down the bed until she can grab one of his hands. "They're all grown up now, and they get to decide where they live, but what you and I do, that's just between the three of us."

"Would I have to change school?"

Stupidly, I hadn't even considered practicalities like where he'd go to school, but Gwen answers this question too. "Yes, if we lived here, we'd be in a different school district, but you're changing school next year anyway to start middle school."

That seems unlikely to convince him. He might be changing schools regardless, but he'll be doing it with his friends if they stay put in their apartment. But Tristan surprises me, his face brightening as he says, "That's cool. I was worried I was going to get Mr. Holland for math next year, and everyone says he's awful."

This kid. Trying not to laugh, I ask, "So does that mean you want to live here?"

Tristan shrugs. "Yeah. It's not that far, so I could still hang out with Rob, right?"

"Absolutely," I say and Gwen is nodding along with me. It's a little hard to accept that he's so blasé about something that's caused so much strife between his mother and me, but I guess that's kids for you.

"Can I have scrambled eggs now?"

"Sure, why don't we all go downstairs and—"

I'm interrupted by Tristan, who throws himself across Gwen's legs with a petulant, "Da-ad!" that is nearly drowned out by her accompanying whine about the stairs.

"This is a peek at my future, isn't it?" I grumble, climbing out of bed. They both think that's very funny and when I return twenty minutes later with scrambled eggs and toast for everyone, they're snuggled in my bed, happily chattering.

"Can I paint my room?" Tristan asks, accepting the plate I've offered him.

"Uh, no." I hand Gwen her plate and then wave one finger between all three of us. "*We* can paint your room, though."

Tristan seems satisfied with that answer, but Gwen is grinning and pointing her fork at her stomach. "Oh, sorry…the fumes. And all that bending and lifting. Whew." She blows out a breath and shakes her head as if just thinking about painting has worn her out. "I'm afraid that's all on you two." Fair, but she doesn't have to look so happy about it. Especially when she adds, "We'll need to pick a room for the nursery, and you'll have to paint that too."

"I already thought about that." Although I didn't really expect Gwen would agree to move in, I've spent more time than I care to admit considering how it might work if she did. Leaning back against the headboard with my plate in my lap, I gesture toward the walk-in closet and the room beyond. "We can use my office."

The entire third floor of my townhouse is taken up by the master suite. The bedroom, bath, walk-in closet, and a mid-sized room the real estate agent called the master sitting room. Since I have no idea what a master sitting room is or why I'd need one, I've always used it as a home office, but now it makes more sense as a nursery.

Gwen stares at me, her fork halfway to her mouth, and states the obvious. "But it's your office."

"Sure, but I can use a different room for that. Maybe the bedroom behind the garage. That's practically empty already, and this way no one has to go upstairs for late-night feedings or whatever." I finish with a shrug, because it seems pretty straightforward to me.

"You're sure you wouldn't mind?"

"Tonight has made me painfully aware of just who will be running up and down the stairs to give bottles or bring you a crying baby. I definitely don't mind."

"Okay." Gwen nods, looking down at her plate before adding, "So we'll have to figure out rent."

What the fuck? Tristan's birthday gift was a promising start on the path to resolving our financial impasse but one civil discussion doesn't mean we should be doing this in front of him. Maybe if she wanted to talk about who would pay for his summer camp or some other smaller, less meaningful thing it would be okay. Maybe. But rent? Odds are better than fifty-fifty that conversation will end in an argument. "We can talk about that later," I suggest, my tone making it sound more like an order.

Gwen just keeps right on talking, though. "I should pay half of your mortgage payment. Although—"

"Gwen."

"I don't know if I can afford that." Her mouth pinches in a worried frown. "Of course, if Willa comes, she'll help—"

"Gwen."

"And maybe if I—"

"Gwen, I don't have a mortgage."

That stops her in her tracks. Tristan is looking back and forth between us and while I don't think he totally understands the gravity of this discussion, he seems eager to hear what his mom might say next too.

After a moment to process this new information, Gwen nods and says, "Okay. I'll bet if I get on Craigslist, I can find other rooms for rent in the neighborhood. Or I could call a real estate agent. They could probably tell us—"

"I am not taking your money."

"I knew you'd say that." She has the nerve to smile at me as she says this.

"Then why did you even bring it up?" I am more confused than ever.

"Because it doesn't matter. I have to pay you rent. It's only fair."

"That's ridiculous. If I were renting to tenants now and had to kick them out to make room, you'd have a point. Maybe. But I'm not, so you don't."

"But you could."

"I'm not running a flop house here, baby. I would sell the place before I took on boarders who weren't you, our kids, or your sisters, and it's not costing me anything for you guys to move in."

"But it is! The utilities will go up. And groceries. And—"

"Right, fine, we can figure out a fair way to split that stuff. But you are not paying me rent, and that's not negotiable." She's run the table on every discussion we've had about money thus far, and I've had to content myself with inconsequential wins, if you can even call them that. But this is my line in the sand. If she refuses to move in because I won't accept rent, so be it.

We stare across the bed at each other in tense silence, both of us apparently unwilling to cede ground. If it were up to the two of us, it's entirely possible we'd be here all night, but Tristan puts an end to our standoff when he asks, "Mom, if you aren't paying rent anymore, can I get—"

"No," we answer simultaneously, and Gwen's lips twitch with humor, the first sign that she might not be irreparably angry with me.

"But you didn't even hear what I was going to ask," Tristan whines, spraying toast crumbs all over my bed.

"Okay, what is it?" I suppose there's some possibility, however minute, that his request isn't unreasonable.

"I want a dog, but mom always said they're too expensive."

Gwen holds up one hand, counting off her reasons for saying no. "They are expensive, they need a yard, and it's not a good time. Pretty soon we'll have a new baby to take care of." Gwen winces on the word "baby" and I know she feels guilty about not telling him the truth, because I do too. "It would be irresponsible to get a dog right now."

"The yard thing isn't a big deal. Lots of people in this neighborhood have dogs. I see them out walking them all the time, and there's a dog park just a couple of blocks over," I say for reasons I don't understand. But seeing the hope kindling in Tristan's eyes I hastily add, "Your mom's right, though. Now isn't a good time."

"But someday?"

"Maybe," Gwen answers, unwilling to commit to even the ambiguous someday.

The conversation devolves into a discussion of what kind of dog we'd get if someday ever arrives, a subject I have very little opinion on but Gwen and Tris have very strong feelings about. She wants something small and fluffy, like a poodle, and he wants something big and dumb, like a Saint Bernard. One minute they're arguing about the relative merits of various dog breeds and the next they've both fallen asleep in my bed. Stacking the dirty plates on my dresser and turning off the lights, I crawl into bed with them, and you know, I don't even mind all the crumbs.

CHAPTER 20

GWEN

"So, today was a good day, yeah?" Stef asks, reaching for her glass of wine. "What's Kim going to say about it in her interview?"

"I guess you'll see when it airs." Mac flashes her a quick grin then tips his head back, taking a long pull from his bottle of beer.

It's impossible not to get a little turned on by the way his throat works when he swallows, and Stef catches me staring, although she seems to misinterpret the reason. "Ugh, I'm sorry. We're assholes to drink like this in front of you, aren't we?"

"No, it's fine." I wave one hand and pull the platter of buffalo wings in the center of the table closer to me. "This is all I need to be happy in life right now. Well, this and more ranch dressing."

"I'm on it," Mac says, excusing himself from the table to track down our waitress or, knowing him, a gallon of ranch dressing. He's been nothing short of heroic in catering to my often bizarre cravings and sometimes random whims, especially the last couple of weeks as I've gotten progressively more uncomfortable. *And I'm not even halfway yet.* It's enough to make a girl cry, and I have, several times already. He was there to rub my back and let me ruin his dress shirts with my mascara-stained tears every time.

It's almost enough to make me think our relationship has grown into something more without either one of us realizing it. But I know better. I love Mac—I've maybe always loved him—and there's no question he cares for me. But I'm only setting myself up for heartbreak if I start thinking my life is like one of those sappy movies on the Hallmark channel.

"Okay, ladies." Stef leans forward in her seat, smiling at me and Cece. "Now that he's gone, spill it."

"No way. I like my job." Cece shakes her head and reaches in front of me to steal a stalk of celery from the plate. I growl at her, and she growls back.

If only everyone was as accommodating as Mac.

"Oh, come on! You guys should all be shouting about this from the rooftops. I don't understand why the campaign hasn't even released a statement yet." Stef throws both hands in the air, clearly exasperated with all of us.

I understand her frustration. Today has been an exceptionally good day for Kim's campaign, mostly because it's been such a bad one for Brett Whitaker. Everyone has known for years that the incumbent president is a trash fire, professionally and personally, and if ever a sitting president was ripe for a primary challenge, it was him. But two separate scandals plus an incident involving Mac's dad and a hot mic rocked Whitaker's campaign, making the primary challenger look nearly as bad as the President.

Stef puts her hands on the table and leans across it, lowering her voice. "Is it because Mac's dad is involved?"

"I don't think so. Just because you don't know about it yet doesn't mean we don't have a strategy," I tease, although I too am in the dark on the campaign's plans to capitalize on Whitaker's latest missteps. And boy were they doozies.

First, Whitaker's adult son from his first marriage, who up until this point had avoided the media, gave an interview in which he thoroughly smeared his father with accusations of cheating, verbal abuse and neglect, and tens of thousands of dollars in delinquent child support still owed to his mother. Since Whitaker's main campaign argument was that he was a more moral version of the incumbent, one who shared the voters' traditional family values, it was a huge blow.

An hour later, Whitaker's younger brother gave a press conference, where he explained how the candidate had cheated him and their sister out of their share of the family fortune. It was clearly a coordinated attack from his own family, and it should have been devastating but these days, given the current President's bullshit, it's hard to guess how voters might react.

The hot mic was the icing on the cake. Between his son's interview and his brother's press conference, Whitaker decided to give an interview himself, attempting to get ahead of the scandal. It might have worked—or at least stemmed the bleeding—if William MacKenzie Sr. hadn't opened his big mouth. He apparently thought the cameras were already off when he lit into a young staffer, viciously berating him, and the reporter couldn't be talked out of airing the footage. Alex was shaken when he saw it, but Mac didn't even flinch.

"If it makes you feel any better, Gwen doesn't know what's up, either," Cece announces, clearly pleased to be the only person at the table with the goods.

Mac returns just in time to overhear Cece. Setting a soup bowl of ranch dressing in front of me, he drops back into his seat. "Doesn't know what?"

Even I don't need that much ranch, and I gawk at the bowl. "Seriously? A bowl? That's, like, half a bottle of ranch."

One corner of his mouth kicks up. "Sorry, baby. No medics on hand to set up an IV for you. I asked."

"You're a dick." I emphasize my point by throwing a baby carrot at him, but he catches it out of the air with a smirk and pops it in his mouth.

"You're all a bunch of dicks." Stef pushes her chair back from the table. "Where's Alex? He'll tell me."

"I owe you a scoop, don't I?" Mac asks, referring to her help acquiring a pregnancy test for me. There's a teasing note in his voice, but Stef settles back in her chair with an eager nod. "When asked, Kim will say that if the allegations are true, they're very troubling, but mostly she's going to focus on the issues, just like she always has. She'll say all the drama with Whitaker and the President is a distraction. That it gets in the way of accomplishing all the real work that needs to be done, and that's what she wants to focus on."

"Sure, that makes sense. Rising above the fray makes her look calm and steady. But there's blood in the water, so her surrogates will go on the attack, right? And you'll run a bunch of ads?" Stef's been covering politics long enough to know the standard playbook.

"Nope, none of that. It doesn't seem to work anymore, not like it used to, and a full-throated attack just makes Kim look like she's sinking to their level, even if it doesn't come directly from her. You all —" he waves a finger at Stef, "—will be like a bunch of dogs with bones, anyway. We don't need to worry about making sure their fuck-ups stay in the news cycle. The media will keep it there for the clicks. So instead of hammering on how unqualified and corrupt the opposition is, we're going to create opportunities to show how different we are without mentioning them at all. Show don't tell, isn't that what all you writer types say?"

Stef snorts. "I think that's more for creative writers."

"Whatever. You get the point."

"I do." She gives him a calculating look, tracing the lip of her wine glass with one finger. "You want to give me an exclusive? You and Alex together? I could get it in the Sunday paper. Just a few softball questions about what it's like to work with your brother, your connection to Kim, and your roles with the campaign."

Mac stiffens, his easygoing demeanor faltering for the first time tonight, but I don't understand why. It's a good suggestion. He and Alex have both done the occasional interview acting as surrogates for Kim, so their connection to her campaign is pretty well known at this point. After the way their father behaved today, people will make assumptions about them too. It isn't fair and it certainly isn't accurate, but it would be wise to remind voters they aren't anything like their dad, and Stef's given us the perfect way to do that. "No. The play here is less Alex and Mac, not more," he finally says, and I wonder again where Alex is. I haven't seen him all night.

Cece makes a strangled sound, like there's something she wants to say but doesn't dare, and I get the distinct feeling they may have discussed something similar—and disagreed—in the team meeting I missed.

"That's a mistake." Stef challenges him without hesitation. I admire her fearless determination, especially in light of their previous relationship. Having his former booty call on the campaign trail could have been disastrous for everyone involved, and I'm still a little surprised how well it's gone. Grateful, but surprised.

Mac doesn't seem to appreciate her tenacity, though, at least not right this second. He looks like he's considering lunging over the table to strangle her. "No one cares about me and Alex. As long as we aren't front and center, people will forget all about the family connection."

"Maybe." It's simple acknowledgment that he might be right, but Stef isn't convinced. He could be wrong too, and she isn't backing down from that. "All I'm saying is, it can't hurt to give your reputation a little spit shine. Just in case."

"She isn't wrong, and you know it. How many times have we sent clients out for interviews as a preemptive measure?" Cece asks.

When he doesn't answer, Stef sighs and crosses her arms over her chest, her gaze cutting to me before settling on him again when she says, "At least give me Gwen."

I'm not all that surprised to be dragged into their argument. She thinks Mac and I are really together. Not just irresponsibly fucking and having kids because we're both too stupid to properly manage birth control, but the kind of together that means we're partners. That we're building a life and a family and a future. And from that vantage point, putting me out there as a stand-in for both MacKenzie brothers makes perfect sense. A few comments about what a doting uncle Alex is and what an attentive partner and father Mac is would go a long way in establishing distance between them and their own dad.

"No." His response is immediate, his voice cold and hard. "She has nothing to do with any of this."

There it is. The reminder I need to keep my head on straight and my heart protected. Well, it's a little late for that last part, but I can try and minimize the damage. I have to, because the truth is, we aren't together at all, not in the way Stef imagines. It doesn't matter that we have a son together and twins on the way or that we're moving in together. It doesn't even matter that he's confided in me and told me things about his dad no one else knows. I'm not a part of that piece of his life, and putting me out there to subtly demonstrate how very different he is from his dad is out of the question. He's let me in as far as he intends to, and I'd be a fool to ever think that's going to change. It isn't a surprise, or it shouldn't be. We've both added bricks to the invisible wall between us. But even so, I can't seem to help the disappointment that swells in my heart.

MAC

THE WORST THING ABOUT REPORTERS, even the ones who are your friends, is that they're persistent. It's like when Jake jokes about his parents being attorneys. He says he spent his entire adolescence being cross-examined because they just couldn't turn it off. It seems it's no different for Stef, but her relentless badgering isn't going to get her anywhere tonight, and she seems to have finally realized it.

"If you change your mind, you know where to find me." The words come out clipped, and the glasses on the table rattle as she pushes away from it. "It's been a long day. I'm off to bed."

Cece and Gwen murmur their goodnights, both of them more subdued than they were earlier, and a twinge of guilt tugs at me. Everyone was in such a good mood earlier, having a good time and enjoying a few relaxing minutes among friends in the otherwise chaotic churn of working on a campaign, and I shit all over it. It's hard not to feel bad about that.

Everyone but Alex, that is. He's been MIA since our meeting broke this afternoon, and it's unlike him to disappear like this. Then again, it's not every day you watch your dad castigate some poor kid on national TV. We were together when we saw it for the first time and I was so ashamed and mortified that it took me longer than it should have to notice his reaction. He looked as if he didn't even recognize the red-faced, shouting man on the screen, and in that moment I wished so badly I could have protected him from this that my knees felt weak.

"Have either of you seen Alex?" They both shake their heads and I stand, looking down at Gwen. "You okay if I go look for him?" He wanted space—needed it—and hell, I can understand that, but it's been hours. I should make sure he's okay, see if he wants to talk.

"I'll go with you." She starts to rise then stops, hands on the table, caught between standing and sitting, her expression wary. "If you don't mind?"

"I don't mind, as long as you feel up to it."

She nods, absently rubbing her lower back as she straightens. "A walk will help, I think."

Tonight's hotel is actually a resort, and there are a lot of public spaces where Alex could be hiding out, although the late hour narrows the possibilities down some. After leaving Cece at the elevator with a promise that she'll check Alex's room, Gwen follows me quietly from place to place, investigating the restaurants and bars. Her quiet mood bothers me. Sure, my argument with Stef put a damper on everyone's fun, but that was work, and Gwen rarely lets that get to her. So something else is bothering her. But what?

"Are you feeling okay?"

We're walking down the wide hallway lined with high-end shops —all thankfully closed at this hour, although it's hard to imagine Alex hanging out in a Coach store anyway. Gwen, on the other hand, seems very interested in the shops, and her steps have slowed as she peers through windows into the dark boutiques beyond. She sounds distracted when she answers. "Yeah, of course. I mean, as okay as I ever feel anymore." One hand comes up to rest on the curve of her stomach and she turns around to give me a frown. "Why did you argue with Stef tonight?"

Huh. So that is what she's been brooding about. "She doesn't work for the campaign. The decisions have been made, and we aren't going to deviate from the plan just because she wants a juicy story. You disagree, I take it?"

Gwen just hums, and I have no idea what that means, but she's started to walk again so I follow. When we reach the end of the corridor, it dumps us into an enormous gallery. A long line of people snakes around the room and through the exterior doors to the sidewalk beyond, waiting to get into the nightclub on the other side. The music filtering out of the club is so loud my bones vibrate with the bass, even though we're still thirty yards from the entrance.

"Do you think they'll let us in just to check for Alex real quick?" Gwen asks, eyeing the three bouncers blocking the door.

I snort and shake my head. "Doesn't matter. There is zero chance my brother is inside that club."

"Then where is he? We've looked everywhere and we haven't heard from Cece, so he must not have been in his room." The concern creeping into her voice makes my stomach twist. She has enough to worry about these days without adding my brother and our family drama to her list.

"We'll look outside. And if we still can't find him, I'll call my mom."

Gwen's lips twitch as I settle my hand on the small of her back and guide her into the warm night air. "Yeah? What's she going to do?"

We're in Chicago tonight, seven hundred miles from home, and as formidable as my mom can be, even she is limited by that kind of distance, so I understand Gwen's skepticism. But that doesn't mean Mom is helpless. "If she calls him, the little shit will actually answer his phone."

Gwen laughs, a bubbling, happy sound that makes some of the tension in my chest ease, and we round the corner of the building, our search over. There's a small outdoor cafe just outside the pro shop and although both are now closed, Alex is seated at one of the wrought iron tables. He's slouched down in his chair, chin on his chest with an open bottle of whiskey on the table, no glass in sight. I almost wonder if he's drunk himself into a stupor, but as we draw closer, I can see he's tracking our approach. His eyes are a little glassy but he's too alert to be that far gone, and his sharp tone confirms it when he snaps, "What do you want?"

"I'm here to rescue you," Gwen declares and even though the patio is only lit by string lights that twinkle like stars, I can see the humorous glint in her eyes.

"From?" Alex squints suspiciously, his gaze darting to me.

Gwen points a finger in my direction. "Him. He was going to call your mom."

"Fuck, I don't want to talk to her tonight."

"Figured. So you can talk to me." It's what siblings are supposed to do, right? It's what Gwen and her sisters would do, I know that much. Maybe with a little effort from both of us, we can have that kind of relationship as well. *Maybe.* Our day at the ballpark has given me some hope, but to be honest, it still feels out of reach.

"I don't want to talk to you, either." Alex scrubs a hand over his face, and I glance at the bottle, trying to gauge how much he's had to drink. Less than a quarter of the bottle, assuming this is his first. Not bad. But then I notice the other items strewn across the table's surface. A lighter. A small black box of rolling papers. A plastic baggie. It's too dark to be certain what's in it, but it isn't very fucking hard to guess.

As far as I know, my brother's never smoked pot in his life, and it seems wrong to start now. If he's going to do it, it ought to be because he wants to, not because our old man showed his ass on national TV. "Are you fucking kidding me, man?"

Alex ignores me, his attention sliding to Gwen. "Make him go away."

She shakes her head, her lips pressed into a firm line. I don't know if he realizes it, but she's struggling not to laugh.

Trying again, I ask, "So, what, you've just been sitting out here drowning your sorrows in whiskey and weed all day?"

"First wine. Then whiskey. No weed." Alex shifts his gaze, staring off into the darkness that covers the golf course. "I tried to roll a joint and accidentally tore the paper and spilled it everywhere. Then I tried again and I don't know, I guess I didn't roll it tight enough or something, because it all just sort of fell out the end."

Christ. Ignoring Gwen's giggling, I reach across the table and grab the bag, holding it up to the light. There's just enough left for one good roll, so I jerk my chin at her and gesture to the other side of the table, upwind of Alex. "You. Over there."

One hand pressed to her mouth, Gwen complies, and I drag a chair closer to Alex.

When I sit down, he asks, "What are you doing?"

"Rolling a fucking joint for you. Least I can do, since I should have taught you how to do this twenty years ago."

"You'd have made fun of me if I asked."

"I would have," I admit. "I'm your older brother—making fun of you is in the job description. But I still would have shown you how to do it."

He shrugs. "It was illegal back then."

"Now you sound like her." I give Gwen a teasing smile across the table and turn my attention back to what I'm doing. "Where'd you get this, anyway?" I ask, carefully transferring the contents of the baggie to a piece of rolling paper.

"Toby."

I should have guessed. Toby's about Olivia's age, I think, and he's spending the summer volunteering for Kim before he heads off to college this fall. He's a good kid but a bit of a goofball, and I'm sort of annoyed he apparently turned Alex loose without telling him what to do.

When I say as much, Alex grimaces. "He did tell me. He made it sound easy." He pauses, watching while I shape and roll the joint. "You make it look easy."

Gwen snorts. "You think that's impressive? He used to be able to do it one-handed. In bed."

I've never really seen Alex like this before, and I'm not sure what to do about it, but her lighthearted joking keeps me from dwelling on it. It brings back an awful lot of fond memories too. Lazy summer afternoons in bed, Gwen tucked against my side while I smoked a joint and we talked about all kinds of ridiculous shit. Even back then, my life was a mess, but those hours I spent wrapped up in her made everything seem so much simpler.

Alex holds up one hand and glares at her. "I don't want to hear anything about what he can do in bed."

Gwen laughs, watching with half-lidded eyes as I lick the seam—at least Toby had the good sense to get papers with adhesive—and use the end of my tie bar to give it a quick final pack. Reaching for the lighter, I ask my brother, "Have you ever smoked a cigarette?" He shakes his head. "A cigar? A pipe? Anything?" Alex is still shaking his head, and Gwen is trying not to laugh again. With an exasperated sigh, I ask no one in particular, "How did I end up surrounded by a bunch of squares?"

Neither of them answers, although even Alex is looking slightly amused. He leans closer, his brow furrowing with concentration, and watches me light the joint. The first hit is better than I remembered, and I hold it for just a second, savoring it, before letting it slip out on a soft breath and passing the joint to him. "Just like that. Breathe it in slow and easy, and exhale it just the same if you don't want to spend all night coughing."

Alex nods and then promptly does exactly the opposite, gulping in a fast, deep breath that sets him to hacking his damn brains out.

Leaning over, I slap him on the back. "What the fuck did I say?"

Still in the throes of a coughing fit, Alex can't really answer, but he rolls his eyes and flips me the bird. Once it passes, I coach him threw his next couple of attempts until he finally manages it without triggering another coughing spasm. I'm not sure how much time passes then, the two of us passing the joint back and forth in silence while

Gwen looks on, but it's long enough that I'm briefly startled when Alex speaks.

"He talked to that kid the way he talks to you."

Yeah, he did. Only difference is, that kid stood there and took it, and I've always fought back. But that's why I don't understand Alex's reaction today. Granted, it's embarrassing as hell to have the outside world see Dad acting that way, and I have my own fucked-up complicated feelings about that, but this isn't new behavior for him. He's always been that guy; he's just kept it out of the public eye until now. That this is apparently some kind of revelation for Alex stings. "And it's okay when he does it to me, but not when he targets an employee, is that it?" I ask, unable to keep my voice even. There isn't enough pot in the world to keep me mellow for this conversation.

"Of course it's not okay," Alex snaps before shaking his head and adding more quietly, "It's just that I thought… I don't know, I never realized he was like that with other people. I guess I always chalked it up to the two of you being so different."

"That's part of it," I concede. For as long as I can remember, Dad and I have never gotten along, so it isn't just the secrets I'm keeping from Alex that fuel our arguments. It's hard to admit that, though, because I know exactly what he'll ask next and I don't know how to answer it.

"And what's the rest of it?"

Gwen makes a small choking sound and starts to rise, I guess because she doesn't think she belongs here for this conversation, wherever it might be headed, but I don't want her to go. I'm so goddamn tired of having this fight with my brother, of dancing around my secrets and being the odd man out in my own family, and for once, with Gwen's quiet presence on the other side of the table, I don't feel quite so alone.

But Alex intervenes before I can. "Stay. You probably already know more about this than I do, and he's nicer when you or Tris are around." He doesn't sound entirely serious, like he's trying to ease some of the tension in the air by taking a playful shot at me, but there's something genuine lurking in his words, and it brings me up short.

"You think I'm mean?"

"I was kidding." He sighs, his shoulders slumping. "Mostly kidding, but I feel like we're playing the same hand of Texas Hold'em, except you already know what's in the river and I haven't even seen the flop yet. I don't know what the fuck you want me to do, because I can't see all the cards. I try to guess sometimes, but it's apparently never the right thing and you inevitably get pissed off, and then you're just... you're dismissive. Like I should have just known what you wanted and why when you've never bothered to show me your hand."

Dismissive? It's a punch to the gut, because I've never really looked at this from that angle before. I've been too self-absorbed to even consider how it made him feel. It doesn't matter that I had good intentions, that I was trying to protect him. All I've done is hurt him in a different way.

The weight of Gwen's stare is so heavy it's oppressive. I don't even have to look at her to know what she's thinking, but my gaze drifts to her anyway and it's there, just as I expected. *Tell him.*

Even if I wanted to—and I don't—I wouldn't know how. It should be easy, right? *Oh, by the way, Amy is our half sister and Dad demanded I convince Jess to have an abortion.* One sentence, and the worst of it would be out. But I can't do it. The words refuse to make the short trip from my brain to my mouth, because I'm a fucking coward. After the way Alex reacted today, I can't fathom how he'd react if I told him everything, and I can't be the one to put him through that. And just as it does so often when I try to think about a future with Gwen and our kids, that treacherous voice in my head—the one that sounds so much like my dad—is there undermining everything. *He wouldn't believe you anyway.*

"Look," I start, but my voice has a weird rasp, and I clear my throat before trying again. "I'm sorry. I never meant to make you feel that way, but that shit is between me and Dad, and I'm not going to drag you into the middle of it. It would do more harm than good. But you're right, it isn't fair of me to expect you to take my side when you don't even know why there are sides. I'll work on that."

Alex nods and gives me a wry smile. "I suppose it was too much to hope that you might actually let me in." He pushes out of his chair and passes the remnants of the joint to me. "Here, I'm going to bed."

"Hold on." Licking the pads of my thumb and forefinger first, I pinch the cherry before offering it back to him. "You can save that for later."

"Keep it." He shoves his hands in his pockets and starts to walk away, calling over his shoulder, "You probably need it more than I do."

CHAPTER 21

GWEN

THE TRIP up to our room is a quiet one. I imagine Mac is still thinking about his conversation with Alex and I am too. Alex deserves to know the truth, and as long as he doesn't, it will always be a fissure in their relationship, no matter how hard they might both try to ignore it.

It isn't like I don't understand why Mac is being so stubborn about it though, especially because in a lot of ways, his secrets aren't really his—they belong to Jess and Amy. But carrying them alone has obviously taken a toll on him and his relationships. I've relied on my sisters over the years—sometimes I think too much—but the inescapable truth is, I never would have made it without them, and everyone deserves to have someone in their life to give them that kind of unwavering support.

After brushing my teeth and changing into my nightshirt, I exit the bathroom to find Mac standing in the center of our room in nothing but his navy boxer briefs with his phone in one hand. Distracted by whatever he's looking at, he doesn't move when I stop behind him and slip my arms around his waist, peeking around him at the screen. The sound is off, but he's watching the clip of his dad again, and my stomach knots. I hate how this is affecting him and how helpless I am to do anything about it.

"Do you ever talk to Jess about it?" All this time, she's been the one other person who knows the truth, and the idea that they might occasionally commiserate together is comforting.

Gently disentangling himself from me, Mac tosses his phone on the table. "About what?"

Was he really so absorbed in his own thoughts that he doesn't understand my question? Or is he evading it? I suspect the latter and that should probably make me angry, but instead it just makes me sad. "All this stuff with your dad."

"Not in years." He's definitely trying to avoid the topic now, because he throws back the covers and gets in bed. "It's been a long fucking day. What do you say we get some sleep?"

I'm exhausted and sore and it would be so easy to let it go in favor of sleep, especially when I crawl into bed next to him and turn the lights off. He pulls the blankets over us and rolls onto his side, his chest to my back, with one strong hand lightly massaging my hip. This is how we fall asleep most nights lately, and the familiarity is reassuring. Ignoring the problem won't make it go away, though. "You know you can talk to me, right?"

Mac sighs, his warm breath puffing against my shoulder. "There's nothing to talk about."

"No? Then how come you were watching the video again just now?"

"I don't want to talk about this, Gwen." He squeezes my hip then slides his hand around to palm my belly. "You have enough to worry about without adding my family's bullshit." He means my pregnancy, and my skin prickles with irritation because it's a copout and he damn well knows it.

It's true I'm often uncomfortable, my hips and back aching so much they keep me awake at night sometimes. I don't remember feeling this way with Tris until much later in my pregnancy, and the prospect of another twenty-two weeks of ever-increasing discomfort is daunting. Of course, the alternative—pre-term labor—would be worse, and although my doctors insist I'm doing well so far, it's a constant worry.

But for all the challenges that make this pregnancy more difficult than my first, it's in some ways easier too. Mac makes it easier. Short of throwing gobs of money at researching sci-fi medical procedures that would allow him to physically carry our babies, he has done everything he can to lighten my load. He's at every doctor's appointment, even if that means flying into DC in the morning and back out the same afternoon. He rubs my sore muscles and indulges my every craving. Even the hormonal rollercoaster that sometimes sends me careening between dramatically opposed emotions doesn't throw him. Sometimes he's baffled, yes, when some internal switch flips and I go from a crying jag to desperately horny in the blink of an eye, but he rolls with the punches and he's always, always there trying his best no matter what I need. It's meant a lot to me and I want to do the same for him, if only the stubborn asshole would let me.

"Don't do that. Being pregnant hasn't made me so fragile I can't handle listening to you vent." Pushing his hand away, I turn over so we're face to face, but it's too dark to make out his expression. "Why are you so dead set on keeping this all bottled up?"

"What do you expect me to say?" Mac demands, the blankets rustling. He moves away from me, and the lights flicker on before he settles on his back to stare at the ceiling. "I fucking enjoy that video, Gwen. It makes me happy. Like, my heart beats a little faster and it's everything I can do not to start laughing like a giddy idiot every time I see it."

"It makes you happy?" I must sound as confused as I feel, because he turns his head on the pillow to arch one brow at me, his expression dark.

He rumbles a sound of agreement. "Takes a pretty awful person to like something like that, doesn't it?"

"I think that depends on why you feel that way."

Mac presses the heels of his palms to his eyes and is quiet for a long time, probably trying to figure out how to end this conversation as quickly as possible. But now that the door is cracked, I'm not letting him close it again.

Scooting closer, I put one hand on his chest, over his heart. "Talk to me, Mac. Please."

"What's the point?" He lowers his arms to give me a stern look. "You can't fix this."

"It isn't about fixing it. You can't fix it when my back hurts, but you still rub it anyway. It's the same thing."

"You said it helps." He sounds equal parts defensive and accusatory, as if I've just been humoring him all this time. *Stupid man.*

"It does—that's the point! The only thing that will fix it is not being pregnant anymore, but that makes it feel better for a while and I like that you care enough to do it. Just because something doesn't solve a problem doesn't mean it won't make it easier to bear."

Staring at the ceiling again, Mac rubs his lip and thinks about that for a minute. When his eyes drift back to mine, his reluctance has been replaced by wary acceptance. "I don't really like the video. I feel fucking terrible for that kid; no one should ever be treated like that. But there's still this ugly, petty part of me that's glad it happened. Even before all the stuff with Jess, Dad and I never got along, and it's always felt like everyone blames me for it. Like I'm the difficult asshole. Maybe it won't make a difference in the long run and maybe no one else will see it or care, but it seems to have opened Alex's eyes a little, and that feels good."

"I think that's a perfectly natural reaction." Alex's shock tonight is only a small snapshot of their interactions over the years, but if it's representative, it isn't hard to see why Mac would be relieved—and yeah, maybe even a little happy—now. It's too complicated a situation, with complex and contradictory emotions, to be captured with one word. We need Olivia and her talent for inventing compound words to give Mac his own version of "happified," although this might be beyond even her considerable creativity.

"Maybe." Mac shrugs. "But it makes me feel like I'm just like him, you know?"

"You're nothing like him." It's hard to keep the anger out of my voice, because the idea that he would ever compare himself to his dad is heartbreaking.

"Don't be so sure," he says with a tight smile.

"Bullshit. You're a wonderful father, and you aren't a slimy cheater. You—"

"I'd have to have a relationship to cheat, and you're the closest I've ever gotten to one of those."

Tensing, the fine hairs on the back of my neck tingle. This is dangerous ground. "Right, and we've agreed on monogamy for however long this lasts, whatever it is. Are you telling me you didn't mean that?"

"No." That one word is a forceful, certain answer, but he sounds less sure when he continues. "I'm just saying you can't compare a man who's been married for more than thirty-five years and cheating for all of them to someone like me. It's a different situation. Who knows what I'd do in those circumstances?"

Alarm bells blare in my head, telling me to let it go, to change the subject, to do something—anything—other than press him on this, but the words tumble out of me before I can stop them. "What's so different? We aren't married but we're monogamous, we have kids together…we're even moving in together."

Mac rolls to his side, gathering me close and cupping my cheek in one hand. "I will always be here for you and Tris and the twins. Always. But I can't promise that *this* will last forever." He gestures between us, and I know he means the physical and emotional intimacy. "Neither of us can. You know that."

Because I've already left him once. Between the two of us, we're carrying around more baggage than a 747 and maybe, if for no other reason than that, he's right. I'm not quite ready to accept that, though. Mac's worth fighting for. I just have to figure out how I'm going to do it.

"Well," I start, forcing a cheerfulness I don't feel into my voice, "for now at least, I'm on your side, and I'm perfectly happy sitting around calling your dad vulgar names with you if that's what you need."

Mac snorts, his lips twitching with the beginnings of a smile.

"Thanks. And if it helps, I'm not trying to shut you out. It's just I've never really had anyone I can talk about this with other than Jess, and it didn't seem fair to unload on her. I don't have a lot of practice at this whole sharing-my-feelings thing."

"You should work on that. You're kind of a dick when you get wound up about this, and at least until after the babies come and my hormones return to something resembling normal, I'm calling dibs on dickish behavior."

Mac kisses my forehead. "That's fair."

"You were supposed to say I'm not a dick," I complain with a slap to his chest.

"You're a delight." He's laughing now, his chest vibrating under my palm.

We're in familiar territory again, the tension in the room dissipating. It's a shame I have to risk pissing him off again, but I do. "Good. Remember that, because in the morning I'm going to text Stef and tell her I'll do an interview." Holding my breath, I wait for his answer.

It comes quickly and, while not exactly positive, it isn't explosive, either. "No."

"I wasn't asking." The lines between work and personal are blurred here and Mac could, technically, forbid me from doing it. He's my boss, after all, and he has Kim's ear. If he really wants to stop me, there won't be much I can do about it. I'm betting he won't go that far, though, and I can try to tilt the odds in my favor. "Stef was right, we need to create distance between you and Alex and your dad in voter's minds. You know as well as I do the click-hungry talking heads will try to use this connection against Kim if we don't."

"Any other day, that might be true, but with Whitaker's own family turning on him so publicly, that'll keep the media occupied. Which makes it a bad idea to draw more attention to Dad's tantrum when there's every chance that part of the story will fly under the radar."

"And if it doesn't?"

"Worst-case scenario, Alex and I go home. If we push back now, when it's possible—likely even—that the story won't get a lot of oxygen, it just makes us look like we're protesting too much, and that will only feed the story."

I hate that he's probably right, but it also demonstrates that he isn't clear-headed about this. If he were, he wouldn't need me to say, "That's why I should do it instead of you or Alex. It's subtler."

Mac gives me a sidelong look, one brow arched sharply. "Putting my obviously pregnant girlfriend in the paper or on TV to talk about how great my brother and I are is your idea of subtle?"

Well, when he puts it that way, I can see his point, but I'm stuck on something else and my voice cracks when I say, "Your girlfriend?"

"Exactly." He points one finger at me and gives me a smug smile, like I've just proven his point, but I'm more confused than ever.

"Exactly what?"

"You have to admit, having the mother of my children react like she's just seen an unsolicited dick pic when she's referred to as my girlfriend isn't going to improve my image."

"Everyone else already says it. You know that, right? And I don't freak out all over the place about it, because the particulars of our relationship are between us. It's you saying it that confused me." Jabbing one finger into his sternum, I glare at him, and it feels like my nerves are popping with angry energy. "You've never said it before, except to say that isn't what I am."

"I'm sorry, I was trying to make a point, and that was a mistake." Genuine apology wars with wariness in his expression, and he reaches for me before abruptly stopping and putting his hand in his lap.

"Can we just agree it doesn't matter what anyone else says? We're on the same page, and that's what counts."

"Yes." He nods, hesitating for a moment. Then, with a great heaving sigh, he says, "I'm not sure it's true, though."

What the hell does that mean? My heart slams in my chest, and it feels like the wind has been knocked out of me. I can't cope with a reality in which Mac says he wants more, and if that's what's about to happen...no. That can't be what he meant.

The one difference between our unlabeled, not-a-relationship-relationship and a real, normal relationship like everyone else has is the future. Outside of Tris and the babies, we don't have one. Somewhere deep inside we both know that, and that's why we never talk about it. Why we never plan or daydream for far-off days that will never come. What we're doing now works for now and when it doesn't anymore, we'll figure out something different, and as much as I love him, as much as I want to share my life with him, I'm not prepared for that change. The inevitability of our end is too obvious, and I refuse to pretend otherwise.

"What does that mean?" My voice is soft, but steady.

He holds my gaze for a long moment and his brown eyes are so dark and intense it almost feels like he's trying to read my mind. It must not work, because he loops one arm around me, pulling me tight to his side, and says, "Forget it. We've got an early flight tomorrow, and we both need to get some sleep."

MAC

I SHOULD BE in a better mood today than I am.

For one thing, we've just stepped off a plane at DCA and we aren't just home for a night or two this time. We'll be here a whole week, during which time Gwen, Tris, and Olivia will move into my townhouse, Kim will have a slew of meetings with potential V.P. picks, and I'll get to sleep in my own bed every single night. Add in Dad and Whitaker's gaffes yesterday, and I should be nothing short of jubilant.

I'm not, though, and neither is Gwen, both of us still apparently sulking after last night's argument. Well, sulking isn't exactly the right word, at least not for what I'm doing, but I don't know what the right word is, either. I'm equal parts stung that she reacted so poorly to my casual use of the word "girlfriend" and relieved that she didn't press me into committing to the term. Whatever else that makes me, cheerful isn't it.

We're standing at baggage claim, waiting for our luggage, when Cece pushes her way between me and Gwen with a determined smile.

"I will pay you to find out the baby's gender at your appointment tomorrow."

Gwen and I were actually in agreement on this particular issue. We'd rather be surprised when the twins come. Cece's having a little trouble accepting that, though, and hell, maybe fucking with her a little will cheer my curmudgeonly ass up. Giving her a sidelong look, I ask, "How much?"

Dropping her chin, she narrows her eyes. "What would it take?"

"More than you could ever afford," Gwen snaps and then, probably realizing she came off sharper than she intended, she softens her voice and asks, "Why do you care so much, anyway?"

"Are you really going to make me spoil the surprise?" When we both stare at her, Cece sighs. "Fine. I want to crochet a baby blanket for him or her, but I don't know what colors to use."

That's never made much sense to me and, now that I've actually done a little research about infants, it makes even less sense. "According to the baby books, newborns can't even see color yet, so I'm pretty sure he or she won't have a particular preference."

Cece tips her head to the side and looks at me like she's never seen me before. "You're reading baby books now?"

"I was as surprised as you are," Gwen admits, patting Cece's shoulder and biting back a smile. Her eyes meet mine, and the playful sparkle in their depths makes my heart skip a beat. It's the first she's actually made eye contact since our argument last night, and it's an encouraging sign.

But there's a serious question lurking under her impish humor. *Should we tell her?*

It isn't a difficult question, not for me, and especially not if Cece is planning on making something. It feels kind of dickish to continue keeping the secret from her in that case. So I take a step closer to my PA and drape one arm around her shoulders, lowering my voice. "We appreciate the gesture more than you know, but you don't need to go to the trouble of making something."

Cece's expression is stern, as if she's offended I would say that.

"Yes, I do. I'm happy and excited for you guys, and that's what families do when they're happy. They share it."

Family? She's my personal assistant and my friend, but family? It's almost enough to derail me, but Gwen clears her throat and gives me an encouraging nod. "Well, then you should know..." I pause for effect, waiting until Cece looks like she might strangle me before continuing, "We're having twins."

Cece's squeal is so loud and shrill, everyone in the general vicinity —and probably within five miles of the airport—turns to look at her. She doesn't notice, though. She's too busy hugging first me, then Gwen, while chastising us for keeping it a secret this long.

"Speaking of the twins," Gwen says when she can finally get a word in edgewise, "We've reached the dance-party-on-my-bladder portion of today's schedule. Can you grab my bags if I run to the restroom?"

"Too much coffee on the plane. I'll go with you," Cece says to Gwen then turns on me with puppy dog eyes that rival Tristan's when he wants something. "Can you get mine too?"

"Sure thing," I agree, in part because I'm one hundred percent certain Cece isn't done with her effusive reaction to our revelation, and I'm happy to let Gwen deal with it. Does that make me a dick? Maybe, but I don't care.

I've just pulled Cece's suitcase off the conveyor belt—and seriously, what the fuck does she have in there? Cement blocks?—when I hear someone shouting my name behind me. It's Alex, and judging by the agitated edge to his voice, something's wrong. Something big.

Spinning to face him, I try to keep my cool. No use jumping to conclusions before I even know what's happened. "What's up?"

Alex shoves his phone at me. "I stopped by the lounge, figured we had some time to kill before our bags turned up, but as soon as I sat down it was all over the TV."

He's so clearly upset, it's a struggle to keep my voice calm when I ask, "What was all over the TV?" I don't believe in premonitions, but apprehension swells in my gut. Kim wasn't on our flight; she took a private jet with Arnie and Jess and a handful of her staff. Did something happen?

He jams his phone in my face, so close I have to lean back to try and focus on what he's showing me. The web browser's loaded one of the news sites, but not one of the old-school traditional outlets. It's one of the trashy, gossip sites where half of what they publish is the dead honest truth and half is Elvis sightings in Kalamazoo, except not always quite that obvious so you can never be sure which is which.

The headline reads *Dunn Public Relations Expert Exposed Having Public Relations.* Below that, a grainy video has begun to play, and it takes me longer than it should to place the location, partly because it's in black and white and not all that clear and partly because I'm still not sure what's happening.

It's security footage from a parking garage and the location seems vaguely familiar, but it isn't until two people stumble into the frame—or rather, one person carrying the other—that I realize exactly what I'm looking at.

There's no sound, but the events unfold exactly the way I remember them. Slamming Gwen's back against my car, I scan our surroundings and, to my current horror, make eye contact with the camera. There's no question it's me and there's no question exactly what we're doing a moment later when I hitch her leg around my hip. Even the moment of her orgasm is obvious, with her hands clawing against the back of my suit coat and her face pressed to my chest, and she's still clinging to me, boneless and spent a few seconds later when I come.

My heart is hammering so hard I almost can't hear Alex when he asks, "That's Gwen, right?"

For a split second, I glare at him over the top of his phone. Who the hell else would I be fucking up against my car in a goddamn parking garage? But then something else hits me, the one small bit of silver lining in what is sure to be a massive shitstorm.

The video cuts off before we step away from each other, and the camera never got a clear shot of Gwen's face. If even Alex wasn't certain it was her, well, that says some awful shitty things about what he thinks of me, and my nerves crackle with anger. But more importantly, it also means no one else will be sure, either. It means I might be able to protect her from the worst of what's to come. It means—

Fuck. I have to find Gwen.

❧

GWEN

"Is Tris excited?"

We're standing at the long row of sinks, washing our hands, but Cece hasn't stopped talking about the twins since she found out. Weirdly, her enthusiasm is infectious, and I'm not nearly as bothered by this conversation as I thought I'd be. Probably because other than the initial hug, she hasn't tried to maul me or otherwise gotten grabby with my stomach. And honestly, when there's so much to worry about, it's just nice to see someone so unreservedly happy. "We haven't told him yet. We're trying to be cautious."

Drying her hands, Cece nods. "That's smart." Her smile widens into a goofy grin and she looks like she might start squealing again but instead, she says, "I'm glad you decided to tell me, though."

"Me too," I admit. I haven't known Cece all that long, but she's never in a bad mood. She's always upbeat and supportive and fun to be around. I'm almost sorry we didn't tell her sooner, and I'm on the verge of saying something stupidly sappy when I'm rescued by a text message.

Olivia: *OMG*

Well that's vague and her follow-up text, which is just a link, doesn't explain anything, either. I've clicked through and am waiting for the page to load when someone bangs on the bathroom door. Who that someone is becomes clear when Mac calls through the still-closed door. "Gwen? Cece? You in there?"

What the hell?

Cece glances at me, then back to the door. "Yeah, we're in here."

The door swings open and then Mac is in the women's restroom, standing in front of me with his brow creased and mouth pressed into a frown. He takes one look at my phone, still clutched in my hand, then snatches it away, tucking it in the inside pocket of his suit.

"Hey!" My temper is hotter than the surface of the sun, and I make a grab for my phone that he easily dodges. "You can't just—"

"Is anyone else in here?" he interrupts, directing his question to Cece. Too shell-shocked by his wildly out-of-character behavior to argue, she shakes her head, and Mac nods. "Good. Go find Alex—he's waiting with our bags and he'll bring you up to speed. I need to talk to Gwen."

Apparently impressed by the gravity of his tone, Cece doesn't argue, instead hustling out of the bathroom with a speed that would be impressive if I weren't so confused. Now that I've had a second to process whatever is happening, that's my dominant reaction. Sure, I'm still irritated he barged into the ladies room and took my phone like some kind of maniac, but that is unusual behavior for him. Whatever provoked that kind of reaction must be big, and it almost certainly isn't good. "What's happening?"

"You remember Super Tuesday? The parking garage?" He waits for my nod, his expression grim. "Footage from one of the security cameras just hit the internet."

"You mean..." But I can't finish the sentence and the room tilts, my stomach shifting with it. I'm going to be sick. Either that or fall flat on my ass.

"Hey, hey." Mac grips my upper arms, steadying me and pulling me into him. "I got you. It's going to be okay."

My tears have come without warning, stinging my nose and garbling my voice. "How is it going to be okay? There's video of us having sex on the internet." What if Tristan sees it? Or my sisters? *Oh, God, no. Olivia's already seen it.* That must be the link she sent, and I don't know how I'll ever face her again.

"There's some good news." His voice is gruff, but his strong hands are reassuring on my arms. "There'll be no denying it's me, but the angle…there isn't a clear shot of your face."

"How does that help?" I've fisted my hands in the front of his shirt, my face pressed to his throat. He's so strong. So steady. It would be easy to believe him. I *want* to believe him.

"We'll say it isn't you. You'll dump my sorry cheating ass, and I'll leave the campaign. It sucks, but it's the best way to protect Kim and, more importantly, you."

"No!" My voice bounces off the tile walls and I jerk out of his embrace. Moments ago, it felt so comforting to have him hold me, but now it's the last thing I want.

He can't do this. I won't allow it. It's Jess and Amy all over again. Him taking it all on his shoulders to protect someone else. Me. But I don't need his protection, and I definitely don't want it, not when I know so well what it costs him. What it would cost all of us.

"Yes. It's for the best. You don't have to like it, but you know I'm right." He takes a step toward me, hands outstretched, and I back away until my ass comes up against the edge of the counter.

"I won't let you do this," I insist, frantically trying to wipe away my tears. "You're overreacting, anyway. It's embarrassing, but nobody is probably even going to care."

Mac grimaces. "You know that isn't true."

He's right. This wouldn't be the first time a scandal in an aide's life impacted the candidate, but most of the other examples I can think of were a lot bigger deal than semi-public sex between consenting adults. They involved activities that were illegal and immoral. We don't have to let this matter, and we don't have to make any rash decisions we might regret. "We need to think this through. We'll figure out the best way to handle it."

But it's like I'm talking to myself, because Mac is shaking his head, a regretful look in his brown eyes. "Do you really want to go into every job interview you have for the rest of your life knowing the person sitting across the desk from you has probably already searched your name and snickered over that video?" He waits for me to answer and when I don't, his expression becomes almost pleading. "I don't want that for you. I love you and I don't want my impulsive, reckless behavior that night to be hanging over your head for the rest of your life. Let me take the hit. Let me protect you."

"You don't love me." My voice cracks and the words are dry and bitter in my mouth. Like ashes. How many times have I wished he loved me? How often have I wanted him to say it? I never expected he would and now he has...while simultaneously trying to burn it all down. For my own good. *Fuck that.*

He seems equal parts hurt and frustrated by my denial and he rakes one hand through his hair before trying again. "I do, actually, which is why—"

Ignoring the way my heart feels like it's shattering into a thousand pieces, I shake my head. "No. I'm not even sure if you know what love is because if you really loved me, you would listen to me. We would be a team and you would care about us as a couple more than about me or you as individuals. And you definitely wouldn't be so damn eager to sacrifice everything we might have for the sake of fucking appearances." It's impossible to keep the scorn out of my tone on the last word so I don't try and, petty though it may be, it's gratifying when he winces. But I'm not finished. "Just so we're perfectly clear, I won't cooperate. Issue a press release that it isn't me in that video and I'll hold a press conference and say it is. Try me, Mac. I dare you. It might be interesting to see what the press does with *that.*"

I can't give him the chance to keep arguing with me about this. I don't want to hear whatever else he might say. So I leave without looking back, the bang of the door smacking closed behind me, but I can't quite seem to purge the image of him standing in the middle of the women's restroom, looking like he's been sucker punched.

Mac and Gwen's story concludes in Undeterred, coming October 2020.
Pre-order your copy now!

ABOUT THE AUTHOR

Liza Gaines grew up in Michigan before moving to Virginia in 2007. She misses her family and the Great Lakes but has otherwise fallen in love with her adopted home state.

A dedicated reader, Liza often has her nose in a book. She also enjoys cooking, baking, knitting, and watching terrible science fiction movies with her husband. Their small farm in Fredericksburg, Virginia is home to an ever-expanding menagerie that currently includes three dogs, five cats, two horses, and three goats.

For the latest updates and sneak peeks:
http://www.lizagaines.com/newsletter